VAMPIRE'S HONEYMOON

VAMPIRE'S HONEYMOON

Cornell Woolrich

CARROLL & GRAF PUBLISHERS, INC.
New York

Published by arrangement with Blazing Publications, Inc., successor-in-interest to Popular Publications, Inc., in cooperation with The Chase Manhattan Bank, N.A., as the Executor of the Estate of Cornell Woolrich.

First Carroll & Graf edition 1985

Carroll & Graf Publishers, Inc.
260 Fifth Avenue
New York, NY 10001

ISBN: 0-88184-132-2

Manufactured in the United States of America

Table of Contents

VAMPIRE'S HONEYMOON

MAY TWENTIETH . . . . I met her last night. She's beside me now, asleep, because I'm afraid to let her out of my sight; afraid I'll lose her again, as mysteriously as I found her, if I don't keep her with me every moment of the time.

I went to the party engaged to one girl, and left it engaged to another. I can't understand how it happened myself, because I've never been a fickle type of man. Sherry Wayne and I had known one another for years, ever since we were kids, and it was always understood between us that we were to be married some day. Finally, when I landed this bridge contract, we both agreed the time had come. I bought the ring and put it on her finger, and she gave this party last night to announce the coming event to all our friends.

I went to the party as much in love with her as ever, even more so if possible. That's one thing I can't understand, when I look back now, less than twenty-four hours later. How could I have been so in love with her at midnight, and then by three. . . ?

The Camerons, friends of Sherry's who were out of town had lent her their penthouse-apartment for the occasion. It had a private terrace high up above the city, and was ideal for her purpose.

She greeted me at the door, lovely as an early-morning sunrise in a spreading gown of fleecy pink. With her golden hair and sky-blue eyes, it was as if she represented Daytime, the Spirit of Light, itself. But her eyes were troubled as I kissed her, and I asked her what the matter was.

"A terrible thing happened a few minutes ago, Dick." She shuddered, hiding her face against my shirt-front. "I found Pasha, the Cameron's cat, out on the terrace. It—it was lying there dead right outside the French windows, with its throat torn and blood on its fur. What do you suppose could have happened to it?"

"Oh, it got into a fight with another cat, I suppose," I tried to reassure her.

"But there aren't any other cats out there; it was the only one in the building. And then the terrace is completely closed off on all four sides, there's no other way of reaching it than through the rooms here. It's almost as though some big bird of prey flew down out of the sky and attacked it. And I don't know what I'll tell the Camerons; they prized it so."

"Don't let that worry you. We'll buy them another after we're married."

"Dick, I hope it's not a bad omen—for you and me, you know."

I laughed outright at that, and we went in to join the party.

By three o'clock the festivities had begun to pall on me slightly, I don't know why. The rooms were stuffy, and I wanted to get a breath of fresh air. After what had happened to the cat, Sherry had kept all the windows closed, although she had ordered sand sprinkled around outside to cover up the bloodstains. When she saw me moving toward the terrace windows, she came running anxiously over. "Dick, don't go out there," she urged plaintively. "Stay in here with the rest of us."

"Why not?" I laughed.

"Oh, I don't know—I just have a funny feeling."

"Are you afraid I'll fall over the edge?"

"No, it isn't that. It's just that it's such a creepy hour of the night, and it's so dark out there. Anything can happen—"

I lost my temper a little. "That thing about the cat's got you all unstrung. Better lie down for a few minutes, you'll feel better. I just want to get away from all this noise and chatter for a few minutes, I'll be right in again."

"Then I'll come, too. I want to be with you."

"Better not, if you're afraid of spooks," I said, half teasingly, and closed the floor-length window after me.

I strolled to the edge of the parapet and lit a cigarette, wondering why Sherry had gotten on my nerves like that just now. It was as though I had come under some other influence, diametrically opposed to hers, without knowing it. I was fed up with pink and blue and gold, the colors of daytime; night and mystery seemed to be calling to me, drawing me to them by some strange magnetic force. I could almost *feel* it in the air around me, without knowing what it was.

The lights of the city-streets were pinpoints twinkling twenty stories below. There was a full moon riding the sky, dusting everything silver-bright. I moved aimlessly away from in front of the lighted windows, down to the lower end of the terrace, and around the side. It was ink-black there; the moon was on the other side, and the penthouse-super-structure cast its shadow over this way. There were no lighted windows on this side, either. That feeling of being drawn toward something kept growing stronger all the time, as I drifted along. It was as though some occult power were pulling irresistibly at me, guiding my footsteps toward it.

I came to the back of the terrace and stopped by the ledge, in the impenetrable shadow cast by the building's water-tank, high above. The spark of my cigarette was the only thing that showed in the gloom. A slight rustling sound came to my ears; at first I thought it was one of the furled terrace-awnings stirring in the before dawn breeze. I turned my head, and as I did so the cigarette fell out of my hand. There was a form, a figure of some sort, standing full-length upon the parapet a few feet to my left. Not leaning over it at elbow-height as I was, but standing erect on the top, with a sheer drop of countless stories below.

My first idea was that it was a would-be suicide. "Wait, don't!" I choked, and took a quick step over. I seized her—it was a woman—with both my arms about her legs and held her fast. A reassuring hand came to rest lightly on my shoulder from above, and a soft voice said: "Don't be alarmed—I am in no danger."

"No danger?" I gasped. "Do you realize where you are standing?"

"Perfectly." There was a hint of mockery in the answer. But she let me guide her by the hand resting on my shoulder, and dropped lightly to the terrace-floor beside me, with a swirl of loose draperies that flicked across my face, and bore a peculiar scent I couldn't analyze, unlike any perfume I had ever detected on Sherry.

"That was a crazy thing to do," I rebuked her. She was standing very close to me, and I thrust my face toward her to see if I could detect any alcohol on her breath. That was the only other possible explanation I could find for such an action. But there was no trace of liquor.

Suddenly, before I knew what had happened, her lips had lightly brushed past my own, and come to rest on the side of my neck, just under the jaw-line. Her arms slowly slid up past my shoulders, linked themselves at the back of my head. I tried to draw away; but only weakly and half-heartedly, for my own senses seemed to be swimming. I could feel the loose garments she wore swirling back and forth before me, lulling me.

I managed to take a step backward, away from her. But already it was against my own inclinations. It was hard to remember that Sherry was inside at this very moment, wearing my ring on her finger.

"Who are you?" I asked. "Come into the moonlight and let me see—"

"Why not stay in the shadows?" But she let me lead her a few steps out of the heavy shadows. To my astonishment, I had never seen her before—and I knew everyone that Sherry had invited here tonight. Perhaps she had been brought by one of the others, unasked, I thought.

"I don't believe we've met inside," I said uncertainly.

"No," she purred. "It's out here—that we've met."

She was beautiful, only hers was the dark beauty of night, just as Sherry's was the bright beauty of daytime. Her hair was raven-black, ending in a sort of widow's peak low on her forehead, and her face and arms were alabaster-white. Her gown was a clinging thing of swirling black, almost like smoke, and two peculiar shoulder-draperies she wore, hanging down loosely and caught at the wrists, almost suggested great triangular wings when her arms were in motion.

Her lips were a red gash in the pallor of her face, and they glistened as though she had daubed them with fresh blood instead of rouge.

"What's your name?" I asked.

"Call me Faustine," she said low. I saw her staring fixedly at me, with a sort of half-smile on her face, but her gaze rested a little lower than my own face. I fingered my neck uneasily. "Is there something on my collar?"

Instead of answering she drew toward me again. Her eyes seemed to grow even larger; my own half-closed, held in helpless thrall. Again my lips sought hers, but she evaded them, and her mouth came to rest softly, caressingly where her gaze had been centered. Again that swirling of her draperies all but effaced a burning needle of pain that was hidden somewhere in her soft, mysterious kiss.

"Dick!" a horrified voice cried out behind us.

She stepped back. I turned slowly, almost dazedly, and Sherry was standing there at the turn of the terrace, looking over reproachfully at us. A choked sob sounded from her, and she ran back inside without another word.

My senses seemed dulled somehow, I couldn't feel the remorse, the self-reproach I should have. I didn't want to go after her and try to explain, I didn't want to leave this bewitching stranger's side even for a moment. "Come in with me," I said vaingloriously, "and let me show you to all of them."

"I don't like it where there is too much light," she objected. "It hurts my eyes." But she let me lead her by the hand around to the front and inside through the French windows to the crowded, brightly-lighted rooms.

"Look whom I've found outside," I cried out to them all. "Look what the night dropped into my lap!"

The laughter and the voices died down, and instead of coming forward, they all drew slowly back, as though a chill had come over the party. No one seemed to know her. I saw one of the lightly-clad women present shiver a little and clasp her own shoulders. "Close the windows," she complained, "it's gotten damp here in the room."

One of the men pointed to my collar. "There's blood on your neck, Manning. You must have tangled with one of the radio antennae out there." I knew it was just rouge.

"I'm intruding," Faustine said softly beside me, with that mocking smile on her glistening lips. "I'd better go." Her hand trailed lightly down my forearm, as if in farewell, but the gesture seemed to draw me after her as she moved wraith-like across the room, toward the foyer where the elevator was.

"If you go, I'm going with you," I called after her defiantly.

Sherry came in from the bedroom just in time to hear me. Her eyes showed plainly she had been crying in there. Nothing could have made me relent; something far stronger than any hold she had on me seemed to be pulling me after Faustine. She only had to look back over her shoulder at me, and I started in her wake.

Sherry tried to bar my way. "What's happened to you?" she breathed in mortal dread. "Who—who is that you brought in here with you?"

"You ought to know—she's one of your own guests," I exclaimed impatiently.

Her face paled. "I never saw her before in my life! How could she get out there without passing through the apartment first?"

Faustine looked back at me a second time, and I had no more time for Sherry. She pulled the engagement-ring off her finger. "If you go with her, Dick, take this with you." I dropped it into my pocket without a glance, brushed past, as Faustine stirred her draperies slightly, where she was standing waiting by the elevator-bank.

Sherry followed me as far as the entrance to the foyer, as if still hoping I would change my mind and remain. The elevator-door Faustine and I were standing before was of polished chromium, bright as a mirror. I saw Sherry looking at it in consternation. Her hand went distractedly to her hair. Her lips parts but no sound came. She fell forward on the carpet in a dead faint, just as the car came up and the metallic barrier shunted aside. Faustine touched me lightly on the arm, as if to dissuade me from going back to help her. Her lightest touch was already an inescapable command as far as I was concerned.

I followed her into the car, and the slide clicked back into place, shutting out the sight of the confusion and heartbreak my actions had wrought. As we dropped swiftly downward, I reached out and took her hand in mine. It was ice-cold to the touch. I slipped the ring Sherry had just returned to me on her finger. "With this ring I pledge my troth to you, my Lady of the Night."

May twenty-fifth . . . We have been at the seashore four days now, spending our honeymoon. A peculiar thing happened this afternoon, something I can't understand. I have never been ill a day in my life. I was riding down alone in the elevator at our hotel—for Faustine will never come out with me during the daytime—and I remember asking the operator not to let the car down so fast, it was making me dizzy. The next thing I knew, they had me stretched out on a settee in the lobby and were applying restoratives. "What happened?" I asked weakly, sitting up. "Was there an accident?"

"No sir, you fainted in the elevator coming down," the desk-clerk explained worriedly.

"*I* fainted!" I gasped. I couldn't believe it; only a few days ago I could have whipped my weight in wildcats. But now as I struggled to my feet, vertigo overcame me and my knees all but folded up under me. Black specks danced in front of my eyes.

"You'd better see a doctor, Mr. Manning," the clerk suggested worriedly. "You don't look well. Shall I notify Mrs. Manning?"

"No, don't disturb her, she's resting," I said. I was ashamed to have Faustine think me a weakling. "Can you recommend one? I'll go to him myself."

"Dr. Lane, across the Inlet, is about the best one down here." They called a taxi for me, but they had to help me even the short distance out to where it was waiting; my legs were as unmanageable as rubber. However, by the time I had gotten out there, the fresh air had restored me somewhat.

Dr. Lane was a wholesome, hearty man with iron-grey hair; one look at him inspired me with confidence. I felt instinctively that he wasn't the type of practitioner who would exaggerate a patient's ailments just to extract all the money he could out of him. What followed was therefore all the more astonishing and inexplicable.

I began by telling him what had happened to me in the elevator just now. He took his stethoscope to my heart, tested my pulse and blood-pressure. Then he nodded encouragingly. "Nothing to worry about. Nothing unusual in your case. You're perfectly sound organically. Just weak from loss of blood. They should have given you a transfusion or two, to speed your recovery along, that's all. Must have been a pretty bad accident, eh? Whereabouts are the scars?"

I stared at him in complete bewilderment. "But doc, I haven't been in any accident!"

"What was it, an operation then?"

"No, no operation either!"

"Are you subject to nosebleeds? That's the only other possible cause I can ascribe—"

"Never had one in my life!" I protested.

His own surprise now equalled mine; exceeded it if anything. He looked me over a second time, more thoroughly; punctured the ball of my thumb with a needle, tested my blood under the microscope. "You're anemic, short on red corpuscles," he told me. "Not naturally so, but due to recent and considerable loss of blood. That explains the spots in front of your eyes, dizziness, and the fainting-spell you just had. There's no possible mistake in my diagnosis. Now—" Suddenly he broke off short and his face stiffened.

"What's the matter?" I asked.

He sounded almost afraid. "Where'd you get those little reddish marks on your neck?" he whispered.

"Oh, those," I shrugged unconcernedly. "Must be giant mosquitoes down here. I've been finding them there when I put my shirt on in the mornings—"

He continued to whisper, as though it were something he were afraid to speak of out loud. "No mosquito-bite ever went that deep." He drew nearer, sat down, staring at me. "Tell me something about yourself, Manning."

"I'm an engineer, just landed a big contract to do the Interstate Bridge—"

"No, I don't mean that. Tell me something about your personal life, your romance and marriage. I'm your doctor, remember."

I couldn't figure what he was driving at, but I did as he asked. When I had told him the little there was to tell, he just stared at me in a stunned, incredulous, horrified sort of way. He asked me a question or two, but what they had to do with my coming here to consult him I couldn't see for the life of me. "Your wife remains asleep all day, you say. Did you ever try awakening her while she's lying there like that?"

"No, why should I be that inconsiderate? We're up all night dancing and night-clubbing. Anyone would be tired out."

"She dresses only in black, never wears any other color?"

"No, but that's part of her charm, she represents the night. I like her that way, why should I try to change her?"

"When she dresses up to go out with you, does she sit in front of a mirror the way most women do?"

"She has an aversion to mirrors. She had them taken out of the room when we arrived. Anyone has her little peculiarities," I defended her, like any loyal husband would. "She's so beautiful, what does she need with mirrors anyway?"

He had been fiddling with his stethoscope while he was sitting talking to me. He dropped it now to the floor. "My God!" he exclaimed. He stood up and his face was haggard. He now looked the more ill of the two of us. "My God!" he repeated, and held his hand to his forehead. I was beginning to think he was a little cracked, and regretted coming to him.

A moment later, as though he had read my mind, he himself said: "I almost wish you hadn't come here, wish I'd never seen you. There are some things even a doctor would be happier without knowing." He was striding aimlessly around the office, one minute starting to dial a number, the next changing his mind. "I don't know what I can do for you," I heard him mutter distractedly. "Who will believe me if I ask for help?"

I was more convinced than ever I had to deal with a lunatic. I shifted uneasily in my chair, anxious to get out of there. "Wait," he said, "don't go yet. At least let me do what little I can—"

I saw him preparing some kind of a salve or unguent, mixing it, then and there, with a little hand-mortar and pestle. He put it in a box and gave it to me. The odor was abominable.

"The moon's on the wane, now, luckily," he mumbled cryptically. "It'll be another month before it's full again. When next it waxes, if you love life, smear some of this on your throat—at night, before retiring. It contains some of the worst-smelling, worst tasting ingredients known to the medical pharmacopia. Above all, don't let anyone see you apply it. Anyone at all. Do it in the dark, as privately as you would say your prayers. Keep it hidden under your mattress or some place. It may make your throat lose the strange attraction it seems to have for—those 'giant mosquitoes' that have been preying on you." And as he spoke, I could read aversion, horror and mortal fear on his face.

"How much do I owe you?" I asked, taking out some money.

"Money? I don't take money from the doomed." Then

as I hurriedly started for the door, he stopped me with a gesture. "Will you do something for me? Give me the name and address of that girl you were to marry."

I wondered for a moment whether I should or not. Judging by his behavior he was absolutely deranged; I still thought enough of Sherry not to want her annoyed or threatened in any way by a crank. "Why?" I asked cautiously. "What do you want with her?"

"I just want to send her a book," was his strange answer.

I gave him what he asked. Then as he made a note of it, I heard him say: "Pray to your God that she still loves you—and that she can read, as much between the lines as *on* the lines. That's your only salvation."

I banged the office-door behind me and took a deep breath of the fresh air. "Crazy as a loon!" I grunted. I fingered the little box of ointment he'd given me, tempted to throw it away then and there. In the end I didn't; after all, it just *might* be an effective remedy against those mosquito-bites that had been troubling me. No harm in trying it out.

June twentieth: The moon was full again last night; I was troubled by a strange dream, so real that it's hard for me to believe even yet that it was just a nightmare and not actuality. In fact when I look at that single drop of blood still visible on the pillow beside where my head rested, the only possible explanation is that my dream had a basis of fact, though not the same fact that I dreamed about. In other words, I dreamed one thing, but something else entirely was the cause of it. I must cling to that belief like a drowning man to a straw, or madness will be the result. I can sense that, without fully understanding the reason for it.

We were retiring, and it was nearly twelve. As I put the room-lights out, a great pathway of beaten silver sprang up, spilling across the floor from the window. The moon was full, a great white wagon-wheel riding the sky. That reminded me of that crackpot Doctor Lane. I smiled pityingly when I thought of him handing out his magic potions like a sorcerer of the Middle Ages.

The stuff he had given me was still in the little drawer of the night-stand, beside my bed. I took it out, out of curiosity, and passed it under my nose. The odor was as unspeakable as ever. Faustine was standing beside the window gazing out at the moon-flooded sky with her back to me, unaware of what I was doing. I couldn't bring myself to apply the stuff, if only because it was so evil-smelling. To me it almost seemed a worse alternative than the mosquitoes themselves. I put the lid hastily back on, slipped the little carton underneath the mattress, and lay down.

Faustine remained there motionless by the window, silhouetted against the moon-bath in her long black gown. I supposed when she had tired looking at the moon she would come to bed, so I didn't disturb her.

What kept me from falling asleep as quickly as I would have ordinarily was that little cardboard-box I had wedged under the mattress. It made a little lump under me and disturbed me, but it was too much trouble to reach out and under and extract it.

The last thing I remember with any clarity was the stroke of midnight tolling from some steeple. I didn't seem to fall asleep, but of course I must have at this point. Then my dream began.

As the twelfth stroke ended, Faustine raised both arms high over her head, as if in salute to the night and the moon. She dropped them, raised them again, dropped them, raised them. The draperies attached to her wrists made her outline seem like that of a great black bird flapping its pinions.

In my dream-state she seemed to come toward me, stand there looking down at me, eyes aglow like green gas-

flames. Slowly she bent down over me. The coverings
seem to draw softly away from my neck and shoulder, as
if of their own accord. The rustle of her garment fanned
me lullingly. I fell into a deeper sleep than before. There
was a needle of pain lurking somewhere in the bottomless
depths of it.

I threshed out deliriously with one arm, eyes tightly
closed, and the back of my hand struck something perched
on the edge of the night-stand a glancing blow. There was
a thud as the telephone fell over and separated. "Sleep,
beloved, sleep," a soft whisper sounded in my ear. Then
the waves of oblivion rolled over me again, and I dreamed
that I was dying, but death was pleasant and I didn't mind.

Suddenly a pounding, an insistent knocking, brought me
up through layers of sleep to consciousness again. A voice
was shouting through the door; "Your phone's off the
hook—anything wrong in there?"

There was a slight creak from the bed. Instantly Faustine
was standing motionless all the way over by the window
again—just as she probably had been all along, except in
my imagination.

A pass-key turned in the lock, the door opened, lights
flashed on. My head was hanging down over the side of
the bed. I felt them raise it, and then I was held propped
up in a sitting position. "Whiskey!" a voice ordered.
"Give him whiskey, quick!" A stinging, life-giving heat
poured down my throat that brought me back life and
strength.

I opened my eyes. It was the night-manager and a
bellboy who had come in. Faustine was still by the window, face hidden in her hands with wifely solicitude.
Some of her rouge had come off on her fingers. She
touched her mouth with her black handkerchief, and threw
it out the window. Then she came toward me, all anxiety
and compassion. "Poor Dick," she crooned. "Again those
horrible mosquitoes. It doesn't agree with you here, let's

go back to the city. You can go now, gentlemen. My husband will be all right.''

They left, closing the door after them. But as I saw them go, leaving me alone in there once more, I struggled to my feet, weak as I was. "I want to tip them for their trouble," I explained, warding her off. I reeled out into the hall after them. "Wait," I panted. "I don't want to go back to sleep again, if it means having any more dreams like that. For God's sake, do as I tell you. Keep ringing this phone at thirty-second intervals for the rest of the night—until it gets light again."

When I went in again, I looked down at the pillow. There was a single, vivid, red drop of blood there, near where my head had rested. How strange, I thought bewilderedly, for a dream to leave actual, visible traces behind.

All night long, every half-minute, the warning peal of the phone sounded in the room. Dawn found me exhausted—but alive.

July twenty-fifth . . . We have been back in the city a month now, and I am running out of the unguent that crackpot Dr. Lane gave me. However, it seems to have done the trick, immunized me. There have been no more of those oversize mosquitoes attacking me. That, of course, may simply be because there are none here in town; maybe I'm giving the doctor's cure-all more credit than it deserves.

However, I now have troubles of another sort. I have reason to believe Faustine has tired of me, doesn't love me any more. She has a lover that she slips out to see at night, when I am asleep, dog-tired from working on my bridge-building job all day long. How long it has been going on, I don't know. It may have just begun.

Last night I happened to wake up. It was the full of the moon again, and its strong light peering in at me may have been what roused me. I had that strange feeling of being

alone in the room, and couldn't shake it off, although at
first I felt sure it was unwarranted. The radium dial of my
watch marked four-thirty. I reached out for the light switch,
and the moment I had cut it on, I found out that I was
right. Faustine was missing. I jumped up and looked for
her, even called her. She wasn't anywhere in the apartment. The front door, I noticed, had been left slightly ajar,
as though to enable her to return without being detected. I
looked into the closet in which she kept her things; her
black evening-gown with the shoulder-draperies was missing; she had donned it for her rendezvous.

I put out the lights again and sat there waiting for
her to return, heartbroken as any young husband would
be at such a deception. Just before the first streak of dawn
paled the sky, there was a soft rustle at the door, and
she had come back. She came in like a wraith, seemed not
to see me as I raised my head accusingly and looked at
her. She was staggering, reeling like a drunken thing.
Yet she didn't smell of alcohol. She wove her way around
me to her own bed, toppled blindly into it, and lay there
torpid, dead to the world. She had put on too much
lipstick; her parted lips were caked with the stuff, there
was even a thread of it down her chin. The first, silver
thread of daylight cleaved the eastern horizon at that
instant.

I leaned over her, anger getting the better of my dejec-
tion. I seized her by the shoulders and shook her until I
was almost in danger of dislocating her neck. "Look at
me!" I gritted in her ear. "Answer me! Where have you
been? Who is he?"

Her eyes never opened, she was as inert as though she
was dead. Unable to rouse her, I finally let her fall back
again on the pillow, and she lay there like a log. A long,
black log.

"She doesn't know I know," I said to myself bitterly.
"Tomorrow night I'll catch her!"

July twenty-sixth: This morning I came across this item in the paper: "Edward Gray, a Princeton student who was spending the week-end at home with his family, was found in a dying condition in his room this morning, suffering from loss of blood. At the hospital, to which he was taken in a state of collapse, transfusions were resorted to, but very little hope was held out for his recovery. Neither he nor the members of his family were able to furnish any clue as to what had caused his condition."

Just a few lines that had nothing to do with me, but I couldn't help noting the strange similarity the case bore to what had happened to me at the seashore-resort. I could feel my face grow taut and pensive as I pored over the thing, but I couldn't make anything out of it. I shrugged it off finally; the other problem was weighing too heavily on my mind.

I watched her closely tonight, without letting her know I was doing it. She was restless, fidgetty, kept going to the window constantly to peer out at the moon, as though it held some strange attraction for her. Toward midnight, I chose a moment when her back was turned to slip under the bedcoverings fully dressed except for my coat and shoes. She turned to look at me once or twice, but didn't leave the window. I made my breathing long and audible as though I were fast asleep, watched her through my lashes.

After an hour's motionless vigil, she suddenly came to life, swept her arms high up over her head and down a few times, turned and glided across the room like a shadow, and was gone—again leaving the outer door ajar behind her.

But this time I was ready. I jumped up, thrust my feet into a pair of soft-soled tennis-shoes I had taken the precaution of hiding under the bed, shrugged on my coat, and went after her, treading as soundlessly as she.

We live in a building without either a doorman or an

elevator-operator; a rarity in a big city, but that had been her preference, I now remembered. Had she already planned these nocturnal sorties then?

She was still in sight when I came out after her, walking rapidly along at the lower end of the street, black against the moonlit buildings. She rounded the corner and disappeared momentarily, and I hurried down to it to avoid losing her. I kept after her, neither increasing the distance between us nor shortening it, taking cover in doorways as much as possible in case she should look back and sight me, but she seemed oblivious of anything but whatever purpose it was that had brought her out at this ungodly hour. Once we passed a policeman, on a late round of duty, and he looked at her curiously as she glided by, evidently taking her for some fashionable woman who had strayed away from a party for a breath of air. But when I came into sight, obviously stalking her, he stopped me. "What're you up to?" he asked gruffly.

"That's my wife," I explained. "She's walking in her sleep, and I'm keeping after her to see that no harm comes to her."

"I thought she looked kind of half-off," he admitted. "Want me to help you take her back where she belongs?" he offered.

"No," I said hastily. "The shock's very bad for her if she's awakened suddenly. Best way is to let her walk it off, till she turns back on her own accord." I went on after her before he had time to make up his mind whether to believe me or not. He just stood there looking after us, puzzled.

I couldn't understand why, if her destination was this far from where we lived, she hadn't ridden to it, instead of going on foot, especially at such an hour. It never occurred to me that she mightn't have a destination, was simply going along looking for one.

We had left our own neighborhood of well-to-do

apartment-buildings far behind by now, were in a zone of old-fashioned private houses, easier to get into and slumbering in false security. Midway down a quiet street a single light shining from a basement-window attracted her; I saw her change her course abruptly and go down toward it. I peered around the corner building-line after her, keeping well back out of sight.

I saw her stand outside the lighted square looking in for a moment or two. Then she stepped down into the areaway before it and the shadows of the high stoop to one side of it hid her. I hurriedly closed in on her, on noiseless, furtive feet. I was just in time to hear the basement-grating under the stoop squeak, as it opened and she went in. It had either been left ajar, or she had forced the lock in some way with a hairpin, for I had heard no key clash.

I peered through the window, which was only protected by net curtains. A young man lay sleeping over in the corner on a daybed, a magazine still clutched in his inert hand. He had evidently fallen asleep while reading it; that explained the room-light left burning. Right as I watched, I saw the door-key, which had been on the inside of the room-door, fall out to the floor. A moment later the door opened cautiously, and Faustine stood there in the opening, replacing something in her sleek, midnight-black hair. She glowered at him for a second, then reached out to the light-switch beside her and plunged the room into darkness. Her two eyes remained, over there by the door; twin flecks of spectral green. Then they began to move forward across the room, and sink lower toward the floor.

This was no rendezvous. It might be one of death, but not of love. She had forced her way into a stange house. I remembered that item I had read in the paper only this morning, and I remembered what had happened to me at the resort-hotel. Was there some horrible, unguessable connection between her and those events after all? My mind reeled with the impact of the idea, but this was no time for conjecture, this was a time for action. There was a life endangered in there, and I was the only one who could save it.

I moved noiselessly down into the area, flattened myself out to one side of the window. I wrapped a handkerchief around my clenched fist, swung it like a battering-ram at the pane. There was an explosive crash and the window shattered into fragments. I held myself motionless against the wall as the basement-grate opened and she whisked by me, like a swirl of black smoke.

A moment later the room-light had gone on again. I peered in. He was sitting dazedly up in bed, touching his neck and then looking at his fingertips. I suppose he thought a piece of flying glass had done it. Anyhow, he was saved.

I turned away and set out after her again, to see what she would do next. For all I knew, she might still make another attempt somewhere else. If I abandoned the chase now, death might still strike some unsuspecting sleeper. Faustine might go on and on.

She had flitted as far as the next corner. But this time, perhaps alarmed by the interruption or guessing what it was, she threw up her arm and signalled a taxi. She got in and it whisked her away. Moments later I was at the same corner, looking frantically this way and that. Luck was with me. A second machine appeared, cruising for fares. I dove into it, told the driver: "See that hack two blocks up, straight ahead of us? Catch it!"

He put on a burst of speed that should have overhauled our quarry. But either she or her driver must have noticed they were being followed. They turned down a side-street, trying to lose us. Then they whisked up Third, under the El pillars. Their red tail-light slowly but surely started to pull away from us. "Can't you do better than that?" I urged frantically. "They're giving us the gate."

"Maybe he don't care what happens to him under these

El pillars, but I do, I got a wife and kids!" was the stubborn answer.

Suddenly something happened. We could hear the crash all the way down where we were, blocks behind them. The red tail ahead blacked out. A black car-shape up there swerved crazily broadside to the avenue, threatened to turn over, came to a stop with its front axles up on the sidewalk.

I jumped out a block below, ran the rest of the way to the scene. The driver of the wrecked machine had gotten out, was sitting dizzily on the curb. He was bleeding from a cut on his forehead but otherwise seemed miraculously unhurt. A cop was running down from one direction, an ambulance-siren already sounding in the distance from another. I threw open the shattered rear door, looked in. The cab was empty. I shook him by the shoulder. "Where is she? What happened to her?"

He was half-senseless with terror, hung onto my arm with both hands. "I *saw* someone get in, I *heard* her tell me to drive fast—but when I looked in the rear-sight mirror just now, to ask her if she didn't think we better slow up a little, it didn't show no reflection. That's what did it! A minute later I piled into one of the El posts—"

I left the scene hurriedly, to avoid a lot of awkward questions, that would have only ended up in my being sent to the psychopathic ward at Bellevue for observation.

I staggered the rest of the way home on foot, groaning aloud from time to time. A hideous realization was slowly dawning on me, and it was almost more than my sanity could bear.

The first pallor of dawn was glimmering in the eastern sky as I tottered back into the apartment, closed the door after me. She was there ahead of me, rigid on the bed, so beautiful, so vile. There was a smile on her face that seemed to mock me. That broke the last thread of my self-control. I knew then that I was going to kill her.

"Go back to hell," I sobbed, "where you came from!"

I found her lovely ivory throat with my ten fingers, circled it, pressed down upon her windpipe. I bent my knee and raised it to her chest, to give me the leverage for murder. I bore down, *crushed;* nothing could have breathed through a grip like that, anything living would have smothered. *Anything living.*

She didn't struggle, made no move at all. And yet when at last, exhausted myself, I desisted, fell back limp to the floor beside the bed, her eyes wavered open for a moment, she turned that mocking, maddening smile on me, then slept more deeply than ever.

My terrified sobbing on the floor died away at last, and consciousness left me, from sheer physical prostration. Sleep is so merciful to humankind.

July twenty-seventh: This is the last entry of a tormented life, nearing its end. Before the ink dries on this diary page, I shall be dead. The blood is flowing faster, darker, all the time. I spared the right wrist, until I've finished writing this; someone may read it, but no one will believe or understand. I'm holding the left wrist, already gashed, out away from me, so the red-black drops that were Dick Manning won't fall on the page. It doesn't hurt much. Maybe that's a sign it's nearly over; I'd better hurry—

She stirred at evening, as the darkness returned. I, too, was awake, but I remained there where I had fallen after my attempt at killing her, on the floor beside the bed. I couldn't make the effort to get up and move about, knowing what I knew now. The will to live was dying out in me, beaten, battered by sheer weight of horror.

She smoothed her hair, draped a gauzy black scarf about her head, adorning herself the way human women do. Then she came and bent low above me. "Tonight," she whispered, "we go out together, as husband and wife should. The time has come to make you—as I am. Is that not what marriage really is—perfect affinity?''

She took my hand and tugged, gently but insistently, until I had gotten to my feet. "Come," she said, "the moon is up. This shall be our true honeymoon, not those night-clubs of the living.''

Though her hand, on mine, had no pull to it, seemed but to guide me, I felt myself being irresistibly drawn after her by it, as though it were some sort of a suction-pump cupped to me. Her glowing eyes, on mine, seemed to rob me of all volition, hold me under the same inescapable spell as that night I had first met her.

I tried, instinctively, to hold onto the door-frame, to keep from being drawn after her like a steel-filing after a magnet. It was useless; she reached down with her other hand and gently, gently but insistently, detached my fingers one by one. "Why fight against it?" she purred. "It must be, sooner or later. Let it be now then. You will not find it so abhorrent—once you know. You will say, Faustine, how blind I was!''

The doorway was slipping past me like water, I could feel myself going out into the night after her, like a sleepwalker, like someone in a trance.

This time she went northward, to the quiet well-to-do residential district called Lenox Hill. She stopped at last before a neat brick house with a lantern glowing over its entrance. It had been divided into small apartments. "Reach up, turn out that light," she cautioned. Then as I hesitated, she did it for me, and we were plunged into blackness. "This time there shall be one for each of us," she promised. "I selected this place ahead of time for your initiation.''

I didn't answer. More dangerous than her strange power over me was a new symptom I was just beginning to discover in myself. A strange unholy curiosity was burning in me. What would it be like? What was its fascination? Would it hurt to try it just once?

"We can get in through a key that you have," she whispered. "You have forgotten it, but I remember." I didn't understand what she meant, but I felt her fingers slip into my vest-pocket and out again, and a moment later the door opened. The hall within was dimly lit. She quickly reached up and turned out that light, too, before I could recognize it—if indeed I had ever been here before. She took the same key to an inner apartment-door, there on the ground-floor to the right. Within all was blackness, and the even breathing of people asleep.

"I will lead you so that you make no noise," she breathed, "for you are yet a neophyte."

Every God-given instinct in me recoiled at the thought of going in there, but yet the glow of her hypnotic eyes, the subtle pressure of her hand on mine, overcame them, drew me on. I felt myself follow her across a small foyer and into a darkened bedroom. She guided my steps toward the blurred outline of a bed, helping me to avoid knocking into an invisible chair or the edge of a table.

We stopped at last. "The other one is inside," she whispered close to my ear. Suddenly her mentor's hand had led mine downward, I felt it resting upon the soft warm contours of a throat. Other flesh, that was not hers.

"Just a stolen kiss," she breathed insinuatingly. "What harm is there in a kiss?"

I felt myself bending over the unknown sleeper. The soft fanning of Faustine's draperies was in the air about the two of us. My lips came diffidently, cautiously to rest upon that velvet-soft throat. The unhallowed curiosity that had been simmering in me all the while suddenly burst into wolfish rapacity, there was a flash of red devil-fire in my brain. The kiss lengthened, grew fiercer, more unreasoning. The air above swirled and eddied with the soothing beat of Faustine's garment. The sleeper stirred just once, then sighed and fell into an ever deeper sleep. Crueler, sharper grew the kiss, minute by minute.

"You have begun," whispered Faustine commendingly, and the two green glints that were her eyes receded across the room into the adjoining one. A door closed soundlessly after her.

The spell, and thrall she held me in, weakened as she left me. Reason tried to reassert itself. I struggled desperately to throw off the horrible hypnosis that gripped me, but couldn't succeed unaided, was held there as in a vise. I couldn't take my lips away, break that demon-kiss. "Pain," I thought despairingly. "Pain will do it." With one hand I reached frantically into my own pocket, felt a cigarette-lighter, brought it out. I flicked it on and a tiny flame rose from the wick. I thrust the palm of my other hand flat down above it. A white-hot stab shot through my hand, shattered the rigor that gripped me. My lips parted, and I toppled back, dropped the lighter to the floor and it went out. Pain had saved me from myself—or whatever baleful influence it was had possession of me.

But that wasn't enough. Faustine was still in the house. I picked myself up, bent down above the sleeper again, but this time only to make doubly sure that she would be saved. "Wake up!" I whispered close to her ear. "For God's sake, wake up, while you still have time!" Then as she stirred uneasily and a sudden tenseness came over her that told me her eyes had opened, I retreated across the room to the door by which I had entered. I slipped out through it, eased it cautiously closed after me, just as her hand reached out to a lamp beside the bed and turned it on. The room was suddenly flooded with light.

In that split second, just as the door was closing after me, I glimpsed her through the crack of it, although she couldn't see me. I saw her clearly: saw the horror on her face as she looked down at her own shoulder, at the ribbon of red that lay on it beside the blue-satin ribbon of her gown. It was Sherry, the girl I had once been about to marry, the girl I had once loved more than anyone in the world! I pressed my hands tightly over my ears as I fled out of the building into the street, but the scream of terror that burst from her lips pierced through them just the same.

I must have roamed dementedly about for a time in the streets. When I at last got back to my own place, Faustine was again there ahead of me, coiled torpid on the bed like a loathsome boa-constrictor. She was already in the never-never land where ghouls like her belonged. I covered her face with one of the pillows, pressed down upon it with the weight of my whole body, held it there until she should have been dead ten times over. Yet when I removed the pillow to look, the black of strangulation was missing from her face. She was still in that state of suspended animation that defied me, a taunting smile visible about her lips.

I had a gun in my valise, from years before when I'd been on an engineering job in the jungles of Ecuador. I got it out, looked it over. It was still in good working order, although it only had one bullet left in it. That one would be enough. She wasn't going to escape me! I pressed the muzzle to her smooth white forehead, mid-center. "Die, damn you!" I growled, and pulled the trigger back. It exploded with a crash. A film of smoke hid her face from me for a minute. When it had cleared again, I looked.

There was no bullet-hole in her skull!

A black powder-smudge marked the point of contact. The gun dropped to the floor with a thud. That ineradicable smile still glimmered up at me, as if to say: "You see? You can't." I rubbed my finger over the black; the skin was unbroken underneath. A blank cartridge, that must have been it. I raised her head; there was a rent in the sheet under it. I probed through it with two fingers. I could feel the bullet lying imbedded down in the stuffing of the mattress.

My reason toppled into that state of flux that precedes self-destruction. That was the only thing left to do now.

That was the only way left to escape from her now. I smiled grimly. That was better than becoming as this thing the night had dropped into my lap.

I went into the bathroom, looking for a way. I saw one of the blades I used to shave with lying discarded on the shelf. I used the edge of a towel to grip it with, shot back my cuff, held out my wrist pulse-up. It didn't take a moment. It didn't hurt much, just one swift slice.

I ran a little warm water over the blade to clean it (a funny thing to do at such a time!). Then I put it back on the shelf. I spared the right wrist, to be able to write one last entry in this diary. This is it. My eyes are blurring from loss of blood and there's a humming in my ears. The lights must have gone out, I can't see the page any more. . . . My name was Dick Man. . . . .

Deposition of Miss Sherry Wayne, accused of the murder of one Faustine Manning, on the morning of June 28th, 1939.*

Two weeks after their marriage I received a book from a man I did not know, a Dr. Lane living near Atlantic City, New Jersey. There was no message with it to show why it had been sent, simply his name and address on the outside of the wrapping. It was a book of medieval lore and superstition; I couldn't imagine why a stranger should send such a thing to me, nor what it had to do with me. When I attempted to communicate with this person to find out why he had done so, he evaded me, as though not wishing to give his reasons. I noticed that certain passages had been underscored, as though meant for me to read to the exclusion of the rest. " . . . They cannot be killed save with a stake driven through the heart as they lie at rest from dawn to dusk within their coffins. The true cross must be held

*Charges were later dismissed.

out toward them at arm's length, and the prayer for the dead repeated: only thus can their souls find release . . .''

Another was, ''. . . They stir only at night, but even then leave no trace upon a glass or mirror that mayhap they shall pass before . . .''

I remembered that woman that had taken Dick away from me. My instincts had told me even that night that she was not a rival in the ordinary sense. The damp mouldy air that had come into the room as she entered; the greenish pallor of her skin, that I had thought was some new shade of face-powder. Above all, the polished metal elevator-panel only giving back his reflection as the two of them stood before it.

This Dr. Lane was evidently trying to tell me something indirectly, by sending me this book. What it was, I could guess. But what was I to do? This was 1939. I couldn't go out and drive a stake through the heart of another woman, no matter how much happiness she had robbed me of. That was murder. I hid the book and didn't tell anyone about it, not even my brother. I was afraid they would think me insane for harboring such thoughts, might even have me sent away.

I couldn't forget Dick; I loved him, you see. But if only he was happy with her, if she would make him a better wife than I would have, then I was content to have it so. I locked my heartbreak up within myself and said not a word. My brother noticed that I was suffering, and knew the reason, but said not a word against him, only, ''It wasn't like him, I can't understand it.''

I could, but I dared not tell him.

Last night, the 27th, the two of us retired at our usual hour. I had a dream that Dick came into the room with me; I couldn't see him in the dark, but I knew in my dream that he was near, and was happy. He seemed to bend over me and kiss me. Then the dream was slowly blotted out and I sank into a deeper sleep than before. Suddenly a voice in my ear roused me. It seemed to whisper warningly, "Wake up! Wake up while you still have time!"

I opened my eyes, turned on the light, and as I did so the door to my room seemed just to have finished closing. To my horror there was a thin trickle of blood on my shoulder. I screamed in mortal terror. I jumped up, threw on something, and ran into the next room to seek my brother's protection.

I couldn't rouse him. There were tiny gashes on his throat, and the same tell-tale trickle of blood as on my own shoulder. I shook him, sponged his face with water, pleaded with him to speak to me. His eyes never opened again from first to last. He murmured pitifully, "Sherry, is that you? I had the strangest dream, and I'm so tired—" And then he put his head against me and he died. He was only nineteen, and all I had left.

The ambulance I'd called in came in a moment or two, but they told me it was too late. Loss of blood, they said. They took him away to the morgue.

They left me alone at my own request. I must have seemed strangely calm to them. I was thinking. I went back into my own room, and it was then I saw the cigarette-lighter lying on the floor beside my bed. It had a familiar look. My brother was on the track-team at college, he didn't smoke. I held it in my hand and saw engraved on it "D. M. from S. W." It was the one I'd given Dick the Christmas before.

I took down the book and I read the marked passages in it once more. Then I got dressed, with icy calm. I opened an old trinket-box that had belonged to my mother, and found a golden cross she had worn around her neck. I looked in the closet and saw an old hockey-stick that had belonged to my brother when he was a boy. I tilted it against something and stamped on it with my foot. The curved end split off and left a sharp point. I took that with me, too.

I didn't know where he—they—lived, but a glance in the directory showed me that. It was a few minutes before dawn when I set out. Not to kill, but to set the suspended laws of mortality into effect years, maybe centuries, after they should have operated. And to save the man I loved, if there was still time.

I knocked on the door when I got there, but only silence answered, and somehow I knew I was already too late for the second half of my purpose. But that only fortified me in my resolve to carry out the first half.

There was a window at the back of the hall, with a fire-escape outside it. I got out on that, and found that it reached one of the windows of their apartment. I forced it up and climbed in through there. The lights were on. He had written a last entry in his diary. He was slumped in the chair, dead, his wrist slashed.

I had two to avenge now, not just one.

She was on the bed, in that state of inanimation the book had told of. I moved relentlessly toward her. I placed the pointed stick upright upon her breast, steadying it with my hand. I looked around, and there was a gun lying upon the floor. I used the flat of that for a mallet. I drove it in until I heard it strike the metal of the bedsprings under her.

Her eyes had flown open. The most horrid shriek ever heard by human ears burst from her. A howl of rage and a death-rattle in one. Nothing earthly could have screamed like that. I was holding out the cross toward her now, saying the prayers for the dead. "Ashes to ashes, dust to dust—"

Her eyelids fluttered closed, she writhed once, then lay still. She seemed to shrink as I looked. Her skin, smooth and white a moment ago, became yellowed, shrivelled. Her lips fell back from her gums. A horrid stench of decay, as from a charnel-house, rose, nearly overcoming me. Some of her sleek black hair loosened, as though it had come out at the roots, and I could see little things moving in the hollows that had been her eyes. It was unspeakably ghastly.

I hadn't killed her; she must have been dead a century or more. The first rays of the sun peered in and glinted from the golden cross I laid upon her brow. I tottered across the room to where the phone was, and called you gentlemen, and waited here for you to come. You know the rest. And now Doctor Lane, after months of research into old records, has forwarded to you an old miniature, unmistakably of this same woman, and documentary proof showing that she was born in Williamsburg, Virginia, in 1759, and died—*the first time*—in 1790.

GRAVES FOR THE LIVING

"THERE HE IS," the grave-keeper whispered, parting the hedge so the two detectives could peer through. "That's the third one he's gone at since I phoned in to you fellows. I was afraid if I tried to jump him single-handed he'd get away from me before you got out here. He's got a gun, see it lying there next to the grave?"

His feeling of inadequacy was understandable; he was not only elderly and scrawny, but trembling all over with nervousness. One of the plainclothesmen beside him un-limbered his gun, thumbed the guard off, held it half-poised for action. The one on the other side of him carefully maneuvered a manacle from his waistband so that it wouldn't clash.

They exchanged a look across the keeper's crouched, quaking back, each to see if the other was ready for the spring. Both nodded imperceptibly. They motioned the frightened cemetery-watchman down out of the way. They reared suddenly, dashed through the opening in the hedge simultaneously, with a great crackling and hissing of leaves.

The figure knee-deep in the grave stopped clawing and burrowing, snaked out an arm toward the revolver lying along its lip. One of the detectives' huge size 12's came down flat on it, pinning it down. "Hold it," he said, and his own gun was inches away from the ghoul's face. A flashlight balanced on a little mound of freshly-excavated soil like a golf-tee threw a thin, ghostly light on the scene. Off to the left one of the other graves was disturbed, wavy with irregular furrows of earth instead of planed flat.

The manacle clashed around the prisoner's earth-clotted wrist, then the detective's. They hauled him up out of the shallow trough he had burrowed almost at full arm-length, like a piece of carrion.

"I though you'd come," he said. "Where'd you put her? Where is she?"

They didn't answer, for one thing because they didn't understand. They weren't supposed to understand the gibberings of a maniac. They didn't ask him any questions, either. They seemed to feel that wasn't part of their job in this case. They'd come out to get him, they'd got him, and they were bringing him in—that was all they'd been sent to do.

One of them stooped for the gun, put it in his pocket; he picked up the torch too, clicked it off. The tableau suddenly went blue-black. They made their way out of the burial-ground with him, the watchman trailing behind them.

Outside the gate a prowl-car was standing waiting; they jammed him into it between them, told the watchman to appear at Headquarters in the morning without fail, shrieked off with him.

He only said one thing more, on the way. "You didn't have to hijack a patrolcar to impress me, I know better than to take you for detectives." They careened through the midnight city streets stonyfaced, one on each side of him, as though they hadn't heard him. "Fiends," he sobbed bitterly. "How can the Lord put things like you into human shape?"

He seemed vastly surprised at sight of the Headquarters building, with its green-globed entrance. When they stood him before a desk, with a uniformed lieutenant at it, his consternation was noticeable. He seemed unable to believe his eyes. Then when they led him into a back room, and a captain of detectives came in to question him, there could be no mistaking the fact that he was stunned. "You—you really are!" he breathed.

"What did you think we were?" one of the detectives wanted to know caustically. "CCC boys?"

He looked about uncomprehendingly. "I thought you were—*them*."

The captain got down to business. "What were you after?" he said tersely.

"Her." He amended it, "My girl, my girl I was going to marry."

The captain sighed impatiently. "You expected to find her in the cemetery?"

"Oh, I know!" the man before him broke out bitterly. "I know, I'm insane, that's what you'll say! I came to you people for help, of my own accord, before it happened— and that's what you thought then, too. I spoke to Mercer, at the Poplar Street Station, only yesterday morning. He told me to go home and not worry." His laughter was horrid, harsh, deranged.

"Quit it, shut up!" The captain drew back uncontrollably, even with the width of his desk between them. He took up the thread of his questioning again. "You were arrested just now in the Cedars of Lebanon Cemetery, in the act of disturbing the graves. The watchman at the Sacred Heart Cemetery also phoned us, earlier tonight, that he had found some of the resting-places in there molested, when he made his rounds. Did you do that too?"

The man nodded vigorously, unashamed. "Yes! And I've also been in two others, since sundown, Cypress Hills, and a private graveyard out beyond the city limits toward Ellendale."

The captain shivered involuntarily. The two detectives in the background paled a little, exchanged a look. The captain let out his accumulated breath slowly.

"You need a doctor, young fellow," he sighed.

"No, I don't need a doctor!" The prisoner's voice rose to a scream. "I need help! If you'll only listen to me, believe me!"

"I'll listen to you," the captain said, without committing himself on the other two pleas. "I think I understand how it is. Engaged to her, you say. Very much in love with her, of course. The shock of losing her—too much for you; temporarily unbalanced your mind. Judging by your clothes—what I can see of them under that accumulation of mold and caked earth, and the fact that you left a car parked near the main entrance of Cedars of Lebanon—robbery wasn't your motive. My men here tell me you were carrying seven-hundred-odd dollars when they caught up with you. Crazed by grief, didn't know what you were doing, so you set out on your own to try and find her, is that it?"

The man acted tormented, distracted. "Don't tell me things I know already!" he pleaded hoarsely.

"But how is it," the captain went on equably, "you didn't know where she was buried in the first place?"

"Because it was done without a permit—secretly!"

"If you can prove that—!" The captain sat up a little straighter. This was getting back on his own ground again. "When was she buried, any idea?"

"Some time after sundown this evening—that's over six hours ago now! And all this time we're standing here—"

"When'd she die?"

The man clenched his fists, raised them agonizedly above his head. "*She—didn't—die!* Don't you understand what I'm trying to tell you! She's lying somewhere, under the ground, in this very city, at this very minute—still breathing!"

There was a choking stillness as though the room had suddenly been crammed full of cotton-batting. It was a little hard to breathe in there; the three police-officials seemed to find it so. You could hear the effort they put into it.

The captain said, brushing his hand slowly across his mouth to clear it of some unseen impediment, "Hold him up." Then he said to the man they were supporting between them: "I'm listening."

To understand about me, you must go back fifteen years, to 1922, to when I was ten years old. And even then, perhaps you'll wonder why a thing like that, horrible as it was, should poison my whole life. . . .

My father was a war veteran. He had been badly shell-shocked in the Argonne, and for a long time in the base hospital behind the lines they thought they weren't going to be able to pull him through.

But they did, and he was finally sent home to us, my mother and me. I knew he wasn't well, and that I mustn't be too noisy around him, that was all. The others, my mother and the doctors, knew that his nerve-centers had been shattered irreparably; but that slow paralysis was creeping on him, they didn't dream. There were no signs of it, no warning. Then suddenly, in a flash, it struck. The nerve-centers ceased to function all over his body. "Death," they called it, in ghastly error.

I wasn't frightened of death—yet. If it had only been that, it would have been all right; a month later I would have been over it. But as it was. . . .

His government pension had been all we'd had to live on since he'd come back. It had been out of the question for him to work, after what that howitzer-shell exploding a few yards away had done to him. Mother hadn't been able to work either; there wouldn't have been anyone to look after him all day. So there was no money to speak of.

Mother had to take any undertaker she could get, was glad to get anybody at all for the pittance that was all she could afford. The fly-by-night swindler that she finally

secured, turned up his nose at first at the sum offered, she
had to plead with him to take charge of the body. Meanwhile the overworked medical examiner had made a hasty,
routine examination, given the cause as a blood-lot on the
brain due to his injuries, and made out the death-certificate
in proper order.

But he was never prepared for burial in the proper way.
He couldn't have been or it wouldn't have happened.
Those ghoulish undertakers must have put him aside while
they attended to other, more remunerative cases, until they
discovered there was no time left to do what they were
supposed to. And, cold-bloodedly figuring no one would
ever know the difference anyway, simply contented themselves with hastily composing his posture, putting on his
best suit, and perhaps giving his face a hurried, last-minute
shave. Then they put him in the coffin, untouched, just as
he was.

We would never have known, perhaps, but mother was
unable to meet even the first monthly payment on the plot,
and the cemetery officials heartlessly gave orders to disin-
ter the coffin and remove it elsewhere. Whether something
about it excited their suspicions, or it was of such flimsy
construction that it accidentally broke open when they
tried to remove it, I don't know. At any rate, they made a
hideous discovery, and my mother was hastily summoned
to come out there. Word was also sent to the police.

Thinking it still had to do with the money due them, she
frantically borrowed it from a loan-shark, one of the early
forerunners of that racket, and in an evil hour allowed me
to go with her out there to the cemetery-grounds.

We found the opened coffin above ground, lying in full
view, with a number of police-officials grouped around it.
They drew her aside and began to question her, out of
earshot. But I didn't need to overhear, I had the evidence
of my own eyes there before me.

The eyes were open and staring; not just blankly as they

had been the first time, but dilated with horror, stretched to their uttermost width. Eyes that had tried vainly to pierce the stygian darkness that he found about him. His arms, no longer flat at his sides, were curved clawlike up over his head, nails almost torn off with futile tearing and scratching at the wood that hemmed him in. There were dried brown spots all about the white quilting that lined the lower half of the coffin, that had been blood-spots flung about from his flailing, gashed fingertips. Splinters of wood from the underside of the lid clung to each of them like porcupine-quills. And on the inside of the lid were even more tell-tale signs. A criss-cross of gashes, some of them almost shallow troughs, against which his bleeding nails had worn themselves off. But it had held fast, had only split now, when it was being taken up, weeks later.

The voice of one of the police-officials penetrated my numbed senses, seeming to come from far away. "This man—your husband—" he was saying to my mother— "was buried alive, and slowly suffocated to death—the way you see him—in his coffin. Will you tell us, if you can—"

But she dropped at their feet in a dead faint without uttering a sound. Her agony was short, merciful. I, who was to be the far greater sufferer of the two, stood there frozen, stunned, without a whimper, without even crying. I must have seemed to them too stupid or too young to fully understand the implications of what we were looking at. If they thought so, it was the greatest mistake of their lives.

I accompanied them, and my mother, back to the house without a word. They looked at me curiously once or twice, and I overheard one of them say in a low voice: "He didn't get it. Good thing, too. Enough to frighten the growth out of a kid that age."

I didn't get it! I was frozen all over, they didn't understand that; in a straight-jacket of icy horror that was crushing the shape out of me.

Mother recovered consciousness presently and—for just a little while, before the long twilight closed in on her—her reason, sanity. They checked with the coroner, the death-certificate was sent for and examined, they decided that neither she nor he was to blame in any way. She gave them the name of the undertaker who had been in charge of the burial preparations, and word was sent out to arrest him and his assistants.

Fate was kind to her, her ordeal was made short. That same night she went hopelessly, incurably out of her mind, and within the week had been committed to an institution. Nature had found the simplest way out for her.

I didn't get off so easily. There was a brief preliminary stage, more or less to be expected, of childish terror, nightmares, fear of the dark, but that soon wore itself out. Then for a year or two I seemed actually to have gotten over the awful thing; at least, it faded a little, I didn't think of it incessantly night and day. But the subconscious doesn't, couldn't, forget a thing like that. Only another, second shock of equal severity and having to do with the same thing, would heal it. Fighting fire with fire, so to speak.

It came back in my middle teens, and from then on never again left me, grew steadily worse if anything as time went on. It was not a fear of death, you must understand; it was a fear of *not* dying and of being buried for dead. In other words, of the same thing happening to me some day that happened to him. It was stronger than just a fear, it grew to be an obsession, a phobia. It happened to me over and over again in my dreams, and I woke up shivering, sweating at the thought. Burial alive! The most horrible death imaginable became easy, preferable, compared to that.

Attracted by the very thing I dreaded, I frequently visited cemeteries, wandered among the headstones, reading the inscriptions, shuddering to myself each time: "But was he—or she—really dead? How often has this thing happened before?''

Sometimes I would unexpectedly come upon burial services being conducted in this or that corner of the grounds. Cringing, yet drawing involuntarily nearer to watch and listen, that unforgotten scene at my father's grave would flash before my mind in all its pristine vividness and horror, and I would turn and run as though I felt myself in danger then and there of being drawn alive into that waiting grave I had just seen.

But one day, instead of running away, it had an opposite effect on me. I was irresistibly drawn forward to create a scene, a scandal, in their solemn midst. Or at least an unwelcome interruption.

The coffin, covered with flowers, was just about to be lowered; the mourners were standing reverently about. Almost without realizing what I was doing, I jostled my way through them until I stood on the very lip of the trench, cried out warningly: ''Wait! Make sure, for God's sake, make sure he's dead!''

There was a stunned silence, they all drew back in fright, stared at me incredulously. The reading of the service stopped short, the officiating clergyman stood there book in hand blinking at me through his spectacles. Even the lowering of the coffin had been arrested, it swayed there on an uneven keel, partly in and partly out. Some of the flowers slipped off the top of it and fell in.

Realizing belatedly what a holy show I had made of myself, I turned and stumbled away as abruptly as I had come. No one made a move to detain me. Out of sight of them, I sat down on a stone bench behind a laurel hedge, and tormentedly held my head in my hands. Was I going crazy or what, to do such a thing?

About half an hour went by. I heard the sound of motors starting up one after the other on the driveway outside the grounds, and thought they had all gone away. A minute later there was a light step on the gravel path before me, and I looked up to meet the curious gaze of a young girl. She wore black, but there was something radiantly alive about her that looked strangely out of place in those surroundings. She was beautiful; I could read compassion in her forthright blue eyes. She had evidently been present at the services I had so outrageously interrupted, and had purposely stayed behind to talk to me.

"Do you mind if I sit here?" she murmured. I suddenly found myself wanting to talk to her. I felt strangely drawn to her. Youth is youth, even if its first meeting-place is a cemetery, and outside of this one phobia of mine, I was no different from any young fellow my age.

"Who was that?" I asked abruptly.

"A distant relative of mine," she said. "Why did you do it?" she added. "I could tell you weren't drunk or anything. I felt you must have a reason, so I asked them not to complain to the guards."

"It happened once to my father," I told her. "I've never quite gotten over it."

"I can see that," she said with quiet understanding. "But you shouldn't dwell on it. It's not natural at our age. Take me for instance. I had every respect for this relative we lost. I'm anything but a hard-hearted person. But it was all they could do to get me to come here today. They had to bribe me by telling me how well I looked in black." She smiled shyly, "I'm glad I did come, though."

"I am too," I said, and I meant it.

"My name is Joan Blaine," she told me as we walked toward the entrance. The sunlight fell across her face and seemed to light it, as we left the city of the dead and came out into the city of the living.

"I'm Bud Ingram," I told her.

"You're too nice a guy to be hanging around graveyards, Bud," she told me. "I'll have to take you in hand, try to get rid of this morbid streak in you."

She was as good as her word in the months that followed. Not that she was a bossy, dictatorial sort of girl, but—well, she liked me, just as I liked her, and she wanted to help me. We went to shows and dances together, took long drives in my car with the wind humming in our ears, lolled on the starlit beach while she strummed a guitar and the surf came whispering in—did all the things that make life so worth living, so hard to give up. Death and its long grasping shadows seemed very far away when I was with her; her golden laughter kept them at a distance. But when I was alone, slowly they came creeping back.

I didn't let her know about that. I loved her now, and like a fool I was afraid if I told her it was still with me, she'd give me up as hopeless. I should have known her better. I never again mentioned the subject of my father, or my fears; I let her think she had conquered them. It was my own undoing.

I was driving along a seldom-used road out in the open country late one Sunday afternoon. She hadn't been able to come with me that afternoon, but I was due back at her house for supper, and we were going to the movies afterward. I had taken a detour off the main highway that I thought might be a short-cut, get me there quicker. Then I saw this small, well-cared-for burial-ground to my left as I skimmed along. I braked and sat looking at it, what I could see of it. It was obviously private. A twelve-foot fence of iron palings, gilt-tipped, bordered it. Inside there were clumps of graceful poplars rustling in the breeze, ornamental stone urns, trim white-pebbled paths twisting in and out. Only an occasional, inconspicuous slab showed what it really was.

I drove on again, past the main entrance. It was chained and locked, and there was no sign of either a gatekeeper or a lodge to accommodate one. It evidently was the property of some one family or group of people, I told myself. I put my foot back on the accelerator and went on my way. Joan wouldn't have approved my even slowing down to look at the place, I knew; but I hadn't been able to help myself.

Then sharp eyes betrayed me. Even traveling at the rate I was, I caught sight of a place in the paling where one of the uprights had fallen out of its socket in the lower transverse that held them all; it was leaning over at an angle from the rest, causing a little tent-shaped gap. My good resolutions were all shattered at the sight. I threw in the clutch, got out to look, and before I knew it, had wriggled through and was standing on the inside—where I had no right to be.

"I'll just look around a minute," I said to myself, "then get out again before I get in trouble."

I followed one of the winding paths, and all the old familiar fears came back again as I did so. The sun was rapidly going down and the poplars threw long blue shadows across the ground. I turned aside to look at one of the freshly-erected headstones. There was an utter absence of floral wreaths or offerings, such as are to be found even in the poorest cemeteries, although nearly all the slabs looked fairly recent.

I was about to move on, when something caught my eye close up against the base of the slab. A small curved projection, like a tiny gutter to carry off rainwater. Then just under that, protected by it, so to speak, and almost indiscernible, a round opening, a hole, peering through the carefully-trimmed grass. It was too well-rounded to be an accidental gap or pit in the turf. And it was right where the raised grave met the tombstone. But that curling lip over it! Who had ever heard of a headstone provided with a gutter?

I glanced around to make sure I was unobserved, then squatted down over it, all but treading on the grave itself. I hooked one finger into the orifice and explored it carefully. Something smooth, hard, lined it, like a metal inner-tube. It was *not* a hole in the ground. It was a pipe leading up through the ground.

I had a penknife with me, and I got it out and scraped away the turf around the opening. A half-inch of gleaming, untarnished pipe, either chromium or brass, protruded when I got through. Stranger still, it had a tiny sieve or filter fitted into it, of fine wire-mesh, like a strainer to keep out the dust.

I was growing strangely excited, more excited every minute. This seemed to be a partial solution to what had haunted me for so long. If it was what I thought it was, it could take a little of the edge off the terror of burial—even for me, who dreaded it so.

I snapped my penknife shut, straightened up, moved on to the next marker. It wasn't close by, I had to look a little to find it, in the deepening violet of the twilight. But when I had, there was the same concealed orifice at its base, diminutive rain-shed, strainer, and all.

As I roamed about there in the dusk, I counted ten of them. Some bizarre cult or secret society, I wondered uneasily? For the first time I began to regret butting into the place; formless fears, vague premonitions of peril, that had nothing to do with that other inner fear of mine began to creep over me.

The sun had gone down long ago, and macabre mists were beginning to blur the outlines of the trees and foliage around me. I turned and started to beat my way back toward that place in the fence by which I had gained admittance, and which I had left a considerable distance behind me by now.

As I came abreast of the entrance gates—the real ones and not the gap through which I had come in—I saw the orange flash of a lantern on the outside of them, through the twilight murk. Chains clanged loosely, and the double gates ground inward, with a horrid groaning sound. Instinctively I jumped back behind a massive stone urn on a pedestal, with creepers spilling out of the top of it.

The gates clanged shut again, lessening my chances of getting out that way, which was the nearer of the two. I peered cautiously out around the narrowed stem of the urn, to see who it was.

A typical cemetery-watchman, no different from any of the rest of his kind, was crunching slowly along the nearest path, lantern in hand. Its rays splashed upward, tinged his face, and downward around the ground at his feet, but left the middle of his body in darkness. It created a ghastly effect, that of a lurid head without any body floating along above the ground. I quailed a little.

He passed by close enough for me to touch him, and I shifted tremblingly around to the other side of the urn, keeping it between us. He stopped at the nearest grave, only a short distance away, set his lantern close up against the headstone, and turned up the oil-wick a bit higher. I could see everything he was doing clearly in the increased radiance now. Could see, but couldn't understand at first.

He squatted down on his haunches just as I had—this, fortunately, wasn't the one I had disturbed with my penknife—and I saw him holding something in his hand that at first sight I mistook for a flower, a single flower or bloom, that he was about to plant. It had a long almost invisible stalk and ended in a little puff or cluster of fuzz, like a pussywillow. But then when I saw him insert it into the little orifice at the base of the slab, move it busily around, that gave me the clue to what it really was. It was simply a wirehandled brush, such as housewives use for cleaning the spouts of kettles. He was removing the day's accumulated dust and grit from the little mesh-strainer in the pipe, to keep it from clogging. I saw him take the brush out again, put his face down nearly to the ground, and blow his breath into it to help the process along. I heard the sound that made distinctly—"*Phoo!*" Even as I watched, he got up again, picked up the lantern, and trudged on to the next grave, and repeated the chore.

A chill slowly went down my spine. Why must those orifices be kept unclogged, free of choking dust, like that? Was there something living, breathing, that needed air, buried below each of those headstones?

I had to grip the pedestal before me with both hands, to hold myself up, to keep from turning and scampering blindly away then and there—and betraying my presence there in the process.

I waited until he had moved on out of sight, and some shrubbery blotted out the core of his lantern, if not its outermost rays; then I turned and darted away, frightened sick.

I beat my way along the inside of the fence, trying to find that unrepaired gap; and maddeningly it seemed to elude me. Then just when I was about ready to lose my head and yell out in panic, I glimpsed my car standing there in the darkness on the other side, and a few steps further on brought me to the place. Arms shaking palsiedly, I held up the loosened paling and slipped through. I stopped a minute there beside the car, wiping off my damp forehead on the back of my sleeve. Then with a deep breath of relief, I reached out, opened the car-door. I slipped in, turned the key. . . . Nothing happened. The ignition wire had been cut in my absence.

Before the full implication of the discovery had time to register on my mind, a man's head and shoulders rose silently, as out of the ground, just beyond the opposite door, on the outside of the road. He must have been crouched down out of sight, watching me the whole time.

He was well-dressed, no highwayman or robber. His face, or what I could see of it in the dark, had a solemn ascetic cast to it. Thee was a slight smile to his mouth, but not of friendliness.

His voice, when he spoke, was utterly toneless. It held

neither reproach, nor threat, nor anger. "Did you—" His stony eyes flickered just once past the cemetery-barrier— "have business in there?"

What was there I could say? "No. I simply went in, to—to rest awhile, and think."

"There was rather a severe wind—and rainstorm up here a week ago," he let me know. "It may have uprooted the sign we had standing at the entrance to this roadway. Thoroughfare is prohibited, it runs through private grounds."

"I saw no sign," I told him truthfully.

"But if you went in just to rest and think, how is it you were so agitated when you left just now? I saw you when you came out. What had you done in there to frighten you so?" And then, very slowly, spacing each word, "What— had—you—seen?"

But I'd had about enough. "Are you in charge of these grounds? Well, whether you are or not, I resent being questioned like this! You've damaged my car, with deliberation. I've a good mind to—"

"Step out and come with me," he said, and here was suddenly the thin, ugly muzzle of a Lüger resting across the doorstep, trained at me. His face remained cold, expressionless.

I pulled the catch out, stepped down beside him. "This is kidnaping," I said grimly.

"No," he said, "you'd have a hard time proving that. You're guilty of trespassing. We have a perfect right to detain you—until you've explained clearly, to our satisfaction, what you saw in there to frighten you so."

Or in other words, I said to myself, just how much I've found out—about something I'm not supposed to know. Something kept warning me: No matter what turns up, don't admit you noticed those vents above the graves in there. *Don't let on you saw them!* I didn't know why I shouldn't, but it kept pounding at me relentlessly.

"Walk up the road ahead of me," he directed. "If you

try to bolt off into the darkness, I'll shoot you without compunction.''

I turned and walked slowly back along the middle of the road, hands helplessly at my sides. The scrape and grate of his footsteps followed behind me. He knew enough not to close in and give me a chance to wrest the gun from him. I may have been afraid of burial alive, but I wasn't particularly afraid of bullets.

We came abreast of the cemetery-gate just as the watchman was letting himself out.

He threw up his head in surprise, picked up his lantern and came over.

"This man was in there just now. Walk along parallel to him, but not too close, and keep your lantern on him.''

"Yes, Brother.'' At the time I thought it was just slangy informality on the caretaker's part; the respectful way he said it should have told me different. As he took up his position off to one side of me I heard him hiss vengefully, "Dirty snooper!''

We were now following a narrow brick footpath, which I had missed seeing altogether from the car that afternoon, indian file, myself in the middle. It brought us, in about five minutes, to a substantial-looking country house, entirely surrounded by such a thick growth of trees that it must have been completely invisible from both roads even in the broad daylight. The lower story was of stone, the upper of stucco. It was obviously not abandoned or in disrepair, but gave no sign of life. All the windows, upper as well as lower, had been boarded up.

The three of us stepped up on the empty porch, whose floor-boards glistened with new varnish. The man with the lantern thrust a key into the seemingly boarded-up door, turned it, and swung the entire dummy-facing back intact. Behind it stood the real door, thick oak with an insert of bevelled glass, veiled on the inside by a curtain through which an electric light glimmered dully.

He unlocked that, too, and we were in a warm, well-furnished hall. The watchman took up his lantern and went toward the back of this, with a murmured "I'll be right in." My original captor turned me aside into a room furnished like a study, came in after me, at last pocketed the Lüger that had persuaded me so well.

A man was sitting behind a large desk, with a reading lamp trained on it, going over some papers. He looked up, paled momentarily, then recovered himself. I'd seen that however; it showed that all the fear was not on my side of the fence. The same silent, warning voice kept pegging away at me: Don't admit you saw those vents, watch your step!

The man who had brought me in said, "I found his car parked beside the cemetery-rail—where lightning struck and loosened that upright the other night. I waited, until he came out. I thought you'd like to talk to him, Brother." Again that "Brother."

"You were right, Brother," the man behind the desk nodded. He said to me, "What were you doing in there?"

The door behind me opened and the man who had played the part of caretaker came in. He had on a business-suit now just like the other two, in place of the dungarees and greasy sweater. I took a good look at his hands; they were not calloused, but had been recently blistered. I could see the circular threads of skin remaining where the blisters had opened. He was an amateur—and not a professional—gravedigger.

"Did he tamper with anything?" the man behind the desk asked him in that cool, detached voice.

"He certainly did. Jerome's was disturbed. The sod—around *it*—had been scraped away, just enough to lay *it* bare." He accented that pronoun, to give it special meaning.

My original captor went through my pockets deftly and swiftly, brought to light the penknife, snapped it open, showed them the grass-stains on the steel blade.

The beat of Death's wings was close in the air above my head.

"I'm sorry. Take him out in back of the house with you," the one behind the desk said flatly. As though those words were my death-warrant.

The whole thing was too incredible, too fantastic, I couldn't quite force myself to believe I was in danger of being put to death then and there like a mad dog. But I saw the one next to me slowly reach toward the pocket where the Lüger bulged.

"I'll have to go out there and dig again, after I got all cleaned up," the one who had played the part of watchman sighed regretfully, and glanced ruefully at his blistered hands.

I looked from one to the other, still not fully aware of what it all portended. Then on an impulse—an impulse that saved my life—I blurted out: "You see, it wasn't just idle curiosity on my part. All my life, since I was ten, I've dreaded the thought of burial alive—"

Before I knew it I had told them the whole story, about my father and the lasting impression it had made.

After I had finished, the man at the desk said, slowly, "What year was this—and where?"

"In New Orleans," I said, "in 1922."

His eyes flicked to the man on my left. "Get New Orleans on long distance," he said quietly. "Find out if an undertaker was brought to trial for burying a paralyzed war-veteran named Donald Ingram alive in All-Saints Cemetery in September 1922."

"The 14th," I said, shutting my eyes briefly.

"You are a lawyer," he instructed, "doing it at the behest of the man's son, because of some litigation that is pending, if they ask you." The door closed after him; I stayed there with the other two.

The envoy came back, silently handed a written sheet of

paper to the one at the desk. He read it through. "Your mother?" he said.

"She died insane in 1929. I had her cremated, to avoid—"

He crumpled the sheet of paper, threw it from him. "Would you care to join us?" he said, his eyes sparkling shrewdly.

"Who—are you?" I hedged.

He didn't answer that. "We can cure you, heal you. We can do more for you than any doctor, any mental specialist in the world. Would you not like to have this dread, this curse, lifted from you, never to return?"

I would, I said; which was true any way you looked at it.

"You have been particularly afflicted, because of the circumstances of your father's death," he went on. "However, don't think you're alone in your fear of death. There are scores, hundreds of others, who feel as you do, even if not quite so strongly. From them we draw our membership; we give them new hope and new life, rob death of all its terrors for them. The sense of mortality that has been crippling them ends, the world is theirs to conquer, nothing can stop them. They become like the immortal gods. Wealth, fame, all the world's goods, are theirs for the taking, for their frightened fellow-men, fearful of dying, defeated before they have even begun to live, cannot compete with them. Is not this a priceless gift? And we are offering it to you because you need it so badly, so very much more badly than anyone who has ever come to us before." He was anything but cold and icy now. He was glowing, fervent, fanatic, the typical proselyte seeking a new convert.

"I'm not rich," I said cagily, to find out where the catch was. And that's where it was—right there.

"Not now," he said, "because this blight has hampered your efforts, clipped your wings, so to speak. Few are who come to us. We ask nothing material from you now. Later, when we have helped you, and you are one of the world's fortunate ones, you may repay us, to assist us to carry on our good work."

Which might be just a very fancy way of saying future blackmail.

"And now—your decision?"

"I accept—your kind offer," I said thoughtfully, and immediately amended it mentally: "At least until I can get out of here and back to town."

But he immediately scotched that, as though he'd read my mind. "There is no revoking your decision once you've made it. That brings instant death. Slow suffocation is the manner of their going, those who break faith with us. Burial while still in full possession of their faculties, is the penalty."

The one doom that was a shade more awful than what had happened to my father; the only one. He at least had not come to until after it had been done. And it had not lasted long with him, it couldn't have.

"Those vents you saw can prolong it, for whole days," he went on. "They can be turned on or off at will."

"I said I'd join you," I shuddered, resisting an impulse to clap both hands to my ears.

"Good." He stretched forth his right hand to me and much against my inclination I took it. Then he clasped my wrist with his left, and had me do likewise with mine. I had to repeat this double grip with each of the others in turn. "You are now one of us."

The cemetery watchman left the room and returned with a tray holding three small skulls and a large one. I could feel the short hairs on the back of my neck standing up of their own accord. None of them were real though; they were wood or celluloid imitations. They all had flaps that opened at the top; one was a jug and the other three steins.

The man behind the desk named the toast. "To our

Friend!'' I thought he meant myself at first; he meant that shadowy enemy of all mankind, the Grim Reaper.

"We are called The Friends of Death," he explained to me when the grisly containers had been emptied. "To outline our creed and purpose briefly, it is this: That death is life, and life is death. We have mastered death, and no member of the Friends of Death need ever fear it. They 'die,' it is true, but after death they are buried in special graves in our private cemetery—graves having air vents, such as you discovered. Also, our graves are equipped with electric signals, so that after the bodies of our buried members begin to respond to the secret treatment our scientists have given them before internment, we are warned. Then we come and release them—and they live again. Moreover, they are released, freed of their thralldom; from then on death is an old familiar friend instead of an enemy. They no longer fear it. Do you not see what a wonderful boon this would be in your case, Brother Bud; you who have suffered so from that fear?"

I thought to myself, "They're insane! They must be!" I forced myself to speak calmly. "And the penalty you spoke of—that you inflict on those who betray or disobey you?"

"Ah!" he inhaled zestfully. "You are buried before death—without benefit of the attention of our experts. The breathing-tube is slowly, infinitesimally, shut off from above a notch at a time, by means of a valve—until it is completely sealed. It is," he concluded, "highly unpleasant while it lasts." Which was the most glaring case of understatement I had ever yet encountered.

There wasn't much more to this stage of my preliminary initiation. A ponderous ebony-bound ledger was brought out, with the inevitable skull on its cover in ivory. I was made to draw blood from my wrist and sign my name, with that, in it. The taking of the oath of secrecy followed.

"You will receive word of when your formal initiation

is to be," I was told. "Return to your home and hold yourself ready until you hear from us. Members are not supposed to be known to one another, with the exception of us three, so you are required to attend the rites in a specially-constructed skull-mask which will be given to you. We are the Book-keeper (man behind the desk), the Messenger (man with the Lüger), and the Grave-digger. We have chapters in most of the large cities. If business or anything should require you to move your residence elsewhere, don't fail to notify us and we will transfer you to our branch in the city to which you are going."

"Like hell I will!" I thought.

"All members in good faith are required to be present at each of the meetings; failure to do so invokes the Penalty."

The grinning ghoul had the nerve to sling his arm around my shoulder in a friendly way as he led me toward the door, like a hospitable host speeding a parting guest. It was all I could do to keep from squirming at the feel of it. I wanted to part his teeth with my right fist then and there, but the Messenger, with the Lüger on him, was a few steps behind me. I was getting out, and that was all that seemed to matter at the time. That was all I wanted—out, and a lungful of fresh air, and a good stiff jolt of whiskey to get the bad taste out of my mouth.

They unlocked the two doors for me, and even flashed on the porch-light so I could see my way down the steps. "You can get a city bus over on the State Highway. We'll have your car fixed for you and standing in front of your door first thing in the morning."

But at the very end a hint of warning again showed itself through all their friendliness. "Be sure to come when you're sent for. We have eyes and ears everywhere, where you'd least expect it. No warning is given, no second chances are ever allowed!"

Again that double grip, three times repeated, and it was over. The two doors were closed and locked, the porch-light snuffed out, and I was groping my way down the brick footpath—alone. Behind me not a chink of light showed from the boarded-up house. It had all been as fleeting, as unreal, as unbelievable, as a bad dream.

I shivered all the way back to the city in the heated bus; the other passengers must have thought I had the grippe. Joan Blaine found me at midnight in a bar around the corner from where I lived, stewed to the gills, so drunk I could hardly stand up straight—but still shivering. "Take him home, miss," she told me afterwards the bartender whispered to her. "He's been standing there like that three solid hours, staring like he sees ghosts, frightening my other customers off into corners!"

I woke up fully dressed on top of my bed next morning, with just a blanket over me. "That was just a dream, the whole thing!" I kept snarling to myself defensively.

I heard Joan's knock at the door, and the first thing she said when I let her in was: "Something happen to your car last night? I saw a mechanic drive up to the door with it just now, as I was coming in. He got out, walked off, and left it standing there!"

There went my just-a-dream defense. She saw me rear back a little, but didn't ask why. I went over to the window and looked down at it. It was waiting there without anyone in or near it.

"Were you in a smash-up?" she demanded. "Is that why you stood me up? Is that why you were shaking so when I found you?"

I grabbed at the out eagerly. "Yeah, that's it! Bad one, too; came within an inch of winding up behind the eight-ball. Gave me the jitters for hours afterwards."

She looked at me, said quietly: "Funny kind of smash-up, to make you say 'Little pipes coming up through the ground.' That's all you said over and over. Not a scratch on you, either. No report of any smack-up involving a car with your license-number, when I checked with the police after you'd been three hours overdue at my house." She gave me an angry look, at least it tried to be. "All right, I'm a woman and therefore a fibber. But I sewed you up pretty this time. I asked that grease-monkey what it was just now, and he said only a cut ignition-wire!"

Her face softened and she came over to me. "What're you keeping from me, honey? Tell Joan. She's for you, don't you know that by now?"

No, it was just a dream, I wasn't going to tell her. And even if it wasn't a dream, I'd be damned if I'd tell her! Worry her? I should say not! "All right, there wasn't any smash-up and there wasn't anything else either. I'm just a heel, I got stiff and stood you up, that's all."

I could tell she didn't believe me; she left looking unconvinced. I'd just about closed the door afer her when my phone rang.

"You're to be complimented, Brother," an anonymous voice said. "We're glad to see that you're to be relied on," and then the connection broke.

Eyes everywhere, ears everywhere. I stood there white in the face, and calling it a dream wouldn't work any more.

The summons to attend came three weeks later to the day. A large white card such as formal invitations are printed on, inside an envelope with my name on it. Only the card itself was blank. I couldn't make head or tail of it at first, didn't even connect it with them. Then down in the lower corner I made out the faintly-pencilled word "Heat."

I went and held it over the steam radiator. A death's head slowly started to come through, first faint yellow, then brown, then black. And under it a few lines of writing, in hideous travesty of a normal social invitation.

Your Presence Is Requested
Friday, 9 P.M.
You Will Be Called For

                                                    F. O. D.

"Call away, but I won't be here!" was my first explosive reaction. "This goblin stuff has gone far enough. The keepers ought to be out after that whole outfit with butterfly-nets!"

Then presently, faint stirrings of curiosity began to prompt me: "What have you got to lose? Why not see what it's like, anyway? What can they do to you after all? Pack a gun with you, that's all."

When I left the office late that afternoon I made straight for a pawnshop over on the seamy side of town, barged in through the saloon-like half-doors. I already had had a license for some time back, so there was not likely to be any difficulty about getting what I wanted.

While the owner was in the back getting some out to show me, a down-and-outer came in with a mangy overcoat he wanted to peddle. The clerk took it up front to examine it more closely, and for a moment the two of us were left standing alone on the customer's side of the counter. I swear there was not a gun in sight on the case in front of me. Nothing to indicate what I had come in for.

An almost inaudible murmur sounded from somewhere beside me: "I wouldn't, Brother, if I were you. You'll get in trouble if you do."

I looked around sharply. The seedy derelict seemed unaware of my existence, was staring dejectedly down at the glass case under him. Yet if he hadn't spoken who had?

He was turned down, took back the coat, and shuffled disheartedly out into the street again, without a glance at me as he went by. The doors flapped loosely behind him. A prickling sensation ran up my spine. That had been a warning from *them*.

"Sorry," I said abruptly, when the owner came back with some revolvers to show me, "I've changed my mind!" I went out hurriedly, looked up and down the street. The derelict had vanished. Yet the pawnshop was in the middle of the block, about equally distant from each corner. He couldn't have possibly—! I even asked a janitor, setting out ashcans a few steps away. "Did you see an old guy carrying a coat come out of here just now?"

"Mister," he said to me, "nobody's come out of there since you went in yourself two minutes ago."

"I suppose he was an optical illusion," I said to myself. "Like hell he was!"

So I went without a gun.

A not only embarrassing but highly dangerous *contretemps* was waiting for me when I got back to my place a few minutes later. Joan was in the apartment waiting for me, had had the landlady, who knew her quite well, let her in. Tonight of all nights, when they were calling for me! I not only had to stay here, but I had to get her out of the way before they showed up.

The first thing my eye fell on as I came in was that damned invitation, too. It was lying about where I'd left it, but I could have sworn I'd put it back in its envelope, and now it was on the outside, skull staring up from it as big as life. Had she seen it? If so, she gave no sign. I sidled around in front of it and pushed it out of sight in a drawer with my hands behind my back.

"Take a lady to supper," she said.

But I couldn't, there wouldn't be time enough to get back there again if I did; they were due in about a quarter of an hour, I figured. It was an hour's ride out there.

"Damn! I just ate," I lied. "Why didn't you let me know—"

"How's for the movies then?" She was unusually persistent tonight, almost as though she'd found out something and wanted to force me to break down and admit it.

I mumbled something about a headache, going to bed early, my eyes fixed frantically on the clock. Ten minutes now.

"I seem popular tonight," she shrugged. But she made no move to go, sat there watching me curiously, intently.

Sweat was beading my forehead. Seven minutes to go. If I let her stay any longer, I was endangering her. But how could I get rid of her without hurting her, making her suspicious—if she wasn't already?

"You seem very tense tonight," she murmured. "I never saw you watch a clock so closely." Five minutes were left.

They helped me out. Eyes everywhere, ears everywhere. The phone rang. Again that anonymous voice, as three weeks before.

"Better get that young woman out of the way, Brother. The car's at the corner, waiting to come up to your door. You'll be late."

"Yes," I said, and hung up.

"Competition?" she asked playfully when I went back.

"Joan," I said hoarsely, "you run along. I've got to go out. There's something I can't tell you about. You've got to trust me. You do, don't you?" I pleaded.

She only said one thing, sadly, apprehensively, as she got up and walked toward the door. "I do. But you don't seem to trust—me." She turned impulsively, her hands crept pleadingly up my lapels. "Oh, why can't you tell me!"

"You don't know what you're asking!" I groaned.

She turned and ran swiftly down the stairs, I could hear her sobbing gently as she went. I never heard the street-door close after her, though.

Moments later my call-bell rang, I grabbed my hat and ran down. A touring-car was standing in front of the house, rear door invitingly open. I got in and found myself seated next to the Messenger. "All right, Brother," he said to the driver. All I could see of the latter was the back of his head; the mirror had been removed from the front of the car.

"Let me caution you," the Messenger said, as we started off. "You went into a pawnshop this afternoon to buy a gun. Don't try that, if you know what's good for you. And after this, see to it that the young lady isn't admitted to your room in your absence. She might have read the summons we sent."

"I destroyed it," I lied.

He handed me something done up in paper. "Your mask," he said. "Don't put it on until we get past the city-limits."

It was a frightening-looking thing when I did so. It was not a mask but a hood for the entire head, canvas and cardboard, chalk-white to simulate a skull, with deep black hollows for the eyes and grinning teeth for the mouth.

The private highway, as we neared the house, was lined on both sides with parked cars. I counted fifteen of them as we flashed by; and there must have been as many more ahead, in the other direction.

We drew up and he and I got out. I glanced in cautiously over my shoulder at the driver as we went by, to see if I could see his face, but he too had donned one of the death-masks.

"Never do that," the Messenger warned me in a low voice. "Never try to penetrate any other member's disguise."

The house was as silent and lifeless as the last time—on the outside. Within it was a horrid, crawling charnel-house alive with skull-headed figures, their bodies encased in business-suits, tuxedos, and evening dresses. The lights were all dyed a ghastly green or ghostly blue, by means of colored tissue-paper sheathed around them. A group of masked musicians kept playing the Funeral March over and over, with brief pauses in between. A coffin stood in the center of the main living-room.

I was drenched with sweat under my own mask and sick almost to death, even this early in the game.

At last the Book-keeper, unmasked, appeared in their midst. Behind him came the Messenger. The dead-head guests all applauded enthusiastically, gathered around them in a ring. Those in other rooms came in. The musicians stopped the Death March.

The Book-keeper bowed, smiled graciously. "Good evening, fellow corpses," was his chill greeting. "We are gathered together to witness the induction of our newest member." There was an electric tension. "Brother Bud!" His voice rang out like a clarion in the silence. "Step forward."

My heart burst into little pieces in my chest. I could feel my legs getting ready to go down under me. That roaring in my ears was my own crazed thoughts. And I knew with a terrible certainty that this was no initiation— this was to be "the punishment." For I was of no value to them—having no money.

Before I had time to tear off my mask, fight and claw my way out, I was seized by half-a-dozen of them, thrust forward into the center of the circle. I was forced to my knees and held in that position, writhing and twisting. My coat, vest and shirt were stripped off and my mask was removed. A linen shroud, with neck-and-arm holes, was pulled over my head. My hands were caught, pulled behind my back, and lashed tight with leather straps. I kicked out at them with my legs and squirmed about on the floor like a maniac—I, who was the only sane one of all of them! I rasped strangled imprecations at them. The corpse was unwilling.

They caught my threshing legs finally, strapped those together at the ankles and the knees, then carefully drew the shroud the rest of the way down. I was lifted bodily like a log, a long twisting white thing in its shroud, and fitted neatly into the quilted coffin. Agonizedly I tried to rear. I was forced down flat and strapped in place across the waist and across the chest. All I could make now were inchoate animal-noises, gurglings and keenings. My face was a steaming cauldron of sweat.

I could still see the tops of their masked heads from where I was, bending down around me in a circle. Gloating, grinning, merciless death's heads. One seemed to be staring at me in fixed intensity; they were all staring, of course, but I saw him briefly hold a pair of glasses to the eyeholes of his mask, as though—almost as though I was known to him, from that other world outside. A moment later he beckoned the Book-keeper to him and they withdrew together out of my line of vision, as though conferring about something.

The face of the Grave-digger had appeared above the rim of my coffin meanwhile, as though he had just come in from outside.

"Is it ready?" the Messenger asked him.

"Ready—and six feet deep," was the blood-curdling answer.

I saw them up-end the lid of the coffin, to close it over me. One was holding a hammer and a number of long nails in his hand, in readiness. Down came the lid, flat, smothering my squall of unutterably woe, and the blue-green light that had been bearing down on me until now went velvety black.

Then, immediately afterwards, it was partially displaced again and the head of the Book-keeper was bending down close to mine. I could feel his warm breath on my forehead. His whisper was meant for me alone. "Is it true you are betrothed to a young lady of considerable means, a Miss Joan Blaine?"

I nodded, so far gone with terror I was only half-aware what I was doing.

"Is it her uncle, Rufus Blaine, who is the well-known manufacturer?"

I nodded again, groaned weakly. His face suddenly whisked away, but instead of the lid being fitted back into place as I momentarily expected, it was taken away altogether.

Arms reached in, undid the body-straps that held me, and I was helped to a sitting-position. A moment later the shroud had been drawn off me like a long white stocking, and my hands and legs were freed. I was lifted out.

I was too spent to do anything but tumble to the floor and lie there inert at the feet of all of them, conscious but unable to move. I heard and saw the rest of what went on from that position.

The Book-keeper held up his hand. "Fellow corpses!" he proclaimed, "Brother Bud's punishment is indefinitely postponed, for reasons best known to myself and the other heads of the chapter—"

But the vile assemblage of masked fiends didn't like that at all; they were being cheated of their prey. "No! No!" they gibbered, and raised their arms threateningly toward him. "The coffin cries for an occupant! The grave yearns for an inmate!"

"It shall have one!" he promised. "You shall witness your internment. You shall not be deprived of your funeral joys, of the wake you are entitled to!" He made a surreptitious sign to the Messenger, and the skull-crested ledger was handed to him. He opened it, hastily turned its pages, consulted the entries, while an ominous, expectant silence reigned. He pointed to something in the book, his eyes beaded maliciously. Then once more he held up his hand. "You shall witness a penalty, an irrevocable burial with the vents closed!"

Crooning cries of delight sounded on all sides.

"I find here," he went on, "the name of a member who has accepted all our benefits, yet steadily defaulted on the contributions due us. Who has means, yet who had tried to cheat us by signing over his wealth to others, hiding it in safe-deposit boxes under false names, and so on. I hereby condemn Brother Anselm to be penalized!''

A mad scream sounded from their midst, and one of the masked figures tried to dash frightenedly toward the door. He was seized, dragged back, and the ordeal I had just been through was repeated. I couldn't help noticing, with chill forebodings, that the Book-keeper made a point of having me stood up on my feet and held erect to watch the whole damnable thing. In other words, by being a witness and a participant, I was now as guilty as any of them. A fact which they were not likely to let me forget if I balked later on at meeting their blackmail-demands. Demands which they expected me to fulfill with the help of Joan's money—her uncle's, rather—once I was married to her. It was the mention of her name, I realized, that had saved me. I was more use to them alive than dead, for the present, that was all.

Meanwhile, to the accompaniment of one last wail of despair that rang in my ears for days afterward, the coffin lid had been nailed down fast on top of the pulsing, throbbing contents the box held. It was lifted by four designated pall-bearers, carried outside to a waiting hearse lurking amidst the trees, while the musicians struck up the Death March. The rest of the murderous crew followed, myself included, held fast by the Messenger on one side, and Book-keeper on the other. They forced me into a limousine between them, and off we glided after the hearse, the other cars following us.

We all got out again at a lonely glen in the woods, where a grave had been prepared. No need to dwell on the scen that followed. Only one thing need be told. As the box was being lowered into it, in complete silence, sounds of frenzied motion could distinctly be heard within it, as of something rolling desperately from side to side. I watched as through a film of delirium, restraining hands on my wrists compelling me to look on.

When at last it was over, when at last the hole in the ground was gone, and the earth had been stamped down flat again on top of it, I found myself once more in the car that had orginally called for me, alone this time with just the driver, being taken back to the city. I deliberately threw my own mask out of the side of the car, in token of burning my bridges behind me.

When he veered in toward the curb in front of my house, I jumped down and whirled, intending to grab him by the throat and drag him out after me. The damnable machine was already just a tail-light whirring away from me; he hadn't braked at all.

I chased upstairs, pulled down the shades so no one could see in, hauled out my valise, and began pitching things into it from full-height, my lower jaw trembling. Then I went to the phone, hesitated briefly, called Joan's number. Eyes everywhere, ears everywhere! But I had to take the chance. Her peril, now, was as great as mine.

Somebody else answered in her place. "Joan can't talk to anyone right now. The doctor's ordered her to bed, he had to give her a sedative to quiet her nerves, she came in awhile ago in a hysterical condition. We don't know what happened to her, we can't get her to tell us!"

I hung up, mystified. I thought: "I did that to her, by asking her to leave tonight. I hurt her, and she must have brooded about it—" I kicked my valise back under the bed. Friends of Death or no Friends of Death, I couldn't go until I'd seen her.

I didn't sleep all that night. By nine the next morning I'd made up my mind. I put the invitation to the meeting in my inside pocket and went around to the nearest precinct-house. I regretted now having thrown my mask away the night before, that would have been more evidence to show them.

I asked, tight-lipped, to see the captain in charge. He listened patiently, scanned the invitation, tapped his lower teeth thoughtfully with his thumbnail. It slowly dawned on me that he considered me slightly cracked, a crank; my story must have sounded too fantastic to be altogether credible. Then when I'd given him the key to my falling in with them in the first place—my graveyard obsession—I saw him narrow his eyes shrewdly at me and nod to himself as though that explained everything.

He summoned one of the detectives, half-heartedly instructed him: "Investigate this man's story, Crow. See what you can find out about this—ahem—country-house and mysterious graveyard out toward Ellendale. Report back to me." And then hurriedly went on to me, as though he couldn't wait to get rid of me, felt I really ought to be under observation at one of the psychopathic wards, "We'll take care of you, Mr. Ingram. You go on home now and don't let it worry you." He flipped the death's-head invitation carelessly against the edge of his desk once or twice. "You're sure this isn't just a high-pressure circular from some life-insurance concern or other?"

I locked my jaw grimly and walked out of there without answering. A lot of good they were going to be to me, I could see that. All but telling me to my face I was screwy.

Crow, the detective, came down the steps behind me leisurely buttoning his topcoat. He said, "An interstate bus'll leave me off close by there." It would, but I wondered how he knew that.

He threw up his arm as one approached and signalled it to stop. It swerved in and the door folded back automatically. His eyes bored through mine, through and through like gimlets, for just a second before he swung aboard. "See you later, Brother," he said. "You've earned the Penalty if anyone ever did. You're going down—without an air-pipe.'' Then he and the bus were gone—out toward Ellendale.

The sidewalk sort of swayed all around me, like jelly. It threatened to come up and hit me flat across the face, but I grabbed hold of a bus-stop stanchion and held onto it until the vertigo had passed. One of them right on the plain-clothes squad! What was the sense of going back in there again? If I hadn't been believed the first time, what chance had I of being believed now? And the way he'd gone off and left me just now showed how safe he felt on that score. The fact that he hadn't tried to hijack me, force me to go out there with him, showed how certain they felt of laying hands on me when they were ready.

Well they hadn't yet! And they weren't going to, not if I had anything to say about it. Since I couldn't get help, flight was all that remained then. Flight it would be. They couldn't be everywhere, omnipotent; there must be places where I'd be safe from them—if only for a little while.

I drew my money out of the bank, I phoned in to the office that they could find somebody else for my job, I wasn't coming in any more. I went and got my car out of the garage where I habitually bedded it, and had it serv-iced, filled and checked for a long trip. I drove around to where I lived, paid up, put my valise in the back. I drove over to Joan's.

She looked pale, as though she'd been through some-thing the night before, but she was up and around. My arms went around her. I said, ''I've got to get out of town—now, before the hour's out—but I love you, and I'll get word to you where I am the minute I'm able to.''

She answered quietly, looking up into my face: ''What need is there of that, when I'll be right there with you—wherever it is?''

''But you don't know what I'm up against—and I can't tell you why, I'll only involve you!''

''I don't want to know. I'm coming. We can get married there, wherever it's to be—" She turned and ran out, was back again in no time, dragging a coat after her with one hand, hugging a jewelcase and an overnight-bag to her with the other, hat perched rakishly on the back of her head. We neither of us laughed, this was no time for laughter.

"I'm ready—" She saw by my face that something had happened, even in the brief time she'd been gone. "What is it?" She dropped the things; a string of pearls rolled out of the case.

I led her to the window and silently pointed down to my car below. I'd had the tires pumped up just now at the garage; all four rims rested flatly on the asphalt now, all the air let out. "Probably emptied the tank, cut the ignition, crippled it irreparably, while they were at it," I said in a flat voice, "We're being watched every minute! Damn it, I shouldn't have come here, I'm dragging you to your grave!"

"Bud," she said, "if that's where I've got to go to be with you—even that's all right with me."

"Well, we're not there yet!" I muttered doggedly. "Train, then."

She nodded eagerly. "Where to?"

"New York. And if we're not safe even there, we can hop a boat to England—that surely ought to be out of their reach."

"Who are they?" she wanted to know.

"As long as I don't tell you, you've still got a chance. I'm not dooming you if I can help it!"

She didn't press the point, almost—it occurred to me later—almost as though she already knew all there was to know. "I'll call the station, find out when the next one leaves—"

I heard her go out in the hall, jiggle the phone-hook for a connection. I squatted down, stuck the pearls back in the case for her. I raised my eyes, and her feet were there on the carpet before me again.

She didn't whimper and she didn't break; just looked through me and beyond as I straightened up. "They mean business," she breathed. "The phone's gone dead."

She moved back to the window, stood there looking out. "There's a man been standing across the way reading a newspaper the whole time we've been talking in here. He seems to be waiting for a bus, but three have gone by and he's still there. We'll never make it." Then suddenly her face brightened. "Wait, I have it!" But her enthusiasm seemed spurious, premeditated, to me. "Instead of leaving here together to try to get through to the station, suppose we separate—and meet later on the train. I think that's safer."

"What! Leave you behind alone in this place? Nothing doing."

"I'll go first, without taking anything with me, just as though I were going shopping. I won't go near the station. I can take an ordinary city-bus to Hamlin, that's the first train-stop on the way to New York. You give me a head-start, show yourself plentifully at the window in case he's one of their plants, then slip out the back way, get your ticket and get aboard. I'll be waiting for you on the station-platform at Hamlin, you can whisk me aboard with you; they only stop there a minute."

The way she told it, it sounded reasonable, I would be running most of the risk, getting from here to the station. I agreed. "Stay in the thick of the crowd the whole way," I warned her. "Don't take any chances. If anyone so much as looks at you cross-eyed, holler blue murder, pull down the whole police-force on top of them."

"I'll handle it," she said competently. She came close, our lips met briefly. Her eyes misted over. "Bud darling," she murmured low, "a long life and happy one to you!" Before it had dawned on me what a strange thing to say

that was, she had flitted out and the door closed after
her.

I watched narrowly from the window, ready to dash out
if the man with the paper so much as made a move toward
her. To get the downtown bus she had to cross to where he
was and wait beside him. He took no notice of her, never
raised his eyes from his paper—a paper whose pages he
hadn't turned in a full ten minutes. She stood there facing
one way, he the other. They could, of course, have exchanged remarks without my being aware of it. The bus
flashed by and I tensed. A minute later I relaxed again.
She was gone; he was still there reading that never-ending
paper.

I decided to give her a half-hour's start. That way, the
train being faster than the bus, we'd both get to Hamlin
about simultaneously. I didn't want her to have to wait
there alone on the station-platform too long if it could be
avoided. Meanwhile I kept returning to the window, to let
the watcher see that I was still about the premises. I—Joan
too for that matter—had long ago decided that he was a
lookout, a plant, and then about twenty minutes after she'd
gone, my whole theory collapsed like a house of cards. A
girl, whom he must have been waiting for the whole time,
came hurrying up to him and I could see her making
excuses. He flung down his paper, looked at his wrist-
watch, took her roughly by the arm and they stalked off,
arguing violently.

My relief was only momentary. The cut phone-wires,
my crippled car, were evidence enough that unseen eyes
had been, and still were watching me the whole time. Only
they did it more skillfully than by means of a blatant
look-out on a street-corner. At least with him I had thought
I knew where I was at; now I was in the dark again.

Thirty-five minutes after Joan had gone I slipped out
through the back door, leaving my car still out there in
front (as if that would do any good), leaving my hat

perched on the top of an easy-chair with its back toward the window (as if that would, either). I followed the service-alley between the houses until I'd come out on the nearest sidestreet, around the corner from Joan's. It was now one in the afternoon. There wasn't a soul in sight at the moment, in this quiet residential district, and it seemed humanly impossible that I had been sighted.

I followed a circuitous zig-zag route, down one street, across another, in the general direction of the station, taking time out at frequent intervals to scan my surroundings with the help of some polished show-case that reflected them like a mirror. For all the signs of danger that I could notice, the Friends of Death seemed very far-away, non-existent.

I slipped into the station finally through the baggage-entrance on the side, and worked my way from there toward the front, keeping my eyes open as I neared the ticket-windows. The place was a beehive of activity as usual, which made it both safer and at the same time more dangerous for me. I was safer from sudden seizure with all these people around me, but it was harder to tell whether I was being watched or not.

"Two to New York," I said guardedly to the agent. And pocketing the tickets with a wary look around me, "When's the next one leave?"

"Half-an-hour."

I spent the time by keeping on the move. I didn't like the looks of the waiting-room; there were too many in it. I finally decided a telephone-booth would be the likeliest bet. Its gloom would offer me a measure of concealment, and instead of having four directions to watch at once, I'd only have one. Then, too, they were located conveniently near to the gates leading outside to the tracks. Passengers, however, were not being allowed through the latter yet.

I took a last comprehensive look around, then went straight at a booth as though I had a call to make. The two on each side of it were definitely empty: I saw that as I stepped in. I gave the bulb over me a couple of turns so it wouldn't flash on, left the slide open on a crack so I could catch the starter's announcement when it came, and leaned back watchfully against the far partition, eyes on the glass in front of me.

Twenty minutes went by and nothing happened. An amplifier suddenly came to life outside, and the starter's voice thundered through it. "New York Express. Track Four. Leaving in ten minutes. First stop Hamlin—"

And then, with a shock like high-voltage coursing through me, the phone beside me started pealing thinly.

I just stood there and stared at it, blood draining from my face. A call to a tollbooth? It must, it *must* be a wrong number, somebody wanted the Information Booth or—! It must have been audible outside, with all I had the slide partly closed. One of the redcaps passing by turned, looked over, then started coming across toward where I was. To get rid of him I picked up the receiver, put it to my ear.

"You'd better come out now, time's up," a flat, deadly voice said. "They're calling your train, but you're not getting on that one—or any other."

"Wh—where are talking from?"

"The next booth to yours," the voice jeered. "You forgot the glass inserts only reach halfway down."

The connection broke and a man's looming figure was shadowing the glass in front of my eyes, before I could even get the receiver back on the hook. I dropped it full-length, tensed my right arm to pound it through his face as soon as I shoved the glass aside. He had a revolver-bore for a top vest-button, trained on me. Two more had shown up behind him, from which direction I hadn't noticed. It was very dark in the booth now, their collective silhouettes shut out all the daylight. The station and all its friendly bustle was blotted out, had receded into the far background, a thousand miles away for all the help it could give me. I slapped the glass wearily aside, came slowly out.

One of them flashed a badge—maybe Crow had loaned him his for the occasion. "You're being arrested for putting slugs in that phone. It won't do any good to raise your voice and shriek for help, try to tell people different. But suit yourself."

I knew that as well as he; heads turned to stare after us by the dozens as they started with me in their midst through the station's main-level. But not one in all that crowd would have dared interfere with what they mistook for a legitimate arrest in the line of duty. The one with the badge kept it conspicuously tilted in his upturned palm, at sight of which the frozen onlookers slowly parted, made way for us through their midst. I was being led to my doom in full view of scores of people.

I tried twice to dig my feet in when we came to ridges in the level of the terraced marble floor, but the point of the gun at the base of my spine removed the impediment each time, I was so used to not wanting to die. Then slowly this determination came to me: "I'm going to force them to shoot me, before they get me into the car or whatever it is they're taking me to. It's my only way out, cheat death by death. I'm to be buried agonizingly alive, anyway; I'll compel them to end it here instead, by that gun. That clean, friendly gun. But not just shoot me, shoot me dead, otherwise—" A violent wrench backwards would do it, compressing the gun into its holder's body, discharging it automatically into me. "Poor Joan," I thought, "left waiting on the Hamlin station-platform—for all eternity." But that didn't alter my determination any.

The voice of the train-dispatcher, loudspeaker and all, was dwindling behind us. "New York Express, Track Four, leave in five more min—"

Sunlight suddenly struck down at us from outside the station portico, between the huge two-story high columns, and down below at the distant bottom of the long terraced steps there was one of those black touring-cars standing waiting. "Now!" I thought, and tensed, ready to rear backward into the gun so that it would explode into my vitals.

A Western Union messenger in typical olive-green was running up the sloping steps straight toward my captors, arm extended. Not a boy though, a grown man. One of *them* disguised, I knew, even as I looked at him. "Urgent!" he panted, and thrust a message into the hand of the one with the badge. I let myself relax again in their hands, postponing for a moment the forcing of death into my own body, while I waited to see what this was.

He read it through once, then quickly whispered it aloud a second time to the other two—or part of it, anyway. "Penalty cancelled, give ex-Brother Bud safe-conduct to New York on promise never to return. Renewed oath of eternal silence on his part accepted. Interment ceremonies will take place as planned—" He pointed with his finger to the rest without repeating it aloud, that's how I knew there was more.

The messenger had already hurried down again to where the car was, and darted behind it. A motorcycle suddenly shot out from the other side of it and racketed off, trailing little puff-balls of blue gas-smoke. A moment later the three with me, scattered like startled buzzards cheated of their prey, had followed him down, at different angles that converged toward the car. I found myself standing there alone at the top of the station-steps, a lone figure dwarfed by the monolithic columns.

I reeled, turned and started headlong through the long reaches of the station behind me, bent over like a marathon runner reaching for the guerdon. " 'Board! 'Board!" was sounding faintly somewhere in the distance. I could see them pulling the adjustable exit-gates closed ahead of me. I held one arm straight up in the air, and they saw me coming and left a little opening for me, enough for one person to dive through.

The train was gathering speed when I lurched down to track-level, but I caught the handrail of the last vestibule of the last car just before it cleared the concrete runway beside the tracks. A conductor dragged me in bodily and I fell in a huddle at his feet.

"You last-minute passengers!" I heard him grumbling, "you'd think your life depended on it—"

I lay there heaving, flat on my back like a fish out of water, looking up at him. "It did," I managed to get out.

I was leaning far out from the bottom vestibule-step at nearly a 45-degree angle, holding on with one hand, when the Hamlin station-platform swept into sight forty minutes later. I could see the whole boat-shaped "pier" from end to end.

There was something wrong; she wasn't on it. Nobody was on it, only a pair of lounging darkies, backs against the station-wall. The big painted sign floated up, came to a halt almost before my eyes: "HAMLIN." She'd said Hamlin; what had happened, what had gone wrong? It *had* to be Hamlin; there wasn't any other stop until tomorrow morning, states away!

I jumped down, went skidding into the little stuffy two-by-four waiting-room. Nobody in it. I dashed for the ticket-window, grabbed the bars with both hands, all but shook them. "A girl—blue eyes, blonde hair, brown coat—where is she, where'd she go? Haven't you seen anyone like that around here?"

"Nope, nobody been around here all afternoon, ain't sold a ticket nor even had an inquiry—"

"The bus from the city—did it get here yet?"

"Ten full minutes ago. It's out there in back of the station right now."

I hurled through the opposite door like something demented. The locomotive-bell was tolling dismally, almost like a funeral knell. I collared the bus-driver despairingly.

"Nope, didn't bring any young women out at all on my last run. I'd know; I like young women."

"And no one like that got on, at the downtown city-terminal?"

"Nope, no blondes. I'd know, I like blondes."

The wheels were already starting to click warningly over the rail-intersections as the train glided into motion; I could hear them around on the other side of the station from where I was. Half-crazed, I ducked inside again. The agent belatedly remembered something, called me over as I stood there dazedly looking all around me. "Say, by the way, your name Ingram? Forgot to tell you, special messenger brought this out awhile back, asked me to deliver it to the New York train."

I snatched at it. It was in her handwriting! I tore it open, my head swivelled crazily from left to right as my eyes raced along the writing.

I didn't take the bus to Hamlin after all, but don't worry. Go on to New York and wait there for me instead. And think of me often, and pray for me sometimes, and above all keep your pledge of silence.

Joan

She'd found out! was the first thunderbolt that struck me. And the second was a dynamite-blast that split me from head to foot. She was in their hands! That gruesome message that had saved me at the station came back to me word for word, and I knew now what it meant and what the part was that they'd kept from me. "Penalty cancelled. Give Brother Bud safe-conduct. Renewed oath on his part accepted—" But I hadn't made one. She must have promised them that on my behalf. *"Interment will take place as planned—"* Substitute accepted!

And that substitute was Joan. She'd taken my place. She'd gone to them and made a bargain with them. Saved me, at the cost of her own life.

I don't remember how I got back to the city. Maybe I thrust all the money I had on me at someone and borrowed their car. Maybe I just stole one left unguarded on the street with the key in it. I don't remember where I got the gun either. I must have gone back to that same pawnshop I'd already been to once, as soon as I got in.

When things came back into focus, I was already on the porch of that boarded-up house at Ellendale, battering my body apart against the doorcasing. I broke in finally by jumping from a tree to the porch-shed and kicking in one of the upper-story windows, less stoutly boarded.

I was too late. The silence told me that as soon as I stood within the room, and the last tinklings of shattered glass had died down around me. They weren't here. They'd gone. There wasn't a soul in the place! But there were signs, when I crept down the stairs gun in hand, that they'd been there. The downstairs rooms were heavy with the thickly cloying scent of fresh flowers, ferns and bits of leaf were scattered about the floor. Folding campchairs were still arranged in orderly rows, as though a funeral service had been conducted. Facing them stood tapers thick as a man's wrist, barely cool at the top, the charred odor of their gutted wicks still clinging to them. And in a closet when I looked I found her coat—Joan's—her hat, her dress, her little pitiful strapped sandals standing empty side by side! I crushed them to me, dropped them, ran out of there crazed, and broke into the adjacent graveyard, but there were no signs that she'd been taken there. No freshly-filled in grave, no mound without its sprouting grass. I'd heard them say they had others. It had grown dark long ago, and it must be over by now. But how could I stop trying, even though it were too late?

Afterwards, along the state highway, I found a couple sleeping overnight in a trailer by the roadside who told me a hearse had passed them on its way to the city, followed by a number of limousines, *a full two hours earlier*. They'd thought it was a strange hour for a funeral. They'd also thought the procession was going faster than seemed decent. And after an empty gin-bottle had been tossed out of one of the cars, they were not likely to forget the incident.

I lost the trail at the city-limits, no one had seen them beyond there, the night and the darkness had swallowed them up. I've been looking ever since. I've already broken into two, and I was in the third one when you stopped me—but no sign of her. She's in some city graveyard at this very minute, still breathing, threshing her life away in smothering darkness, while you're holding me here, wasting precious time. Kill me, then, kill me and have it over with—or else help me find her, but don't let me suffer like this!

The captain took his hand away from before his eyes, stopped pinching the bridge of his nose with it. A white mark was left there between his eyes. "This is awful," he breathed. "I almost wish I hadn't heard that story. How could it be anything else but true? It's too farfetched, too unbelievable."

Suddenly, like a wireless-set that comes to life, crackling, emitting blue sparks, he was sending out staccato orders. "For corroborating evidence we have her note to you sent to Hamlin station; we have her clothing at the Ellendale house, and undoubtedly that ledger of membership you first signed, along with God-knows what else! You two men get out there quick with a battery of police-photographers and take pictures of those campchairs, tapers, everything just as you find it. And don't forget the graveyard. I want every one of those graves broken open as fast as you swing picks. I'll send the necessary exhumation-permits after you, but don't wait for them! Those grounds are full of living beings!''

''Joan—Joan—'' Bud Ingram whimpered as the door crashed after them.

The captain nodded tersely, without even having time enough to be sympathetic. ''Now we stop thinking like policemen and think like human beings for this once, departmental regulations to the contrary,'' he promised. He spoke quietly into his desk-phone. ''Give me Mercer at Poplar Street. . . .'' And then, ''This man Crow of yours . . . He's off-duty right now, you say?''

''He's at the wake, he's beyond your reach,'' Ingram moaned. ''He won't report back until—''

''Sh!'' the captain silenced him. ''He may be one of them, but he's a policeman along with it.'' He said to Mercer, ''I want you to send out a short-wave, asking him to call in to you at his precinct-house at once. And when he does, I want you to keep him on the wire, I want that line kept open until his call has been traced! That man must not get off until I've found out where he's talking from and had a chance to get there, and I'll hold you responsible, Mercer. Is that clear? It's a matter of life and death. You can make whatever case he's on at present the excuse. I'll be waiting to start out from here the minute I hear from you.'' And then, into the desk-transmitter: ''I want an emergency raiding-party made up at once, two cars, everyone you can spare. I want shovels, spades and picks, plenty of them. I want a third car, with an inhalator-squad, oxygen-tent and the whole works. Yeah, motorcycle escort—and give orders ahead: *No sirens, no lights.*''

Ingram said. ''The short-wave mayn't reach him—Crow. And if it does, he may not answer it, pretend he didn't get it.''

''He's got his car,'' the captain said, ''and he's still a policeman, no matter what else he is.'' He held the door open. "There it goes out." A set outside in one of the other rooms throbbed: "Lawrence Crow, detective first grade. Lawrence Crow, detective first grade. Ring up Mercer at your precinct-house immediately. Ring up Mercer—"

Ingram leaned against the door in silent prayer. "May his sense of duty be stronger than his caution!"

The captain was buttoning on a coat, feeling for the revolver at his hip.

"It's no use, she's dead already," Ingram said. "It's one in the morning, seven hours have gone by—"

The desk-phone buzzed ominously, just once. "Hold him!" was all the captain rasped into it, and thrust Ingram out ahead of him. "He's calling in—get out there to the car!"

And as the car-door cracked shut after them outside the building, he gave a terse: "All-night drugstore, Main on the 700-block!" They started off like a procession of swift silent black shadows, the only sound of their going the muffled pounding of motorcycles around and ahead of them.

Crow's car was standing there outside the lighted place as they swept up, and he was still inside. Two of them jumped in, hurried him out between them. The captain stood facing him.

"Your badge," he said. "You're under arrest. Where was she taken, this girl, Joan Blaine? Where is she now?"

"I don't know who she is," he said.

The captain drew his gun. "Answer me or I'll shoot you where you stand!"

Ingram said hopelessly, "He's not afraid of death."

"No, I'm not," Crow answered quietly.

"He'll be afraid of pain, then!" the captain said. "Take him back inside. You two come with me. The rest of you keep out, understand?"

The glass door flashed open again after they'd gone in

and the drugstore nightclerk was thrust out on the side-walk, looking frightened. A full-length shade was suddenly drawn down behind him.

Ingram stayed in the car, head clasped in his arms, bowed over his lap. A muffled scream sounded somewhere near at hand in the utter stillness. The door suddenly flew open and the captain came running out alone. He was stripping off a rubber glove; the reek of some strong acid reached those in the car. Through the open door behind him came the sound of a man sobbing brokenly like a little child, a man in pain.

"Inhalator-squad follow my car," the captain snapped. "Greenwood Park, main driveway. The rest of you go to a large house standing in the middle of its own grounds over on the South Side near Valley Road. Surround it and arrest every man and woman you find in it."

They separated; the captain's and Ingram's car fled silently westward along the nightbound boulevard toward the immense public park on that side of the city.

Trees, lawns, meadows, black under the starlight, suddenly swept around them, and to the left there was the faint coruscation of a body of water. A bagpipe of brakes and a puff of burnt-rubber stench and they had skidded to a halt.

"Lights!" ordered the captain, stumbling out. "Train the heads after us—and bring those tools and the oxygen-tanks!" The sward bleached vividly green as the two cars backed sideways into position. It was suddenly full of scattered, moiling men, trampling about, heads down like bloodhounds.

The one farthest afield shouted: "Here's a patch without grass!"

They came running from all directions, contracted into a knot around him.

"That's it—see the oblong, see the darker color from the freshly-upturned—!" Coats flew up into the air like waving banners, a shovel bit in, another, another. But Ingram was at it with his raw, bared hands again, like a mole, pleading. "Be careful! Oh be careful, men! This is my girl!"

"Now keep your heads," the captain warned. "Just a minute more. Keep him back, he's getting in their way."

A hollow sound, a *Phuff!* echoed from the inch of protruding pipe, and the man testing it, flat on his stomach, lifted his face, said, "It's partly open all the way down."

The earth parted like a wave across the top of it, and they were lifting it, and they were prying at the lid, gently, carefully, no blows. "Now, bring up the tanks—quick!" the captain said, and to no one in particular, "What a night!" They were still holding Ingram back by main force, and then suddenly as the lid came off, they didn't have to hold him any more.

She was in a bridal gown, and she was beautiful, even as still and as marble-white as she was, when they lifted the disarranged veil—when they gently drew aside the protecting arm she'd thrown before her eyes. Then she was hidden from Ingram by their backs.

Suddenly the police-doctor straightened up. "Take that tube away. This girl doesn't need oxygen—there's nothing the matter with her breathing, or her heart-action. She needs restoratives, she's in a dead faint from fright, that's all!"

Instantly they were all busy at once, chafing her hands and arms, clumsily yet gently slapping her face, holding ammonia to her nose. With the fluttering of her eyelids came a shriek of unutterable terror, as though it had been waiting in her throat all this time to be released.

"Lift her out of that thing, quick, before she sees it," the captain whispered.

Back raced the cars, with the girl that had come up out of her grave—and beside her, holding her close, a man who had been healed of all his fears, cured—even as the Friends of Death had promised.

"And each time I'd come to, I'd go right off again," she whispered huskily.

"That probably saved you," the doctor on the other side of her said, "lying still. You'll be all right, you've had a bad fright, that's all."

Bud Ingram held her close, her head upon his shoulder, eyes unafraid staring straight ahead now.

"I never knew there could be such a love in all this world," he murmured.

She smiled a feeble little smile. "Look in my heart sometime—and see," she said.

There were sensational disclosures the next day, when the Friends of Death appeared in court. A number of leading citizens were among them—men and women whom the weird society was draining of their wealth. Others, there were, who claimed they had been brought back from the grave—and, indeed, there were doctor's certificates and burial permits to testify to the truth of this. Only later, at the trial of the leaders of the cult, did the whole story come to light. The people who had "died" and been buried were those chosen by the leaders for their reputations for honesty and reliability. They were then slowly poisoned by a member planted in their household by the society for this purpose—sometimes it was a servant, sometimes a member of the person's own family. But the poison was not fatal. It induced a state of partially suspended organic functions which a cursory medical examination might diagnose as death, the rest was handled by doctors and undertakers—even civil employees—who were members of the "Friends." Then the victim was resuscitated, persuaded he had been restored to life by the secret processes of the society, and initiated as a member. His testimony, after that, was responsible for gaining many new members, without the dangerous necessity of "killing" and reviving more than the first few. And the "penalties" inflicted upon recalcitrant members made those remaining, participants in capital crime—and made the society's hold on them absolute.

But the greatest hold of all—the one which made the vast majority of the members rejoice in their bondage, and turn into rabid fiends at the least suspicion of disloyalty in the organization—was the infinitely comforting knowledge that no longer need they fear death.

And, in the words of the state prosecutor, most of them had been punished sufficiently for their sins in the terrible awakening to the realization that they were not immortals—and that somewhere, sometime, their graves awaited them. . . .

I'M DANGEROUS TONIGHT

THE THING, WHATEVER it was—and no one was ever sure afterwards whether it was a dream or a fit or what—happened at that peculiar hour before dawn when human vitality is at its lowest ebb. The Blue Hour they sometimes call it, *l'heure bleue*—the ribbon of darkness between the false dawn and the true, always blacker than all the rest of the night has been before it. Criminals break down and confess at that hour; suicides nerve themselves for their attempts; mists swirl in the sky; and—according to the old books of the monks and the hermits—strange, unholy shapes brood over the sleeping rooftops.

At any rate, it was at this hour that her screams shattered the stillness of that top-floor apartment overlooking the Parc Monceau. Curdling, razor-edged screams that slashed through the thick bedroom door. The three others who shared the apartment with Maldonado—her maid, her secretary, her cook—sat bolt upright in their beds. They came out into the hall one by one. The peasant cook crossed herself again and again. The maid whimpered and seemed ready to add her own screams to those that were sounding in that bedroom at the end of the hall. The secretary, brisk, business-like, modern, and just a little metallic, wasted no time; she cried out, "Somebody's murdering *madame!*" and rushed for the bedroom door.

She pounded, pushed at it; it wouldn't open. But then they all knew that Maldonado habitually slept with her door locked. Still, the only way to reach her was through this door. The screams continued, a little less violently now than at first.

"Madame Maldonado!" the secretary cried frantically. "Open! Let us in! What is the matter?"

The only answer was a continuation of those long, shuddering moans of terror. "Come here and help me!" the secretary ordered the cringing cook. "You're strong. Throw your weight against the door. See if you can break it down!"

The husky Breton woman, strong as an ox, threw her shoulder against it again and again. The perpendicular bolt that held it was forced out of its groove in the sill, the two halves shot apart. Something streaked by between the legs of the three frightened women—Maldonado's Persian cat, a projectile of psychic terror, its fur standing like a porcupine's quills, its green eyes lambent, its ears flat-hissing, spitting.

The secretary was the first to enter. She was an intelligent young woman of the modern breed, remember. She believed only what her eyes saw, what her ears heard, what her nostrils smelled. She reached out quickly, snapped the light switch. The screams died with the darkness, and became instead a hoarse panting for breath. Eve Maldonado, greatest of all Paris designers, lay crouched across the bed like a terrified animal. There was no sign of a struggle anywhere in the big room. It held no intruder in it, no weapon, no trace of blood or violence. Maldonado was very much alive, unbruised and unhurt, but her face was the color of clay, and her whole body trembled uncontrollably. She couldn't speak for a long time.

Her overtaxed vocal chords refused to respond.

But there were things in the room that should not have been there—a thin diaphanous haze of smoke, as from a cigarette, suspended motionless halfway between floor and ceiling. The bowl beside the bed was crammed with cigarette-ends, but none of those butts in it were smoldering any longer, and both windows overlooking the Parc were wide open. The fresh before-dawn breeze blowing through them should have dissipated that haze long ago. Yet it was plainly visible in the electric light, as though it had been caused by something heavier than burnt paper and tobacco. There was a faintly noticeable odor also, an unpleasant one. A little like burnt feathers, a little like chemicals, a little like—sulphur or coal gas. Hard to identify, vague, distinctly out of place there in that dainty bedroom.

"*Madame!* What was it? What has happened?" the secretary asked anxiously. The other two were peering in from the doorway.

A steel gleam on the night-stand beside the bed caught her eye. She put out her hand and quickly hid the needle before the other two had seen it. "Madame," she whispered reproachfully, "you promised me—!" Maldonado had been in a severe automobile accident a year before. To relieve the pain she had suffered as an after-effect it had been necessary for awhile to—

The young woman went over and hid the needle swiftly in a drawer. Coming back, something on the floor touched her foot. She stopped to pick up some kind of triangular cape or cloak. It was black on one side, a bright flame-red on the other. At first glance it seemed to be brocaded satin, but it wasn't. It glistened. It was almost like the skin of a snake. An odor of musk arose from it.

Maldonado affected exotic negligeés like this one; she must have dropped it in the throes of her nightmare just now. But then as the secretary prepared to fling it back across the foot of the bed, she saw that there was already one there, an embroidered Chinese thing. At the same instant the designer caught sight of what she was holding; it seemed to renew all her terror. She screamed once more, shrank away from it. Her voice returned for the first time.

"That's it! That's *it!*" She shuddered, pointing. "Don't bring it near me! Take it away. Take it away, I'm afraid of it."

"But it's yours, *madame,* isn't it?"

"No!" the woman groaned, warding it off with both hands and averting her head. "Oh, don't—*please* take it away."

"But it must be yours. How else did it get here? You must have brought it home with you from the atelier. You've forgotten, that's all."

Maldonado, beside herself, was holding her head between her two hands. "We have nothing like that at the shop," she panted. "I *saw* how it got in here! I *saw* how it came into this room!"

The secretary, holding the thing up by one hand, felt a sudden inexplicable surge of hatred well up in her. A hatred that was almost murderous. She thought, "I'd like to kill her!" And the craving was literal, not just a momentary resentment expressed by a commonplace catch-phrase. She could feel herself being *drawn* to commit some overt act against the whimpering woman on the bed. Crushing her skull with something, grasping her throat between her hands and throttling her. . . .

It must have shown in her face. Maldonado, staring at her, suddenly showed a new kind of fear, a lesser fear than before—the fear of one human for another. She drew back beyond the secretary's reach.

The secretary let the thing she was holding fall to the floor. The impulse died with it. She passed the back of her hand dazedly before her eyes. What had made her feel that way just now? Was Maldonado's hysteria catching—one of those mass-psychoses to which women, in particular, are sometimes susceptible? This woman before her was her employer, her benefactress, had always treated her well. She admired her, respected her—and yet suddenly she had found herself contemplating killing her. Not only contemplating it, but contemplating it with delight, almost with an insatiable longing. Perhaps, she thought, it was the reaction from the severe nervous shock Maldonado's screams had caused them all just now. But even so, to take so horrible a form—

Something was affecting the other two, too; she could see that. Some sort of tension. The maid, who was a frivolous little soul, kept edging toward the door, as if she didn't like it in here, without knowing why. The Breton cook had her underlip thrust out belligerently and the flesh around her eyes had hardened in hostility, but against whom, or what was causing it, there was no way of telling.

Maldonado said, "Get them out of here. I've got to talk to you." The secretary motioned and they went.

The maid returned for a moment, dropped the fugitive cat just over the threshold, then closed the door on it. The animal, perfectly docile in her arms until then, instantly began to act strangely. Its fur went up and its ears back, it crouched in wary retreat from the inanimate piece of goods on the floor, then finding that its escape was cut off, sidled around it in a wide circle and slunk under the bed. No amount of coaxing could get it out again. Two frightened green eyes in the shadows and a recurrent hissing were all that marked its presence.

Maldonado's face was ghastly. "That," she said, pointing below the bed where the cat lurked, "and that"—pointing to what lay on the floor—"proves it was no dream. Do dreams leave marks behind them?"

"What was no dream?" The secretary was cool, patient. She had humored Maldonado before.

"What I saw—in here." She caught at her throat, as

though still unable to breathe properly. "Get me some cognac. I can speak to *you* about it. I couldn't in front of them. They'd only say I was crazy—" She drank, put the thimble-glass down. A trace of color returned to her face. "There was someone in this room with me!" she said. "I was lying here wide awake. I distinctly remember looking at my watch, on the stand here next to me, just before it happened. I can even recall the time. It was 4:35. Does one look at the time in one's sleep?"

"One could dream one had," the secretary suggested.

"That was no dream! A second later, as I put the watch down, there was a soft step on the balcony there outside my window, and someone came through it into the room—"

"But it's seven floors above the street, there's no possible way for anyone to get on it! It's completely cut off!" The secretary moved her hands. "It didn't occur to me to scream at first, for that very reason. It seemed impossible that anyone *could* come in from there—"

"It is," said the secretary levelly. "You've been working too hard."

"It was no burglar. It seemed to be someone in an opera-cloak. It made no hostile move toward me, kept its back toward me until it had gone all the way around here, to the foot of the bed, where you found that—thing. Then it turned to look at me—" She shuddered spasmodically again, and quickly poured out a few more drops of cognac.

"And?" the secretary prompted.

Maldonado shaded her eyes with her hand, as though unable to bear the thought even now. "I saw its face—the conventional face that we all have seen in pictures and at plays. Illuminated from below with the mot awful red light. Unspeakably evil. Little goat-horns coming out of here, at the side of the skull—"

The secretary flicked her thumb toward the bureau drawer where she'd hidden the needle. "You'd used—that, just before this?"

The secretary's glance was piercing.

"Well, yes. But the cat didn't. And how do you explain what—you picked up from the floor? Whatever it was, it was all wrapped in that thing. It took it off, kept swirling it around there in the middle of the room—a little bit like matadors do in a bullfight. I distinctly felt the *breeze* from it in my face, coming from that way, toward the windows, not away from them! And then he, it—whatever the thing was—spoke. I heard it very clearly. There were no sounds from the street at all. He said. 'Why don't you create a dress like this, Maldonado, and dedicate it to me? Something that will turn whoever wears it into my servant. Here, I'll leave it with you.' That was when I at last found my voice and began to scream. I thought I'd go insane. And even through all my screaming I could hear Rajah over there in the corner with his back up, spitting madly—"

The secretary was getting a little impatient with this preposterous rigamarole. Maldonado was supposed to be one of the brainiest women in Paris, and here she was driveling the most appalling nonsense about seeing a demon in her room. Either the sedatives she was using were breaking down her mind, or she was overworked, subject to hallucinations. "And did this visitor leave the same way, through the window?" the secretary asked ironically.

"I don't know. I was too frightened to look."

The secretary tapped her teeth with her thumbnail. "I think we'd better tell Dr. Ranard that that"—she indicated the drawer—"is beginning to get a hold on you. He'd better discontinue it. Suppose you take another swallow of cognac and try to get some sleep—"

She brushed the fallen cloak aside with the point of her toe, then stopped, holding it that way. Again that sudden urge, that blind hatred, swept her. She wanted to swing the cognac-decanter high over her head, to brain Maldonado with it, to watch the blood pour out of her shattered head.

She withdrew her foot, staggered a little. Her mind cleared.

Maldonado said: "Take that thing out of here! Don't leave it in here with me! How do we know what it is?"

"No," the secretary said weakly, "Don't ask me to touch it any more. I'm almost frightened myself now. I'm going back to my room, I feel—strange." She pulled the door open, went out without looking back.

The cat, seeing an avenue of escape, made a belated dash from under the bed, but the door was already closed when the animal reached it again. The cat stood up on its hind paws, scratching and mewing pathetically. Maldonado slipped off the bed and went to get it. "Come here, come here," she coaxed. "You seem very anxious to leave me—" She picked it up and started back with it in her arms, stroking it. As she did so she trod unwittingly on the cloak, lying there coiled on the floor like a snake waiting to strike.

Her face altered; her eyebrows went up saturninely, the edges of her fine white teeth showed through her parted lips; in an instant all tenderness was gone, she was like a different person altogether.

"Well, leave me then, if you want to so badly!" she said, as the cat began to struggle in her arms. Her eyes dilated, gazing down at it. "Leave me for good!" She threw the animal brutally on the bed, then with a feline swiftness that more than matched its own, she thrust one of the heavy pillows over it, bore down with her whole weight, bands turned inward so that the fingers pointed toward one another. Her elbows slowly flexed, stiffened, flexed, stiffened, transmitting the weight of her suspended body to the pillow—and to what lay trapped below it.

The little plumed tail that was all that protruded, spiraled madly, almost like the spoke of a wheel, then abruptly stopped. Maldonado's foot, unnoticed, was still caught in a fold of the cloak, had dragged it across the floor after her.

Hours later, the secretary returned to tell her she was giving up her job. She was putting on her gloves and her packed valise stood outside in the hall. The little maid had fled already, without the formality of giving notice. The pious cook was at Mass, trying to find an answer to her problem: whether to turn her back on the perfectly good wages she was earning, or to risk remaining in a place where inexplicable things took place in the dead of the night. As for the secretary herself, all she knew was that twice she had been tempted to murder within the space of moments. There was some unclean mystery here that she could not fathom. She was modern and sensible enough to realize that the only thing to do, for her own sake, was remove herself beyond its reach. Before temptation became commission.

What had precipitated her decision was a phone call she had made to the workshop in an effort to trace the cape that was the only tangible evidence of the mystery. Their answer, after an exhaustive check-up had been made, only bore out Maldonado's words: there had never been anything answering its description in the stockroom, not even a two-by-four sample. An account was kept of every button, every ribbon. So whatever it was, how it had got into Maldonado's room, it hadn't come from the shop.

The secretary saw at a glance that a change had come over Maldonado, since she had left her several hours before. A shrewd, exultant look had replaced the abysmal terror on her face. Whatever unseen struggle had taken place in here in the interval, had been won by the forces of evil. Maldonado was sitting at her desk, busy with pencil and sketch-pad doing a rough draft. She had the cape draped around one shoulder.

"Three times I took this thing to the window, to throw it out into the street," she admitted, "and I couldn't let go of it. It seemed to cling magnetically to my hands. The idea wouldn't let me alone, it kept my hypnotized, until finally I had to get it down on paper—''

A cry of alarm broke from the secretary. ''What happened to Rajah?'' She had just seen the lifeless bedraggled tail hanging down below the pillow. ''Take that off him, he'll suffocate!''

Maldonado paid no attention. ''He has already suffocated.'' She held up the sketch. ''Look, that's just the way—what I saw last night—carried it. Call the car. I'm going to get to work on it at once. There's money in it, it'll be worth a fortune—'' But her eyes, over the top of the sketch, had come to rest on the secretary's slim young throat. There was a sharp-pointed ivory paper cutter lying on the desk. As she held the drawing up with one hand, the other started to inch uncontrollably toward it, like a crawling five-legged white beetle.

Inching, crawling—

The secretary, warned by some sixth sense, gave a muffled cry, turned and bolted down the long hallway. The street-door of the apartment slammed after her.

Maldonado smiled a little, readjusted the cape over her shoulder, went on talking to herself as though nothing had happened while she studied the finished sketch. ''I'll advertise it as—let's see—'*I'm Dangerous Tonight—a dress to bring out the devil in you!*' ''

And so a deadly thing was born.

*   *   *

She was standing on a small raised turntable, about two feet off the floor, which could be revolved in either direction by means of a small lever, on the same general principle as a mobile barber's chair. She had been standing on it since early afternoon, with short rest periods every half-hour or so; it was eleven at night now.

They were all around her, working away like ants, some

on their knees, some standing up. The floor was littered with red and black scraps, like confetti. She had eyes for only one thing in the whole workroom: a pair of sharp shears lying on a table across the way from her. She kept looking at them longingly, moistening her lips from time to time. When they were closed, like they were now, they came to a sharp point, like a poniard. And when they were open, the inner edge of each blade was like a razor. She was digging her fingernails into her own sides, to keep from jumping down to the floor, picking them up, and cutting and slashing everyone within reach with them. She'd been doing that, in her brain, for hours; she was all black-and-blue from the pinch and bite of her own nails. Once, the seamstress kneeling at her feet had saved her. She'd already had one foot off the stand, on her way over to them, and the latter had stuck a pin in her to make her hold still. The pain had counteracted the desperate urge she kept feeling. It did no good to try to look at anything else; her eyes returned to the shears each time.

The funny part of it was, when she was at rest, off the stand in just her underthings, and had every opportunity of seizing them and doing what she wanted to, she didn't seem to want to. It was only when she was up there with the dress on her that the urge swept over her. She couldn't understand why her thoughts should take this homicidal turn. She supposed it was because she was due to meet Belden at the Bal Tabarin at midnight, and just tonight they'd picked to work overtime, to finish the thing, keeping her here long after she should have been out of the place.

Meeting him wasn't like meeting anyone else; he was living on borrowed time; he couldn't stick around any one place too long waiting for anyone. He was wanted for murder in the States, and there was an American detective over here now, looking for him; he had to lie low, keep moving around fast, with this Government man always just a step behind him, creeping up slowly but surely. Twice now, in the past two weeks, he'd just missed Belden by the skin of his teeth. And Belden couldn't get out of town until the fake passports his friend Battista was making for him were ready. He'd have them by the end of this week, and then he was going to head for the Balkans—and take her with him, of course. Until then, he was caught in a squirrel cage.

He was a swell guy; suppose he did run dope from France into the States? *She* was for him. She'd rather part with her right arm than see him arrested and taken back to die.

He'd killed one of their Department of Justice agents, and they'd never rest until they'd evened things up. They sat you in a chair over there, he'd told her, and shocked you to death with electricity. It sounded awful, a million times worse than the swift and merciful guillotine.

She was crazy about him, steadfast with that utter loyalty only a woman in love can know. She'd have gone through fire and water to be with him, anytime, anywhere. She was ready to be a fugitive with him for the rest of her life—"Whither thou goest, I will go; thy people shall be my people"—and when a Parisienne is ready to leave Paris behind forever, that's something. She hadn't seen him in five days now; he had to keep moving—but last night he'd got word to her along the underworld grapevine: "The Bal au Diable, Wednesday at twelve." And here it was after eleven, and she wasn't even out of the shop yet! Wouldn't that look great, to keep him waiting, endanger him like that?

She couldn't hold out any longer. Pinching herself didn't do any good, her sides were numb now. Her eyes fastened on the shears; she started to edge toward the edge of the stand, her hand slowly stroking her side. One good jump, a grab, a quick turn—and she'd have them. "I'll take

Maldonado first,'' she decided, as she reached the edge of the platform. "The sewing-woman's so fat, she can't get out of the room as fast—'' Her knees started to dip under her, bracing for the flying jump.

The designer spoke. "All right, Mimi, take it off. It's finished.''

The sewing woman pulled; the dress fell to the floor at the mannequin's feet, and she suddenly stopped eyeing the scissors, wavered there off-balance, got limply to the floor. Now she could get at them easily—and she didn't try, seemed to have forgotten.

She staggered into the little curtained alcove to put on her street clothes.

"It's been a hard job,'' Maldonado said, "You all get a bonus.'' She went downstairs to her car. They started putting the lights out. The rest of the staff, the piece workers, had gone home hours ago. The sewing woman stayed behind a moment to stitch in the little silk label: *I'm Dangerous Tonight, by Maldonado*. Without that label it was just a dress. With it, it was a dress worth twenty thousand francs (and if the buyer was an American, twenty-five thousand.)

Mimi Brissard looked at the junk she wore to work. Stockings full of holes, sloppy old coat. And it was too late now to go back to her own place and dress decently for him. She'd never make it; she lived way out at Bilancourt. She'd look fine, showing up in these rags to meet a swell guy like Belden! Even if he was a fugitive, even if the Bal au Diable was an underworld hangout, he'd be ashamed to be seen with her. He might even change his mind about taking her.

The sewing-woman had finished the label, hung the dress up. "Coming, Mimi?''

"Go ahead,'' the girl called through the curtain, "I'll lock up.'' She'd been with them for five years, they trusted her. There was no money or anything kept up here anyway, just clothes and designs.

"Don't forget the lights." The old woman trudged wearily down the curved stone staircase to the street.

The girl stuck her head out around the curtain, eyed the dress. "I bet he'd be proud of me if I dared wear that! I could bring it back before we open up tomorrow, and they'd never even know." She went over to it, took the hanger down. The dress swept against her. Her eyes narrowed to slits. Her indecision evaporated. "Let anyone try to stop me, and see what they get!" she whispered half audibly. A minute later she had slipped the red dress over her lithe young body and was strutting—there is no other word for it—before the mirror. She hadn't heard the step on the stairs, maybe because the watchman wore felt-soled shoes to make his rounds. He must have come up to see what was taking her so long.

"Eh? Wait, where do you think you're going in that? That's the firm's property." The old man was standing there in the doorway, looking in at here.

She whirled, and the tiny arrow-headed train, that was like a devil's tail, spun around after her. The shears were still lying there on the table, midway between them.

"Where do you think I'm going? I'll tell you where *you're* going—right now! To the devil, and you're not coming back!"

There was no excuse for it. The rebuke had been paternal, half humorous. He was a good-natured, inoffensive old man, half crippled with rheumatism. He was certainly no match for her young and furious strength. And the lust to kill—this dynamic murder-voltage charging her—that gave her the force and determination of two able-bodied men.

Her hand gave a catlike pounce, and the shears clashed; the blades opened, then closed spasmodically, like a hungry mouth, as her fingers gripped the handle. They came up off the table point-foremost.

He saw in her eyes what was coming. "Wait, *mademoiselle!* Don't! Why—?"

She couldn't have told him even if she wanted to. There was a murderous frenzy in her heart. She closed in on him as he tried to retreat, facing her because he was too horrified to turn his back. There was a spasm of motion from her hand, too quick for the eye to follow, and the point of the shears suddenly sank into his chest.

He gave a cough, found the wall with his back, leaned against it. His head went down and his old black alpaca cap fell off. He could still talk. "Have pity! I've never harmed you! I'm an old man! My Solange needs me—"

The shears found his throat this time. He fell down on top of them and was silent.

Something dark like mucilage glistened where he lay.

She had jumped back—not in remorse, but to keep the bottom of her skirt clear of his blood.

Tensed, curved forward from the waist up, peering narrowly at him like something out of a jungle that kills not for food but for love of killing, she executed strange gestures, as though her arms were those of a puppet worked by strings by some master-puppeteer. Stretched them full-length up over her head, palm to palm, as if in some unholy incantation. Then let them fall again and caressed her own sides, as though inordinately pleased.

At last she moved around him, retrieved the ring of keys that he carried beneath his blouse. She would need them to come back into the building later on. She found the lightswitch, plunged the room—and what it contained—into darkness. She closed the door, and moved down the circular stone-stairs with a rustling sound, such as a snake might make on a bed of dry leaves.

The *bal* was not on the list of synthetic Apache dens that guides show visitors to Paris. It was too genuine for that;

sightseers would have been disappointed, as the real thing always makes a poorer show than the fake. It did not pay those who frequented it to advertise themselves or be conspicuous. Nothing ever seemed to be going on there. People would come in, slump down in a chair; no one would pay any attention to them; they would sometimes sit for hours, seemingly lost in dreams; then as suddenly be gone again, as unnoticed as they had come.

There was an accordion fastened to the wall, and a man who had lost an arm in the trenches would occasionally come in, sit down by it, and play softly sentimental ballads with his one hand only, pulling in in and out of the wall.

The *bal* consisted of simply a long, dingy, dimly lighted, smoke-filled semi-basement room; no one ever spoke above a low murmur. If the police never bothered anyone, possibly it was because that was the smartest thing to do. The *bal* often came in handy as a convenient starting-point for a search for any wanted criminal at any given time; it was a focal point for the Paris underworld.

When Mimi, in her red-and-black dress, came down the short flight of stone steps from the street-level, Belden wasn't there. At one table was a soiled glass in a china-saucer stamped: *1Fr50*. As she passed by she glanced into it; in the dregs of vermouth-and-cassis floated a cigarette end. That was Belden's unmistakable trademark; that was where he'd been sitting. He never drank anything without leaving a cigarette in the glass or cup.

She sat down one table away. She knew all the faces by sight, but she gave no sign of recognition, nor was any given to her. No. . . . There *was* one face there she didn't know. Out in the middle of the room, only its lower half visible under a snapdown hat-brim. It didn't have the characteristic French pallor. The chin was squarer than Gallic chins are apt to be. There was a broadness of shoulder there, also, unknown on the Continent.

The man had a stale beer before him. But that was all

right; no one came in here to eat or drink. He was staring at the red-and-white checks of the tablecloth, playing checkers on the squares with little *sou*-pieces. He looked at nothing, but he saw everything; it was written all over him. The atmosphere was tense, too. Without seeming to, all the others were watching him cautiously; they scented danger. His presence was a threat. . . .

Petion, the proprietor, found something to do that brought him past her table. Carefully he removed the neglected glass and saucer from the one ahead.

"Where's Belden?"

Petion didn't seem to hear. The corner of his mouth moved in Apache argot. "Get out of here fast, you little fool. That bird over there is the one that's after him. The American *flic*. Luckily Belden saw him arrive. We got him out the back way. He's up at your place, waiting for you. His own room is too hot." Petion couldn't seem to get the grimy cloth at Belden's table straight enough to please him.

The man in the middle of the room jumped a five-*sou* piece with a ten-*sou* piece. You could almost *feel* the eyes peering through the felt of the shadowing brim.

"Now, watch out how you move—you may draw him after you without knowing it and put him onto Belden."

There was a fruit-knife on the table. She glanced at it, then her eyes strayed to Petion's fat neck, creased above his collar. He caught the pantomine, gave her a surprised look, as much as to say, "What's got into *you*? He been feeding you some of his product?"

He straightened the empty chair and said aloud: "Well, what are you hanging around for? I tell you the dog is a United States Government agent."

"All right, clear away," she breathed impatiently, "I can handle this."

She got up and started slowly toward the stairs to the street. Death by electrocution, the thing she'd always dreaded so, ever since Belden had first told her what he had coming to him. Death by electricity—much worse than death at the point of a pair of shears or a table knife. She veered suddenly, as uncontrollably as though pulled by a magnet, turned off toward that table in the middle of the room, went directly over to it. She was smiling and her eyes were shining.

There was a small, nervous stir that rustled all over the room. One man shifted his chair. Another set his glass of *vin blanc* into a saucer, too noisily. A woman laughed, low in her throat.

He didn't seem to see her, not even when her fingertips were resting on the edge of the table.

"Soir, m'sieu."

He said in English: "Wrong table, *petite. Pas libre ce soir."*

She'd learned some English from Belden. So now she pulled a second chair out, sat down, helped herself to one of his cigarettes. Her hand trembled a little, but not from nervousness. In the dim recesses of the room whispers were coursing along the walls: "She's giving him the come-on, trying to get him somewhere where Belden can finish him. That's the kind of girl to have!"

"She'll trip herself up. Those fish are no fools."

She began to speak quietly, her eyelids lowered. "I am Mimi Brissard, and I live at Bilancourt, number 5 rue Poteaux top floor front."

The line of his mouth hardened a little. "Move on. I told you I'm not int—"

"I am Belden's girl," she continued as though she hadn't heard him, "and he is up there right now, waiting for me. Now, are you interested?"

He pushed his hat back with a thumb and looked at her for the first time. There was no admiration in his eyes, not any gratitude, only the half-concealed contempt the police always have for an informer. "Why are you welshing on him?" he said warily.

She couldn't answer, any more than she could have answered the old watchman when he had asked her why she was stabbing him to death. She fingered the dress idly, as thou she sensed something, but it eluded her.

"You better go back and tell him it won't work," he said drily. "He's not getting me like he got Jimmy Fisher in New York, he's not dealing with a green kid now. I'm getting him—and without the help of any chippy either!"

"Then I have to prove that this is no decoy? Did you see that vermouth-glass with the cigarette in it over there? That was he. This goes with it." She palmed a scrap of paper at him: *Bal au Diable 24th.* "I was to meet him here. You spoiled it. He's up there now. He's armed and he'll shoot to kill, rather than go back—"

"What did you think I expected him to do, scatter petals at my feet?"

"Without me you haven't got one chance in ten of taking him alive. But through me, you can do it. And you want him alive, don't you?"

"Yep," he said curtly. "The man he killed—Jimmy Fisher—was my brother. . . ."

She squirmed eagerly inside the glistening cocoon that sheathed her. But a change had come over him meanwhile. Her nearness, her presence at the table, seemed to be affecting him on some way. He had come alive, menacingly, hostilely, and he was . . . dangerous, too. His jaw line set pugnaciously, a baleful light flickered in his gray eyes, his upper lip curled back from his teeth. His hand roamed down his coat toward the flap of his back-pocket. "I never wanted to kill anyone so much in my life," he growled throatily, "as I do you right now!" He started tugging at something, at the small of his back.

She looked down, saw that a flounce of her dress was

brushing against his knee. She moved her chair slightly back, and the contact broke.

His hand came up on the table again, empty. His face slowly slipped back into its mask of impassivity. He was breathing a little heavily, that was all, and there was a line of moisture along the crease in his forehead.

"So he's at Bilancourt, 5 rue Poteaux," he said finally. "Thanks. You're a fine sweetheart. Some other dame, I suppose."

"No," she said simply. "I loved him very much only an hour ago, at eleven o'clock. I must have changed since then, that's all. I don't know why. Now I'd like to think of him being electrocuted and cursing my name as he dies. . . . Follow me there and watch which window lights up. Keep watching. My window-shade's out of order. Tonight it will be especially so. I'll have trouble with it. When you see it go up, then come down again, you'll know he's ready for the taking."

"Okay, Delilah," he murmured. "When I first hit Paris I thought there was no one lower than Belden. He shot an unarmed kid of twenty-five—in the back, without giving him a chance. But now I see there's someone lower still— and that's his woman. He, at least, wouldn't turn you in; I'll give him that much. But let me warn you. If you think you're leading me into a trap, if I have to do any shooting, you get the first slug out of this gun! That's how you stand with me, little lady."

She smiled derisively, stood up. She didn't bother to reply to his contempt. "Don't leave right after me, they're all watching you here. I'll wait for you under the first streetlight around the corner. She added dreamily: "I couldn't think of anything I wanted to do more than this. That's why I'm doing it."

She went slowly up the stone steps to the street-door, her pointed train wriggling after her from side to side. She turned her head and flashed a smile over her shoulder. Then she went out and the darkness swallowed her.

Frank Fisher rinsed his mouth with beer and emptied it out on the floor.

The room was dark and empty when she stepped into it from the hall outside. The dim light shining behind her outlined her; her silhouette was diabolic, long and sinuous and wavering. Two ridges of hair above her ears looked almost like horns. Something clicked warningly somewhere in the room, but that was all. She closed the door.

"Chéri?" she whispered. "I'm going to put up the light. It's all right. *C'est Mimi.*"

A bulb went on, and its rays, striking out like yellow rain, touched off a gleam between two curtains pulled tightly together across a doorless closet. The gleam was black in the middle, holed through. It elongated into a stubby automatic; and a hand, an arm, a shoulder, a man, came slowly out after it toward her.

Steve Belden was misleadingly unogre-like, for a man who had poisoned thousands of human lives with heroin. In repose his face was almost pleasant looking, and his eyes had that directness of gaze that usually betokens honesty.

The girl glanced quizzically at the gun as he continued to point it at her. "Well, put it way, Chéri," she protested ironically. "Haven't you seen me some place before?"

He sheathed it under his arm, scowled. "What took you so long? D'you know he nearly jumped me, waiting for you at the *bal* just now? Petion got me out the back way by pretending to shake out a table cloth, holding it up at arms's length for a screen. For a minute we were both in the same room, he and I! I hope you haven't steered him over here after you without knowing it."

"He wasn't there any more. Must have looked in merely, then gone away again."

"What's the idea of that dress? I nearly took a shot at you when you opened the door just now."

"It's what they kept me overtime working on tonight. I left it on to save time. I'll sneak it back first thing in the morning—"

"You'll have to have some reach, if you do. Battista finally came through with the passports. We're taking the Athens Express at daybreak. Matter of fact I could have made the night-train to the Balkans, if it hadn't been for you. I waited over so I could take you with me—"

"So four hours more in Paris does the trick?" she said, looking at him shrewdly.

He frowned.

"Yeah, and then we're all set. Fisher's extradition-writ's no good in Greece, and Panyiotis pulls enough weight there to fix it so we both disappear for good. If I've outsmarted him for three weeks now, I can outlast him the few hours there are left. What'd you say?"

She said, "If—" in a low voice. "When did you get any sleep?"

"Night before last."

"Well, take off your coat, lie down here, rest up a while. I'll keep watch. I'll wake you in time for the train. Here, let me have that, I'll keep it trained on the door."

"What do *you* know about these things?" he grinned, but he passed the gun over to her, stretched himself out. "Put out the light," he said sleepily. He began to relax, the long-sustained tension started to go out of his nerves; he could trust her. She was the only one. . . .

The gun was not pointed at the door, but at him—at the top of his head from behind, through the bars of the bed. Her face was a grimace of delight. Then slowly she brought the gun down again. A bullet in the brain—You didn't feel anything, didn't know anything. But electrocution—what anguish, what terror preceded it! Electrocution was a much better way.

A sharp click from the gun roused him, after he had already begun to doze off. He stiffened, looked at her over his shoulder. "What was that?"

"Just making sure it's loaded." She kicked something along the floor with the tip of her foot, something metalically round. It rolled under the bed.

His eyes closed again. He turned his head toward the wall. His breathing thickened.

A warning *whirr* of the shade-roller roused him a second time. He raised half upright on his elbows. His free hand clawed instinctively at his empty shoulder-holster.

She was reaching for the cord, pulling the shade all the way down again to the bottom.

"What're you doing?" he rasped. "Get away from that window! I told you to put the light out, didn't I?"

"It slipped. It needs fixing," she murmured. "It's all right, there's no one down there. Here goes the light—"

The last thing he said, as he lay back again, was: "And take that damn dress off too, while you're about it. Every time I lamp it on you, it throws a shock into me all over again. I think I'm seeing things—"

She said nothing.

He drowsed off again. Then in the dark, only seconds later, she was leaning over him, shaking him awake. Her breath was a sob that threatened to become a scream. The whiteness of her form was dimly visible. She must have discarded the dress while he slept.

"Steve. *Mon* Steve!" she was moaning, "Get up!" She pulled him frenziedly erect with both arms. "*Sauves-toi!* Out! *File—vite!* maybe you can still make it by way of the roof—"

He was on his feet, clear of the bed, in an instant. "What's up? What's up?"

"I've sold you out!" the groan seemed to come from

way down at the floor, as though she was all hollow inside. "I tipped him off at the *bal.* I signaled him with the shade just now—"

The light flashed on.

"Oh, don't stand there looking at me. Quick, get out this door, he has four flights to climb—"

He was usually very quick, but not this time. He stood there eyeing her as though he couldn't believe what he heard. Then at last, he grasped what she had told him. He pulled the gun from her unresisting hand, turned it the other way around, jabbed it at her heart. It clicked repeatedly, almost like a typewriter.

"I—the bullets—" she shuddered. "Under the bed— Oh, get, Steve—save yourself now—"

A warped floorboard groaned somewhere outside the room.

"Too late!"

Belden had dropped down on one knee, was reaching out desperately toward the bullets. There was no pounding at the door; a shot exploded into it, and splinters of wood flew out on the inside. The china knob fell off and lay there like an egg. The door itself ricocheted back off the flat of someone's shoe.

"All right, don't move, Belden. You're through."

Fisher came in slowly; changed gun-hands with a sort of acrobatic twist, and brought out handcuffs.

"Pull your finger joint out of that trigger hole," he added.

The automatic turned over, fell upside down on the floor.

Fisher didn't speak again until the manacles had closed. Then he said, "Got a hat or anything you want to take with you?" He seemed to see Mimi for the first time. He nodded, said curtly: "Nice work, *Mademoiselle Judas.*"

She stood shivering. The dress lay on the floor behind her, but she made no move to reach out for it.

Belden took his capture calmly enough. He didn't say a word to Mimi Brissard; didn't even look at her. "It's a pleasure," he said bitterly, as Fisher motioned him forward, "if only because it means getting out of a town where there are—things like this." He spat on the floor at her feet as he went by.

Fisher hung back a minute to look her almost detachedly, up and down. He pocketed his gun, took out a wallet with his free hand, removed some lettucelike franc-notes. "What was it—money?" he said. "You haven't asked for any, but I suppose that's it. Here, go out and buy yourself a heart."

The wadded bills struck her lightly in the center of the forehead, and fluttered down her to the floor. One caught upon her breast, just over her heart, and remained poised there, like a sort of badge.

She stood there with her eyes closed, perfectly motionless, as though she were asleep standing up, while the man she'd loved and his captor began their long descent side by side down the four flights of stairs that led to the street.

When they came out of the house a moment later, they had to force their way through the crowd of people standing there blocking the entrance.

Fisher thought for a moment that it was his own shot at the lock upstairs in the house that had attracted them. But they were all turned the other way, with their backs to the building. Out in the middle of the narrow cobbled street two or three of them were bending anxiously over something. Some broken white thing lying perfectly still at their feet. One of the men was hurriedly opening and separating the leaves of a newspaper—but not to read it.

Mimi Brissard had atoned, in the only way she had left.

*   *   *

Do I dare?'' Mrs. Hiram Travis said aloud, to no one in particular, in her stateroom on the *Gascony* the night before

it reached New York. Or if to anyone at all, to the slim,
slinky red-and-black garment that the stewardess had laid
out for her across the bed under the mistaken impression
that she would wish to wear it. A stewardess who, although she had assured Mrs. Travis she was not susceptible in the least to seasickness, had come out of the cabin
looking very pale and shaken after having taken the dress
down from its hanger. Mrs. Travis had noticed the woman
glaring daggers at her, as if in some way *she* were to
blame. But this being Mrs. Travis' first trip abroad, or
anywhere at all except Sioux City, she was not well versed
in the ways of stewardesses, any more than in those of
French couturieres.

In fact she hadn't really known what that Maldonado
woman was talking about at all; they had had to make
signs to each other. *She* had wanted just a plain simple
little dress to wear to the meetings of her Thursday Club
back home in Dubuque, and then the next morning *this*
had shown up at the hotel all wrapped up in crinkly paper.
She hadn't wanted Hiram to think she was a fool, so she'd
pretended it was the one she'd ordered, and good-natured
as always, he'd paid for it without a word. Now here she
was stuck with it! And the worst part of it was, if she
didn't wear it tonight, then she'd never have another chance
to. Because she really didn't have the nerve to wear it in
Dubuque. Folks would be scandalized. And all the *francs*
it had cost!

"Do I dare?" she said again, and edged a little closer.

One only had to look at Mrs. Hiram Travis to understand the reasons for her qualms. She and the dress didn't
match up at all. They came from different worlds. She was
a youngish forty, but she made not the least attempt to
look any younger than that. She was very plain, with her
chin jutting a little too much, her eyes undistinguished,
and her mouth too flat. Her hair was a brown-red. She had
never used rouge and she had never used powder. The last

time she'd smoked a cigarette was behind her grandmother's barn at the age of fourteen. She'd never drunk anything stronger than elderberry wine in her life, until a week ago in Paris, just for the look of things, she'd tried a little white wine with her meals. She made swell pies, but now that Hi had made so much money in the lawnmower business, he wouldn't let her do her own cooking any more. He'd even retired, taken out a half-a-million dollar life-insurance policy, and they'd made this trip to Paris to see the sights. Even there the latest they'd stayed up was one night when they had a lot of postcards to write and didn't get to bed until nearly eleven-thirty. About the most daring thing she'd done in her whole life was to swipe a fancy salad fork from a hotel for a souvenir. It was also the closest she'd ever come to a criminal act. That ought to give you the picture.

She was mortally afraid of about eight million things, including firearms, strange men, and the water they were traveling on right now.

"Golly," she clucked, "I bet I'll feel like a fool in it. It's so—kind of vampish. What'll Hi say?" She reached out and rested her hand on the dress, which lay there like a coiled snake ready to strike. . . .

She drew her hand back suddenly. But she couldn't help reaching out again to touch the dress with a movement that was almost a caress.

Instantly her mind filled with the strangest thoughts—odd recollections of instants in her past that she would have said she had completely forgotten. The first time she'd ever seen her father wring a chicken's neck. The day that Hiram—way back in high school—cut his arm on a broken window. A vein, he'd cut. He'd bled . . . a lot; and she'd felt weak and sick and terrified. The automobile smash-up they'd seen that time on the State highway on the way back from Fair . . . that woman lying all twisted and crumpled on the road, with her head skewed way around like it shouldn't be—couldn't be if the woman lived.

It was funny. . . . When those things had taken place, she'd felt terrible. Now—remembering them—she found herself going over every detail in her mind, almost—lovingly.

In a magazine she had once seen a picture of Salomé kneeling on the ground holding on a great tray the head of Baptist John. The woman's body was arched forward; there was a look of utter, half-delirious absorption on her face as her lips quested for the dead, partly open mouth. And quite suddenly, with a little shock of revelation, Sarah Travis knew what Salomé had felt.

The dress slipped from her fingers. She hurried to put it on. . . .

Georges, the *Gascony's* chief bartender, said: "Perhaps *monsieur* would desire another. That's a bad col' you catch."

The watery-eyed red-nosed little man perched before him had a strip of flannel wound around his throat neatly pinned in back with two small safety-pins. He glanced furtively around over his shoulder, the length of the glittering cocktail lounge. "Mebbe you're right," he said. "But the missus is due up in a minute, I don't want her to catch me at it, she'll lace it into me, sure enough!"

Sarah, of course, wouldn't dream of approaching the bar; when she came they'd sit decorously at a little table over in the corner, he with a beer, she with a cup of Oolong tea, just to act stylish.

Hiram Travis blew his long-suffering nose into a handkerchief the size of a young tablecloth. Then he turned his attention to the live canary dangling over the bar in a bamboo cage, as part of the decorations. He coaxed a few notes out by whistling softly. Then he happened to look in the mirror before him—and he recoiled a little, his eyes bugged; and part of his drink spilled out of his glass.

She was standing next to him, right there at the bar itself, before he'd even had time to turn. An odor of musk enveloped him. The canary over their heads executed a few pinwheel flurries.

His jaw just hung open. "Well, fer—!" was all he could say. It wasn't so much the dress she was wearing, it was that her whole personality seemed to have subtly changed. Her face had a hard, set look about it. Her manner was almost poised. She wasn't fluttering with her hands the way she usually did in a room full of people, and he missed the nervous, hesitant smile on her lips. He couldn't begin to say what it was, but there was something about her that made him a little afraid of her. He even edged an inch or two away from her. Even Georges looked at her with a new professional respect not unmixed with fear.

"*Madame?*" he said.

She said, "I feel like a drink tonight," she said, and laughed a little, huskily. "What are those things—cocktails—? Like that woman over there has."

The bartender winced a little. "That, *madame*, is a double Martini. Perhaps something less—"

"No. That's what I want. And a cigarette, too. I want to try one."

Beside her, her husband could only splutter, and he stopped even that when she half turned to flash him a smile—the instinctive, brilliant smile of a woman who knows what feeble creatures men can be. You couldn't learn to smile like that. It was something a woman either knew the minute she was born, or never knew at all.

Georges recognized that smile.

"I can't believe it's you," Hiram Travis said, stupefied.

Again that smile. "It must be this dress," she said. "It does something to me. You have to live up to a gown like this, you know. . . ." There was a brief warning in her eyes. She picked up her cocktail, sipped at it, coughed a little, and then went on drinking it slowly. "About the dress," she said, "I put my hand on it and for a moment I couldn't take it away again, it seemed to *stick* to it like glue! Next thing I knew I was in it."

As the bartender struck a match to light her cigarette, she put her hand on his wrist to steady it. Travis saw him jump, draw back. He held his wrist, blew on it, looked at her reproachfully. Travis said: "Why, you scratched him, Sarah."

"Did I? And as she turned and looked at him, he saw her hand twitch a little, and drew still further away from her. "What—what's got into you?" he faltered.

There was some kind of tension spreading all around the horseshoe-shaped bar, emanating from her. All the cordiality, the sociability, was leaving it. Cheery conversations even at the far ends of it faltered and died, and the speakers looked around them as though wondering what was putting them so on edge. A heavy leaden pall of restless silence descended, as when a cloud goes over the sun. One or two people even turned and moved away reluctantly, as though they hadn't intended to but didn't like it at the bar any more. The gaunt-faced woman in red and black was the center of all eyes, but the looks sent her were not the admiring looks of men for a well-dressed woman; they were the blinking petrified looks a blacksnake would get in a poultry yard. Even the barman felt it. He dropped and smashed a glass, a thing he hadn't done since he'd been working on the ship. Even the canary felt it, and stood shivering pitifully on its perch, emitting an occasional cheep as though for help.

Sarah Travis looked up, and saw it. She took a loop of her dress, draped it around her finger, thrust it between the bars. There was a spasm of frantic movement inside, too quick for the eye to follow, a blurred pinwheel of yellow. Then the canary lay lifeless at the bottom of the cage, claws stiffly upthrust. Its heart had stopped from fright.

It wasn't what she had done—they could all see that contact hadn't killed it—it was the look on her face that was so shocking. No pity, no regret, but an expression of savage satisfaction, a sense of power to deal out life-and-death just now discovered. Some sort of unholy excitement seemed to be crackling inside her; they could all but see phosphorescent flashes of it in her eyes.

This time they began to move away in numbers, with outthrust lower lips of repugnance and dislike turned her way. Drinks were left half-finished, or were taken with them to be imbibed elsewhere. She became the focal-point for a red wave of converged hate that, had she been a man, would surely have resulted in some overt act. There were sulky whispers of "Who is that?" as they moved away. The bartender, as he detached and lowered the cage, looked daggers at her, cursed between his teeth in French.

There was only one solitary drinker left now at the bar, out of all the amiable crowd that had ringed it when she first arrived. He kept studying her inscrutably with an expressionless face; seemingly unallergic to the tension that had driven everyone else away.

"There's that detective again," she remarked with cold hostility. "Wonder he doesn't catch cold without that poor devil being chained to him. "Wonder where he's left him?"

"Locked up below, probably, while he's up getting a bracer," Travis answered mechanically. His chief interest was still his own problem: what had happened to his wife in the ten brief minutes from the time he'd left her preparing to dress in their stateroom until the time she's joined him up here? "I suppose they asked him not to bring him up with him manacled like that, for the sake of appearances. Why are you so sorry for his prisoner all of a sudden, and so set against him? Only last night you were saying what an awful type man the other fellow was and how glad you were he'd been caught.''

"Last night isn't tonight," she said shortly. "People change, Hiram." She still had the edge of her dress wrapped around her hand, as when she'd destroyed the canary. "I don't suppose you ever will, though." Her voice was low, thoughtful. She looked at her husband curiously, then deliberately reached out toward him with that hand and rested it against him.

Travis didn't go into a spasm and fall lifeless as the bird had. He displayed a sudden causeless resentment toward her, snapped, "Take your hand away, don't be pawing me!" and moved further away.

She glanced disappointedly down at her hand as though it had played a dirty trick on her, slowly unwound the strip of material, let it fall. She stared broodingly into the mirror for awhile, tendrils of smoke coming up out of her parted lips.

She said, "Hi, is that half-million-dollar insurance policy you took out before we left in effect yet or still pending?" and narrowed her eyes at her image in the glass.

"It's in effect," he assured her. "I paid the first premium on it the day before we left Dubuque. I'm carrying the biggest insurance of any individual in Ioway—"

She didn't seem particularly interested in hearing the rest. She changed the subject abruptly—or seemed to. "Which one of the bags have you got that gun in that you brought with you for protection? You know, in case we got robbed in Europe."

The sequence of questions was so glaringly, so unmistakably meaningful, that he did what almost anyone else would have done under the circumstances, ascribed it to mere coincidence and ignored it. Two separate disconnected chains of thought, crowding upon one another, had made her ask first one, then the other, that was all. It just would have *sounded* bad to a stranger, to that professional crime-detector over there for instance, but of couse *he* knew better. After all he'd been married to her for eighteen years.

"In the cowhide bag under the bed in the stateroom," he answered calmly. "Why? Every time you got a peek at it until now you squeaked, 'Throw it away, Hi! I can't stand to look at them things!' "

She touched her hand to her throat briefly and moistened her lips.

Travis noticed something, and said: "What's the matter, you seasick? Your face is all livid, kind of, and you're breathing so fast—I coulda told you not to monkey 'round with liquor when you're not used to it."

"It isn't either, Hiram. I'm all right. Leave me be." Then, with a peculiar ghastly smile lighting up her face, she said, "I'm going down below a minute to get something I need. I'll be back."

"Want me to come with you?"

"No," she said, still smiling. "I'd rather have you wait for me here, and then come out on the deck with me for a little stroll when I come back. That upper boat-deck. . . ."

The little undulating serpentine train of her dress followed her across the cocktail lounge and out. Hiram Travis watched her go, wondering what had happened to change her so. Georges watched her go, wondering what what had gone wrong at his bar tonight. Frank Fisher watched her go, wondering who it was she kept reminding him of. He had thought of Belden's sweetheart in Paris at once, but discarded her, because the two women didn't resemble one another in the least.

Fifteen was the number of her stateroom, and she knew that well, yet she had stopped one door short of it, opposite seventeen, and stood listening. The sound was so faint as to be almost indistinguishable, a faint rasping, little more than the buzz of an angry fly caught in the stateroom and trying to find a way out. Certainly it was nothing to attract the attention of anyone going by, as it had hers. It was as though her heart and senses were turned in to evil tonight, and the faintest whisper of evil could reach her.

She edged closer, into the little open foyer at right-angles to the passageway, in which the door was set. None of the stateroom-doors on the *Gascony* opened directly out into the public corridors. There was a food-tray lying outside the door, covered with a napkin, ready to be taken away. She edged it silently aside with the point of her foot, stood up closer to the door. The intermittently buzzing fly on the other side of it was more audible now. *Zing-zing, zing-zing, zing-zing.* It would break off short every so often, then resume.

Mrs. Hiram Travis, who had been afraid of strange men and who had shuddered at the mere thought of criminals until twenty minutes ago, smiled knowingly, reached out and began to turn the glass doorknob. It made no sound in her grasp, but the motion must have been visible on the other side. The grating sound stopped dead, something clinked metallically, and then there was a breathless, waiting silence.

The faceted knob had turned as far as it would go in her hand, but the door wouldn't give. A man's voice called out: "Come on, jailer, quit playing hide-and-seek! Whaddya think you're going to catch me doing, hog-tied like I am?"

She tried the knob again, more forcefully. The voice said: "Who's there?" a little fearfully this time.

"Where's the key?" she whispered.

"Who are you?" was the answering whisper.

"You don't know me. I'd like to get in and talk to you—"

"What's the angle?"

"There's something you can do—for me. I want to help you."

"He's got the key, he took it up with him. Watch yourself, he'll be back any minute—'' But there was a hopeful note in the voice now. "He's got both keys, the one to the door and the one to these bracelets. I'm cuffed to the head of the bed and that's screwed into the floor—''

"I left him up at the bar," she said, "If I could get near enough to him maybe I could get hold of the keys.''

There was a tense little silence while the man behind the door seemed to be thinking things over.

"Wait a minute," the voice said, "I've got something here that'll help you. Been carrying it around in the fake sole of my shoe. Stand close under that open transom, I'll see if I can make it from here—''

Presently a little white, folded paper packet flew out, hit the wall opposite, landed at her feet.

She stooped swiftly to pick it up, scarcely conscious of the unaccustomed grace of her movement.

"Get it? Slip it into his drink, It's the only chance you've got. Now listen, the cuff-key is in his watch-pocket, under his belt; the door key's in his breast-pocket. He turned his gun over to the purser when we came aboard, said he wasn't taking any chances of my getting hold of it while he was asleep. I don't know who you are or what the lay is, but you're my only bet. We dock tomorrow. Think you can do it?''

"I can do anything—tonight," Mrs. Hiram Travis of Dubuque answered as she moved away from the door.

Fisher looked at her a full half-minute while she stood beside him holding her cigarette poised. "Certainly," he said at last, "but you won't find the matches I carry any different from the ones your husband and the bartender both offered you just now—and which you refused." He struck one, held it for her.

"You see everything, don't you?"

"That's my business." He turned back to the bar again, as though to show the interruption was over.

She didn't move. "May I drink with you?"

He stiffened his finger at the Frenchman. "Find out what the lady is having." Then turned to go. "If you'll excuse me—"

"*With* you, not *on* you," she protested.

"This isn't a pleasure trip," he told her briefly. "I'm on business. My business is downstairs, not up here. I've stayed away from it too long already. Sorry."

"Oh, but a minute more won't matter—" She had thrust out her arm deftly, fencing him in. She was in the guise of a lady, and to be unnecessarily offensive to one went counter to a training he had received far earlier than that of the Department. It was ingrained in the blood. She had him at a disadvantage. He gave in grudgingly, but he gave in.

She signaled her husband to join them, and he came waddling up, blowing his nose and obviously beginning to feel his liquor. Tonight was one night Sarah didn't seem to give a rap how much he drank, and it was creeping up on him.

Georges set down three Martinis in a row. Mrs. Travis let a little empty crumpled white paper fall at her feet.

"Y'know," Travis was saying. "About this fella you're bringin' back with you—"

"Sorry," said Fisher, crisply but pleasantly, "I'm not at liberty to discuss that."

Mrs. Travis raised Fisher's drink to her lips with her left hand, moved hers toward him with her right. Georges was busy rinsing his shaker.

"Last Spring one of you fellas showed up in Dubuque, I remember. He was lookin' for some bank-robber. Came around to the office one day—" Travis went into a long, boring harangue. Presently he broke off, looked at Fisher, and turned a startled face to his wife.

"Hey, he's fallen asleep!"

"I don't blame him much," she said, and brushed the lapel of Fisher's coat lightly, then the tab of his vest. "Spilled his drink all over himself," she murmured in explanation. She took her hand away clenched, metal gleaming between the finger-cracks. "Take him outside on the desk with you, Hi," she said. "Sit him in a chair, see if the air'll clear his head. Don't let anyone see him like this in here. . . ."

"You're right," said Travis, with the owl-like earnestness of the partially-intoxicated.

"The boat-deck. No one goes up there at night. I'll join you—presently." She turned and walked away.

She dangled the handcuff-key up and down in the palm of her hand, standing back just beyond his reach. He was nearly tearing his arm out of its socket, straining across the bed to get at it.

There was something oddly sinister about her, standing there grinning devilishly at him like that, something that made Steve Belden almost afraid. This ugly dame was really bad. . . .

"Well, come on, use that key! What'd you do, just lift it to come down here and rib with me it? That knockout-powder ain't going to last all night. It's going to pass off in a few minutes and—"

"First listen to what I have to say. I'm not doing this because I'm sorry for you."

"All right, let's have it! Anything you say. You're holding the aces."

She began to smile and it was a terrible thing to see. Poisonous . . . the pure distillation of evil . . . like a gargoyle-mask.

"Listen," she began. "My husband—there is a half-a-million dollar insurance policy on his life—and I'm the sole beneficiary. I'm sick of him—he's a hick—never will be anything but a hick. I've got to be rid of him—got to. And I want that money. I've earned it. I'll never get another chance as good as now, on this boat. I don't want that half-a-million when I'm sixty and no good any more. I want it now, while I'm young enough to enjoy it. But even if there wasn't any insurance at all, I'd still want to do it. I hate the way he talks and the way he walks and the way he eats his shredded-wheat and the way he always is getting colds and talking like a trained seal! I hate everybody there is in the world tonight, but him most." And she gave the handcuff key one final fillip, caught it again, blew her breath on it—just beyond his manacled reach.

He rubbed his strained shoulder, scowled at her. "What do you have to have me for?" he asked. "Not that it means anything to me to put the skids to a guy, even a guy that I've never set eyes on before; but for a dame that can get Fisher's stateroom and bracelet-keys out of his pocket right under his eyes—why do you have to have help on a simple little stunt like that?"

"I'll tell you why," she said. "You see, mister, I had him with me when I came aboard, and so I have to have him with me when I go ashore tomorrow. That's why I need you. You're going to be—Hiram bundled up in his clothes, with your neck bandaged, and a great big handkerchief in front of your face. You won't have to speak. I'll do all the talking. If I just reported that he disappeared at sea, I'll never be able to prove that he's dead, I'll never get the half-a-million. . . ."

"But suppose I do go ashore with you, how you gonna prove it then?"

"I'll—I'll find something—I don't know just yet. Maybe a—a body from the morgue—or something." She gave him a peculiar searching look.

Steve Belden was no fool. That look made him think that maybe he was slated to play the part of the "remains" in question, when the time came. But he was in no position to bargain. The important thing was to get these cuffs open and get off the ship. And he'd need her help for that. Then later—

"And do I get a cut of the five hundred grand?"

She laughed mirthlessly. "Why, no," she said. "I don't think so. I'm saving your life, you see, and I think it's enough. Your life—for his. . . ."

"All right," he said. "No harm in asking. Now get busy with that key."

A quick twist of her wrist, a click, and the manacle dangled empty from the bed-rail. The murderer of Frank Fisher's brother was free again. His first words, as he chafed his wrist and stamped back and forth like a bear on a rampage, were not of gratitude—the underworld knows no gratitude—but low growls of revenge.

"A week in that filthy pig-pen of a French prison! Four days in this coop, chained up like an animal. Chained to him while I ate, chained to him while I slept, chained to him even while I shaved. *He's* never getting off this ship alive—!"

"Of course he isn't," the woman agreed. "How can we let him? The whole idea would be spoiled if he does. That'll be your job. I'm attending to—Hiram myself."

Belden waved his fists in the air. "If I only had a gun!"

"There's one in my cabin, in a cowhide suitcase under the bed—" Then as he turned toward the door: "Wait a minute. You can't do that. You'll bring the whole ship down on us, the moment you show your face, and there'll be a general alarm raised. Now if you go into my cabin next door, you can hide in the bath. I'll go up and find a way of bringing him down there with me—after I—Somehow your—Mr. Fisher—we have to get him in there before he comes back here and finds you gone. Now wait a minute, we can fix this bed in case he takes a quick look in here first."

She pushed pillows together under the covers, made a

long log-like mound. "Give me your coat," she said. "You'll be wearing Hiram's clothes, anyway." She extended the empty sleeve out from the coverings, locked the open manacle around its cuff. "You went to bed fully-dressed, waiting for him to come down and tuck you in!"

"Hurry up," he kept saying. "We ain't got all night! We must be near Ambrose Lightship already."

"No. We mustn't rush," the lady from Dubuque, who had been afraid of strangers and weapons and violence, said quietly. "Follow me, and I'll get the gun out for you and rig you up in Hiram's things." She eased the door open, advanced to the mouth of the foyer, and glanced up and down the long passageway. "Come on."

She joined him a moment later, unlocked her door for him. She crouched down, pulled out the valise, found the gun and held it up. "You'll have to use this through pillows," she said, "or you'll make a noise." She was handling the weapon almost caressingly. It pointed at his chest for a moment, and her eyes grew misty.

Belden jumped aside out of range, pulled the gun angrily away from her. "What's the matter with you anyway?" he barked. "You kill-crazy? I thought it was Fisher and your husband you were out to get!"

"Yes," she said sullenly. That was the greater treachery, so it had first claim on her. "But I told you, I hate everyone in the world tonight. Everyone—you hear?"

"Yeah? Well, we need each other, and until we're out of this squeeze, let's hang together. Now go on up there and get that dick down here. I'll be just behind the bathroom door there, waiting for him."

She grabbed up a long gauzy handkerchief and sidled out of the room. Behind her Belden wiped his beaded brow. He'd never run into a woman like her before and—hard-bitten as he was—he never wanted to again.

*   *   *

Travis looked up from a deck-chair at the shadowy figure looming before him on the unlighted deck. "That you, Sarah? What took you so long? I don't think it's so good for my cold, staying up here in the wind so long."

"This is going to cure your cold," her voice promised him raspingly.

He motioned to the inert form in the chair beside him. "Hasn't opened his eyes since he came up here. Sure must be dead for sleep. Guess he ain't been getting much rest, chained to that fella down there—" He tittered inanely. "Wonder what they did when they wanted to turn over in bed?"

She bent over Fisher, shook him slightly, ever so slightly, one hand above his breast-pocket, the other at the tab of his vest. Then she straighted again. "I didn't know they ever slept like that—did you?"

She turned toward the rail, went and stood beside it, outlined dimly against the stars. The wind fluttered her gown about her. She held the long gauzy handkerchief in one hand like a pennant. "What a lovely night," she said. "Come here and look at the water."

There was no one on this unroofed boat-deck, but the two of them—and Fisher.

"I can see it from here," her husband answered. " 'Twouldn't be good for my cold to lean way out into the wind like that." He blinked fearfully into the gloom. "You look just like—some kind of a bogey-man standing there like that, with the wind making great big bat-wings grow behind your back. If I didn't know it was you, I'd scared out of ten years' growth—"

She opened her fingers and the handkerchief fluttered downward like a ghostly streamer. A wisp of cloud passed over the new moon just then.

"Hiram," she called in a silvery voice, like the sirens on the rock to Ulysses, "I've lost my handkerchief. Come quickly, it's caught around the bottom of the railing. Hurry, before it blows loose—!''

Hiram Travis heard the voice of the woman he had been married to for eighteen years, asking him a common favor, and the obscured moon and the simulated bat-wings and the chill foreboding at the base of his skull became just the playthings of an overwrought imagination. He got up awkwardly from the deck-chair, waddled across to the rail beside her, peered down. His eyes were watery from his cold and blurred from unaccustomed liquor.

"You sure it's still there?" he said uncertainly. "Thought I saw it go all the way down."

"Of course it's still there, can't you see it? Bend over, you can see it from here—" Then as he prepared to squat on the inside of the guardrail and peer through it from there, she quickly forestalled him with a guiding hand at the nape of his neck. "No, lean over from above and look down on the outside, that's the only way you can see it. I'll hold you."

On the deckchair behind them the unconscious Fisher stirred a little, mumbled in his drugged sleep. He seemed to be on the point of awakening. But the stupor was too strong for him. He sighed heavily, became inert once more.

"Blamed if I can see a dratted thing!" Travis was piping. He was folded almost double over the rail, like a clothespin, with his wife's hand at his shoulder. He made vague groping motions with one hand, downward into space; the other was clasped about the rail.

"You're nearly touching it. It's just an inch away from your fingertips—"

"Get one of the stewards, Sarah, I'm liable to go over myself first thing I know, doing this—"

It was the last thing he said in this world. The last thing she said to him was: "We don't need a steward—*for this*, darling."

She crouched down suddenly beside him, took her hand away from his shoulder. She gripped his bony ankles with both hands, thrust viciously upward, broke their contact with the deck, straightening as she did so. He did a complete somersault across the guard-rail; the arm that had gripped it was turned completely around in its socket, torn free. That was the last thing she saw of him—that momentary appeal of splayed white hand vanishing into the blackness. His screech was smothered in the sighing of the wind.

She thrust out her arms wide, in strange ritual of triumph, as Mimi Brissard had in Paris. She was a black, ominous death-cross against the starlight for a moment. Then she turned slowly, her eyes two green phosphorescent pools, toward where the helpless secret service man lay.

Fisher blinked and opened his eyes. He was still groggy from the dreams he had been having. Dreams in which long, skinny black imps out of hell had pushed people over the side of an immense precipice down into a bottomless abyss below. He'd been chained down, unable to help them, though they screamed to him for assistance. Over and over it had happened. It had been the worst form of torture, the most ghastly nightmare he had ever had. Then toward the end the imps had concentrated on him himself. They had tugged and pulled, trying to get him to the edge of the precipice, and he had held back, dug his heels in, but inch by inch they had been overcoming him. . . .

He saw that he was partly off the chair he had been sleeping on. One leg, one arm and shoulder, hung down over the side, as though somebody had actually been tugging at him. But the lady from Dubuque, the harmless, inoffensive, eccentric middlewestern lady from Dubuque was the only person around, stretched out there in the chair beside his. His mouth lasted like cotton wool, and everything looked warped, like am image in a corrugated mirror. He fell down on his knees when he tried to get off the chair.

Instantly she was all solicitude, helping him get to his feet. She said, "Well, what*ever* happened to you? My husband and I have been taking turns watching over you. We didn't like to call any of the stewards, because—well, because of your position. People talk so on these ships—"

He could feel the drug-dilated pupils of his eyes slowly contract until they were normal again. The lines of the things he looked at resumed their straightness. But even then, the "kicks" wouldn't go away altogether; he had a regular hangover from them. There was cement on his eyelids and it took all the strength he could muster to keep them open. He said surlily: "Where is he? I remember vaguely coming up here with him, leaning on him the whole way—"

She said, "He went below just a few minutes ago, to fix you up a bromo-seltzer. It's just what you need, it'll clear your head marvelously. Come on down with me a minute, and let him give it to you."

He could feel a sense of resentment toward her stir through him, as when you rub a cat's fur the wrong way. Yet she wasn't doing or saying anything to antagonize him. "Why don't you stay out of my business?" he blurted out uncontrollably, "What is this? I never saw you before until tonight—" And then as though the word *business* had reminded him of something, he stabbed his hand toward his watch-pocket, then upward to his breast-pocket.

"Did you lose something?" she asked innocently.

"No," he scowled, "and it's no thanks to myself I didn't, either! I ought to be shot."

She bared her teeth momentarily at that, as though she found the phrase privately amusing, for some reason of her own.

He stood up abruptly, stalked toward the faintly outlined

white staircase leading to the deck below. She came hurrying after him. "Will you help me down the stairs please? They're hard for me to manage on these high heels—"

Grudgingly, he cupped his hand to the point of her elbow, guided her down the incline after him. Yet at the contact his antagonism rose to such a pitch it was all he could do to keep from throwing her bodily down past him, to break her neck or back. He took his hand away, jumped clear, to keep from giving in to the impulse, and a moment later she had gained the safety of the lower deck.

He didn't wait. The muscular lethargy that had gripped him was slowly wearing off. Suddenly it broke altogether, and he was normal again. By that time he was hurrying along the inner passageway toward his stateroom, to see to his prisoner. Behind him, like something in a bad dream that couldn't be shaken off, came the rustle and the slither of Mrs. Travis' dress as she followed him.

He unlocked the door, threw it open, turned on the light switch. Belden lay there sound asleep. The covers up over his head, one arm stiffly held in place by the manacle. Fisher let out a deep breath of relief.

Before he could get in and close the door after him, the rustle and the slither had come to a stop directly behind him. He turned his head impatiently. This woman was worse than a burr.

She said, "We're right next door. Won't you stop in a moment and let Mr. Travis give you the bromo-seltzer before you retire? He came down, 'specially to mix it for you."

"That's good of him," he said shortly, "but I could get one from the steward just as well." An odor of musk enveloped him, at her nearness. Again his early training intervened in her favor, wouldn't let him slam the door in her face and end her importunities once and for all.

She suddenly reached past him and gently closed the

door. "*He's* all right," she purred. "He'll keep a moment longer. He's not running away." She took him by the hand, began to lead him gently but persistently down toward the next foyer.

The contact, as on the stalls just now, again inflamed with nearly uncontrollable and entirely murderous anger. His hands on her throat. . . . He pulled his hand away, face whitening with the effort to overcome it. "I can walk—"

She threw open her own door, called out loudly: "Hiram, here's Mr. Fisher for that bromo. Did you mix it yet?"

The stateroom was empty. A cowhide valise had been pulled partly out from under the bed, allowed to remain there with its lid up.

"He's in the bathroom, I guess," she said. She moved unobtrusively around behind Fisher and closed the stateroom door.

A frog-croak from the direction of the bathroom answered, "I'm mixing it now." Fisher glanced over that way. A blurred reflection created a flurry of movement across the mirror-panel set in the bathdoor, which was turned outward into the room.

She distracted his attention by standing in front of him, turning him around toward her, smiling that same saturnine smile that had been on her lips so often tonight.

He gave her a searching look, wary, mistrustful. "There's something about you—" The back of his hand went out and flicked her shoulder. "Where'd you get that dress? All night long it's kept reminding me of—"

"Paris," she said. "It's a Maldonado. . . ." The blur on the mirror-panel had become a shadow that lengthened as it crept out over the floor into the room. "See, I'll show you." She turned an edge of the shoulder over, revealed a little silk tab with lettering on it. "Can you read what it says?"

He bent his head, peered intently, off-guard.

I'm Dangerous Tonight

Her arms suddenly flashed around him like white whips, in a death-embrace, pinning his own close to his sides. "Now, Belden, *now!*" he heard her cry.

The lurking shadow in the background sprang forward, closed in. The white oblong of a pillow struck Fisher between the shoulders, as though this were no more than a friendly pillow-fight. Then through it came a muffled detonation.

Fisher straightened suddenly, stood there motionless. The woman unclasped her arms, and he collapsed to the floor, lay there at her feet, eyes still open.

From over him came Belden's voice: "Go tell your brother you weren't so hot yourself!"

"Close his eyes," she said, "you've only stunned him!" as though she were talking about some insect.

The pillow fell across him again, and Travis' revolver and Belden's fist plunged into the soft middle of it. There were two more shots. Little goose-feathers flew up and settled again. When Belden kicked the scorched pillow aside, Fisher's eyes were closed.

"They don't come any deader than that!" he said.

She was crouched beside the door, listening.

She straightened up finally, murmured triumphantly: "We did it! It could have been champagne-corks, or punctured party-balloons. Half of them are drunk tonight, anyway!" Her lip curled.

"Let's get going," Belden answered impatiently. "We must be passing the Narrows already. We dock in a couple hours; we want to clear off before they find this guy—"

"All right, get in there and put on Hi's things, while I'm changing out here. Better put on two coats one over the other, he had more of a bulge than you. Turn your collar up around your face and hold a big handkerchief under your nose, you've got a bad cold. I'll pin one of those cloths around your neck like he had. I've got the passports and everything we need.''

Belden disappeared into the bath with an armful of Travis' clothing. She stood before the mirror, started to tug at the dress, bring it down off her shoulders. It looped at her waist, fell down to the floor with a slight hiss. She stepped clear of the mystic ring it had formed about her feet, and as she did so the contact between it and her body broke for the first time since ten the night before.

She staggered against the wall, as though some sort of galvanic shock had pushed her. Her mouth opened like a suffocating fish out of water, slowly closed again. She was as limp and as inert as the bullet-riddled man bleeding away on the floor.

Her hands went dazedly up to her hair, roamed distractedly through it, dragging it down about her shoulders. She was just Sarah Travis again, and the long bad dream was over. But darkness didn't give way to light, darkness gave way to perpetual twilight. Something snapped.

She had one more lucid moment. Her eyes found the opened closet door, where some of Travis' things could still be seen hanging on the rack. ''Hi,'' she breathed soundlessly, ''My husband.'' Then she began to shake all over. The shaking became low laughter, that at first sounded like sobbing.

Belden came out, in Travis' camel-hair coat, cap pulled down over his eyes. ''Are you nearly—? What's the matter, what're you giggling about?''

The laughter rose, became full-bodied, a terrible thing in continuous crescendo.

''I'm getting out of here, if I gotta swim for it!'' He could make it, he told himself; they were far enough up the Bay now. And he knew just where to go to lie low, until he could get word to—

The door closed behind him, muffling her paeans of soulless mirth, that throbbed there in that place of death.

When the ship's doctor was summoned, shortly after the *Gascony* had docked and lay motionless alongside one of the new piers at the foot of the West Fifties, he found her crouched on her knees like a Geisha, back to the wall, one arm extended, pointing crazily to the motionless form lying outstretched on the floor. The rise and fall of her ceaseless wrenching laughter was unbearable.

The doctor shook his head. "Bring a straitjacket," he said tersely, "she's hopelessly insane."

"Is he gone?" they asked, as he examined Fisher.

"Just a matter of minutes," was the answer. He's punctured like a sieve. Better call am ambulance. Let him do his dying ashore."

*   *   *

Fisher's nurse at the Mount of Olives Hospital, Miss Wellington, was a pleasant young person with sleek auburn hair and a small rosette of freckles on each polished cheekbone. She wore rimless hexagonal glasses that softened, instead of hardened her eyes. She came down the gleaming, sterilized corridor in equally gleaming, sterilized white, carrying a tray containing a glass of milk, a cup of cocoa, and a geranium. Every convalescent's breakfast-tray in the hospital always had one flower on it. Miss Wellington remembered, however, that it had had a queer effect on the patient in Room Ten. He had growled he was not dead yet, the last time she had brought one in, and heaved it out of the open window with so much energy that his scars had reopened and begun to bleed again.

MissWellington wisely removed it from the tray, hid it in her uniform-pocket, and replaced it with two smuggled cigarettes. Fisher was a favorite of hers; she disliked tractable, submissive patients, and she was something of a philosopher anyway. A hundred years from now it would be all the same, whether the poor devil smoked or didn't.

She freed one hand to turn the knob and was about to enter Ten, when an alarmed, "Hold it! Just a minute!" was shouted at her from inside. Miss Wellington, undeterred, calmly barged right in.

"Oh, so that's it," she remarked, setting the tray down. "And where do you think you're going, young man?"

Fisher was hanging onto the foot of the bed with one hand, to keep his balance, and belting his trousers around his middle with the other. He had on one shoe, one sock, and his hat.

"Listen," he said, "I got a job to do, a report to make, and you can have my bed back. You can keep the slugs you took out of me, too; I'm generous that way."

"You get back there where you belong," she frowned with assumed severity. "D'you realize that they could put a new roof on this entire wing of the building, just with the lead that was taken out of you? And there was enough left over to weatherstrip the windows, at that! You don't deserve hospitalization, any of you young huskies, the way your crowd your luck—"

He sat down shakily on the edge of the bed. His knees had gone rubbery. "I certainly don't," he agreed. "Any guy that falls down on his job—what good is he, tell me that? They should have left me where they found me, bleeding to death on the *Gascony*. That's all I had coming to me. That's all I'm worth."

"That's right, cry into your soup," she said. She struck a match, held it for him. "Here, smoke this—on an empty stomach; you've broken every other rule of the place, you may as well go the whole hog."

"You don't know what it means. The men I work with—not to be able to look any of them in the face—to have to go around tagged a failure for the rest of my life. That's all anybody has, Wellington, his pride in his job—"

She sighed. "I guess we'll have to let you go. It's better than having you die on our hands. If we try to keep you here you'll probably pine away. And I'm getting worn to a shadow pushing you back in bed every morning at eight, regularly. I'll get MacKenzie in, have him look you over. Put out that cigarette."

MacKenzie looked him over, said: "I'd strongly advise you to give it a week more—if I thought it would do any good. But if you're going to be rebellious and mentally depressed about it, it might do you more harm in the long run. There's really no reason for keeping you here any longer, only to stay off your feet as much as you can—which I know you won't do anyway."

"Sure, and stay out of drafts," Fisher smiled bitterly, "and live to be a hundred. What for?" He put on his coat and tie. "Where's my gun?"

"You'll have to sign for that downstairs, on your way out."

At the door he turned and looked around the room, as though he was just seeing it for the first time. "Who paid for all this?"

"Somebody named Trilling."

Fisher nodded glumly. "He's my boss. Why did he bother?"

MacKenzie and the nurse exchanged a look.

Fisher picked up his hat and walked out, head down, staring at the floor. Along the corridor outside he had to steady himself with one arm against the wall, but he kept going until he'd stumbled into the elevator.

Miss Wellington touched the outside corner of an eye with her finger, stroked downward. "We didn't do that boy any good," she murmured. "The bullets were in his soul. Wonder what it'll take to get 'em out?"

At the local FBI headquarters half an hour later Fisher's face was ashen, but not entirely from the effort it had cost

him to get there. He stood facing Trilling across the desk,
a proffered chair rejected in the background.

"I haven't come to make excuses," he said quietly,
"the facts speak for themselves. He got away. I hashed up
the job. I let you down. I begged, I pleaded with you to
give me the assignment. I not only put you to considerable
expense with nothing to show for it; but through me
Belden even got back into the country, which he never
could have done by himself."

He laid it down before him on the desk. Jealously close
to him, though, as if afraid to have it taken from him.
"You want this—back?" he said huskily. There was almost a prayer in his eyes.

"I'm sorry," Trilling said, and drew it the rest of the
way across the desk. It fell into an open drawer, dropped
from sight. "I don't, but Washington does, and I take my
instructions from them. They seem to want results. What
damned you was, not that he got away, but some story
about a woman being involved—"

Fisher just stood there, his eyes on the desk where the
badge had last been visible. His Adam's apple had gone up
just once, and stayed high. After awhile, when he could
speak again, he said: "Yes, I wonder what that story is,
myself. I wonder if I'll ever know."

Trilling had turned his head away from the look on
Fisher's face. He was on his way to the door now, his
former superior knew. The voice came from further away.
"There's no use standing here," it said. "I never did like
a guy that crawled, myself. I guess you know what this
means to me, though."

Trilling said, "I ought to. I'm in the same outfit. I'm
you—a couple of notches higher up, that's all. Let's not
consider this irrevocable, let's just call it temporary. Maybe
it will be straightened out in a few months. And again I
say, this isn't me. This is word from Washington." He

fumbled embarrassedly with a wallet inside his coat-pocket. "Fisher, come here a minute—" he said.

But the door had opened already. He heard Fisher say, to no one in particular: "That was my whole life. This is my finish now." The frosted-glass panel ebbed shut almost soundlessly, and his blurred shadow faded slowly away on the outside of it.

Trilling resignedly let the wallet drop back in his pocket. Then he caught sight of a wire-wastebasket standing on the floor beside his swivel-chair. He delivered a resounding kick at it that sent it into a loop, with the inexplicable remark: "Damn women!"

The honkytonk bartender, who doubled as bouncer, waiter, and cashier, was in no mood to compromise. Mercy was not in him. He came out around the open end of the long counter, waddled threatening across the floor in a sullen, red-faced fury and began to shake the inanimate figure lying across the table with its head bedded on its arms. "Hey, you! Do your sleeping in the gutter!"

If you gave these bums an inch; they took a yard. And this one was a particularly glaring example of the *genus* bar-fly. He was in here all the time like this, inhaling smoke and then doing a sunset across the table. He'd been in here since four this afternoon. The boss and he, who were partners in the joint—the bartender called it jernt—would have been the last ones to claim they were running a Rainbow Room, but at least they were trying to give the place a *little* class, keep it above the level of a Bowery smoke-house; they even paid a guy to pound the piano and a canary to warble three times a week. And then bums like this had to show up and give the place a bad look!

He shook the recumbent figure again, more roughly than the first time. Shook him so violently that the whole reedy table under him rattled and threatened to collapse. "Come on, clear out, I said! Pay me for what you had and get outa here!''

The figure raised an unshaven face from between its arms, looked at him, said something.

The bartender raised his voice to a bellow, perhaps to bolster his courage. There had been a spark of something in that look. Just a spark, no more, but it had been there. ''Oh, so you haven't got any money! So you think you can come in here, do your drinking on the cuff, and get away with it! Well, I'll show you what we do to bums that try that!''

He gripped the figure by his coat collar, took a half-turn in it, brought him erect and held him that way, half-strangled. Then, treacherously, he began to pump short jabs into the man's unguarded face, the muscles of his great beefy arm tightening and pulling like knotted ropes. Blood came, but the man couldn't fall; he was held tight by the nape of the neck. Heads in a long row down the bar turned to watch in idle amusement, not a hand was lifted to help him.

Then something happened. The bartender was suddenly floundering back against the opposite wall, the line of his jaw white at first, then turning a bruised red. He held it, steadied himself against the wall, spat out pieces of tooth-enamel. The figure across the way—the width of the narrow room separated them no—was holding onto an edge of the table for support, acting as though he'd fall down in another minute. He was holding, not his face where the barman had pummeled him, but his chest as if something hurt him there.

The bartender shrieked, ''You will, will ya? Sock me, will ya? *Now* ya gonna get it! *Now* I'll cut ya to *pieces!*'' He reached behind the bar, caught up an empty bottle from one of the lower shelves. Liquor dispensaries are supposed to break their bottles once they're emptied. This was the kind of place that didn't.

He gripped the bottle by the neck, cracked the bottom of it against the bar so that it fell off, advanced murderously upon his victim with the jagged sharp-toothed remainder in his hand for a weapon. And even yet, no one in the place made a move to interfere. He was only a bum; what difference did it make what happened to him?

The bum made no move to try to bolt for the door and get out of the place. Perhaps he sensed an outstretched leg would trip him if he tried it. Perhaps he was unequal to the effort. Perhaps he didn't care. He even smiled a little, adding fuel to the blazing fire of the bartender's cowardly rage. "Matter, can't you use your hands?"

The bartender poised the vicious implement, to thrust it full in his face, grind it around, maim and maybe kill him.

And then suddenly a girl stood in between them, as though she had dropped from the ceiling. No one had seen where she had come from. A beautiful girl, shabbily dressed. Cheap little blouse and threadbare skirt; golden hair like an angel's, cascading out from under a round woollen cap such as boys wear for skating. She set down the little black dressing-case she'd brought out of the back room with her, caught the bartender's thick wrist in her slim fingers, pushed it back.

"Put that down, Mike!" she said in a cold, angry voice. "Let this man alone!"

The bartender, towering over her five-feet-four of determination, shouted wrathfully: "What do you know about it? He's a bum, and he's going to get what's coming to him! You stick to your canarying and I'll handle the front room here!"

Her voice was like a whip. "He's not a bum. You're the bum. So much of a bum that you can't tell the difference any more! *I* still can, thank heavens, and I'm going to get out of here for good before I lose the ability to distinguish!"

The bartender retreated a step or two, put the shattered

bottle shame-facedly behind his back. A sallow-complected, chunky man, with his hair all greasy ringlets, was standing at the entrance to the inner room. The girl turned her head toward him briefly. "Find someone else to do your canarying, Angelo. I'm not showing up Wednesday." She faced the bartender again. "How much does he owe you?"

The latter had had all the ground cut away around him. "Couple dollars," he mumbled indistinctly. "He's been riding along all evenin'—"

She snapped open a ridiculous little envelope-sized bag. There were five dollars in it; she'd just been paid tonight. She took two of them out. She didn't hand them to him, she dropped them disdainfully on the floor before him, with a million dollars worth of contempt.

Somewhere in back of her, Fisher spoke. "Let him use the bottle. You're only pushing me down a step lower, doing this."

She said without turning her head, "You're sick. Your mind's sick. I've watched you every night. No one's pushing you down, you're pushing yourself down."

The ringleted man in the doorway said, "Don't do this, Joan, what's matter with you? Why you quit?"

She didn't answer. She picked up the kit-bag standing at her feet, put two fingers behind Fisher's seedy coat-sleeve, said: "Come on, shall we? We don't belong in here— either of us."

Behind them, as they went out into the darkness side by side, the crest-fallen bartender was saying to anyone who would give him an ear: "She must be crazy, she don't even know the guy, never saw him before!" And then with a guilty look at his partner: "She was the best singer we ever had in here too."

A block away they stopped, in the ghostly light of an arc lamp. He turned toward her. "A man doesn't thank a woman for doing a thing like that," he blurted out. "That was the finishing touch you gave me in there just now.

Hiding behind your skirts. Letting you buy them off for me.''

She said, almost impatiently, ''You're so easy to see through! Looking at you, listening to you, almost I know your whole story—without actually knowing any of it. A code is doing this to you. A code of your own that you've violated, or think you have. You'll go down under its weight, let it push you down into what that mug mistook you for. But you won't, you can't, slur its weight and responsibility off you.'' She shrugged as though that was all there was to be said. ''Well, aren't you worth saving— from bottle glass?''

He smiled derisively.

She went on, ''You didn't see me slowly walking around that inside room with my mouth open, from table to table, three nights this past week. You didn't hear me. But I saw you. I watched you through the cheap music. You sat there at that little table just outside the door, looking my way but seeing ghosts. Your eyes were the only ones in the place turned inward. You drank until your head fell down, but you weren't drunk—you couldn't get drunk.''

She picked up the little kit that contained her costume, made to move on once more. ''My name's Joan Blaine,'' she said, ''and I like people with personal codes, because I've got one, too. But handle it right. Don't go down under it; make it push you, lift you up, instead. Come back with me awhile and I'll make you a cup of coffee. I can see that you've been ill recently, and you've probably been sleeping around on park benches lately.''

He moved weakly after her, shaking his head. ''You're a funny girl. How do you know I won't turn on you, rob you, maybe even murder you?''

''Faces don't lie,'' she answered. ''Why didn't you run out with your tail between your legs when he came at you with the bottle? A real bum would have. You faced him, hardly able to stand up. Besides, *some*thing, *some*one's, got to come out right for me.''

"Most of it didn't?" he said, in the pitiful little thread-bare room, with its single fly-blown bulb, its white-painted cot with the iron showing through.

"Most of it didn't." She handed him a chipped cup of steaming black coffee. "I didn't come to New York to sing in a Third Avenue honkytonk at five dollars a throw. You'll never know how many tears and busted hopes this room of mine has seen. I was letting it get me down, too. The sight of you pulled me up short. That's why I quit my job so easily just now. Don't blame yourself for that. You've helped me, and perhaps I'm going to be able to help you before I'm through. Fisher—that what you said your name was?—you're going back and tackle this thing that threw you, all over again.''

"Yeah," he said slowly. "Yeah, I am." There was a steely glint in his eyes that hadn't been there before. "It isn't over, Why didn't I see that before? Just round one is over. But round one's never the whole fight. Even though I'm on my own now—''

She didn't ask him what he meant. "Then the credit and the glory'll be all your own too, look at it that way.''

"I'm not doing it for the credit and the glory. I'm doing it because it was my job, and I can't find rest or peace until my job is done. And even though it's been taken away from me, I'll see it through—no matter what—!" He balled a fist and swung it with terrific emphasis around him where the shadows had been. Shadows that a man could fight, even though he couldn't understand them.

She smiled as though she'd gained her secret point. "All right, then," she said. "Tonight—there's a vacant room, little more than an attic, over me. Without a stick of furniture in it, without even a lock on the door. I'm going to give you one of the blankets from my bed, and you roll yourself up in it on the floor up there. No one needs to know. Tomorrow you and I are going out. You're going to get a shave and a necktie, and you're going after this thing that threw you, whatever it is. And I'm going to find the kind of a singing job I came to New York for, and lick it to a standstill when I do! Tomorrow—the world starts over for both of us, brand new."

He looked at her and he said once more what he'd said out on the street: "You're a funny girl. But a lovely one, too."

It didn't work itself out in no time at all, in an hour or a day or even a week, it never does. He'd slipped further down than he'd realized, and there were certain realities to be met first of all—to keep his head above water; to keep a roof over his head; to get his gun back out of hock. But he had to have money. He wasn't on the Bureau's payroll any more. So to have money he had to have a job. He knew he could have gone to Trilling or any of the other men that had worked with him, and written his own ticket. But his pride wouldn't let him. He would have worked for nothing, without salary, but—"Washington wants results," Trilling had said. He would have swept streets, waded through the filth of sewers, if only he could have had one thing back again—that little metal disk that had dropped so emphantically from the desk top into a drawer that day, pulling the sun and the moon and the stars down out of his sky after it.

So he sought Sixth Avenue and the melancholy Help-Wanted cards tacked up so thickly on its doorways, that usually mean only an unproductive agency fee. There was plenty that he could do—and agent's training is nothing if not painstaking, but most of it was highly specialized and in the upper brackets; there seemed to be more demand for waiters and dishwashers along here than for dead-shots, jiu-jitsu experts.

As he moved from knot to knot of dejected employment

seekers gathered before each doorway to scan the cards, he became aware of a face that seemed to keep up with his own migrations from group to group. Which was not unusual in itself, since scores of people were moving along in the same direction he was. But this particular man seemed to be studying him rather than the employment cards. Was it somebody who had recognized him from the old days, when he was with the Bureau? Fisher had a good memory for faces. He studied the man stealthily at first—he was a slimy, furtive-looking customer; but his clothes were both flashy and expensive. Fisher took care to keep his glance perfectly expressionless, to see if he could get the man to tip his hand. The man returned the look in a sort of questioning way, as though he were trying to ask him something.

Fisher took a chance, gave his head a slight nod in the affirmative. The man instantly left the group, strolled slowly on for a few yards, then halted with his back to the window of an empty store, obviously waiting for Fisher to join him.

Fisher moved as he had moved, with seeming aimlessness and unconcern, and stopped by him. The man turned his head the other way, away from him, then spoke through motionless lips even while he did so.

"Could you use any?"

Fisher understood instantly. A peddler, the lowest cog in that devil's hierarchy whose source of supply had been Belden, and whose capstone was lost somewhere in the nebulous clouds overhead. There had been a day when Fisher had hoped that pulling Belden out from under would bring the top man toppling within reach; that hope had been blasted. Fisher had to start over, single-handed now, at the lowest pier of the structure, work his way up. This slimy individual who tramped Sixth Avenue pavements probably no more knew who the ringleader was then Fisher did himself. But he was a means to an end.

Fisher understood the reason for the mistake the peddler had made, that only a short while before would have been so irretrievable. But then only a short while before, it wouldn't have been made. Now he, Fisher, still had the telltale pallor and gauntness of his wounds and hospitalization. A misleading pallor, coupled with a suit whose cut suggested that he was not altogether penniless. So the peddler had jumped to the wrong conclusion. But then if anything backfired, the *could-you-use-any* gag could always be switched to shoelaces, razor blades, or anything equally harmless. Fisher knew many peddlers carried just such articles around with them in their pockets, just for an out. They never had the real thing; peddlers always traveled clean, to guard against sudden seizure and search. A second appointment was always necessary, no matter how well known both parties were to each other.

He answered the surreptitious question in a manner equally covert. "I could," he said, and saw to it that his hand trembled unnecessarily as he lit a cigarette. That wasn't wasted on the peddler.

"Who's been handing it to you?" he said, "I never saw you before."

Fisher pulled a name out of his mental card-index as you do a card in a card-trick. Someone that he knew had been rounded up while he was in Paris, was in a Federal Pen now. "Revolving Larry," he said.

"He's at the Boarding House. So are half the others," the man told him. "What's your dish?"

Fisher knew the different underworld abbreviations for the deadly stuff—usually a single letter. "C," he said promptly.

"We're getting forty for it now. The lid went down something fierce six months ago."

Fisher whistled. "I'll never make it."

"That's what they all say. Ain't you got some gold teeth in your mouth or something?" Then he relented a little. "I'll get it for you for thirty-five, bein' you're an old buyer of Larry's."

Things must be pretty tough, Fisher knew, for it to come to that; Trilling and the rest must be doing a grand job. Only he—he alone—had fumbled.

"I'll raise it somehow," he said. Ironically enough, he wasn't any too certain of being able to. Which was just the right attitude; too ready a supply of money would have immediately raised the other's suspicions.

"Go to Zillick's down the block. It has three booths at the back. Go in the middle one and wait. When you lamp me turning the pages of the directory outside, shove your money in the return-coin slot and walk out. Take it easy. Don't let the druggist see you. Your stuff'll be there when you go back for it. If you're even a dime short don't show up, it won't do ya no good. Twelve o'clock tonight."

"Twelve o'clock," Fisher agreed.

They separated. How many a seemingly casual street-corner conversation like that on the city's streets has just such an unguessed, sinister topic. Murder, theft, revenge, narcotics. While the crowd goes by around it unaware.

He didn't have thirty-five dollars. Go to Trilling or any of the others for it he could not and would not. Not because of any possible risk attached—he'd played and looked his part too well just now for the peddler to bother keeping him under observation.

He'd looked his part *too* well—that gave him the answer. He went back to the Mount of Olives, asked for MacKenzie. "So you want to borrow a hundred dollars?" MacKenzie said. He insisted on giving him a thorough physical examination first, as part of the bargain. Probably figuring it was the only way he could have got Fisher to submit to one. The results didn't seem to please him any too much.

"What've you been doing to yourself?" he snapped. "Not eating, and by the looks of you—See here, Fisher, if this is for liquor, you don't get it."

Fisher wondered what he'd have said if he knew what part of it was actually to be for. He said, "If it was for that, why would I have to have a hundred? Ten would be enough. I don't go around giving my word of honor these days. All I can say is, it's not for liquor."

"That's sufficient," MacKenzie said briskly, and counted out the money. "For Pete's sake, soak a finn of it into a good thick steak. And don't be in any hurry about returning it. You working?"

Fisher smiled. "I'm starting to again—tonight at twelve." The full story of how he had been shot on the *Gascony* had of course never been divulged—either at the hospital or to the newspapers. Trilling had seen to the former, the *Compagnie Transatlantique* to the latter.

Wellington, who had been in the room watching him closely, said after he had gone: "He's had a close shave, but it looks like somebody's beginning to probe for those bullets in his soul I spoke about."

"I think you love the guy," MacKenzie said testily, perhaps to get the fact that he'd loaned a hundred dollars out of his system.

"Sure I do," was the defiant reply. "You just finding out? I love every slug we ever took out of him, but what good does it do? He doesn't know a woman from a fire-hydrant."

But he was beginning to, even if he didn't know it himself yet. There was a difference to Joan's knock on his room door that evening, as though she too had had a break that day. It was the twenty-third day after they'd met in the honkytonk. He had his gun out, was sitting there cleaning it and going over it lovingly. It was like a part of him.

He'd got it out about an hour before, with part of the hundred. He jumped nervously, thrust it out of sight under his mattress. The door of his room didn't have a lock yet, but she wasn't the kind would walk in on him, luckily, or she might have wondered, jumped to the wrong conclusions. He hadn't told her anything about himself yet, out of old habit and training that died hard. What he'd been, nor what it was that had thrown him. He'd tell her everything when—and if—the second payoff came. And he had a long way to go yet before he reached that. Until then—

He went over and opened the door. She was standing there glowing. It always surprised him all over again, each time he looked at her, how beautiful she really was. Blond hair, blue eyes, and all the rest; somehow it all blended together into a gem. But that was for other men, not for his business. A shield in Trilling's desk drawer—that was *his* gem.

She said, "I brought in a can of spaghetti with me. Come on down. I've got news for you." And down in her room, while he pumped a can-opener up and down and—of course—gashed his knuckle, she asked: "What luck?"

"I'm on my way, that all I can say."

"Great. Looks like I am too. It's been on the fire for several weeks now, but I'm superstitious; I didn't want to say anything for fear I'd jinx it. Some fellow—he's new to show business—is opening up a road house tomorrow night. He has a spot for a specialty singer. Lots of backing and he doesn't care what he pays for his talent. I've already auditioned for him three separate times; I'm beginning to wonder if it's my voice he's interested in or if he just likes to have me around. He's not using a floor show, you see—just a band, and a combination singer and hostess. So by tomorrow I'll know definitely whether I've clicked or not."

"You'll click," he assured her, "unless the guy's stone blind."

She opened her mouth in pretended amazement. "The great block of ice is actually beginning to thaw!"

The phone booth was cramped and stuffy, so small that the pane of glass kept clouding with his breath. He cleared it off each time with the point of his elbow, holding a dead receiver to his ear for a stall. At 12:10 the peddler was suddenly standing there at the little rack outside, wetting his thumb as he busily flicked the leaves of a city directory. He didn't look up.

Fisher took out the three tens and a five he'd prepared, wedged them tightly into the return-coin slot. He came out, walked by to the front of the store, lingered there by the door. The peddler seemed to find the elusive number he was looking for just then, went in the booth, came out again a moment later, and brushed by Fisher without so much as a glance.

It wasn't really necessary for Fisher to have the little package that was back there in the booth now. This was not a decoy sale for the purpose of getting enough evidence to make an arrest. Fisher no longer had the authority to make an arrest, and even if he did have, he lacked witnesses. But he retrieved the packet nevertheless, to prevent its falling into the hands of some innocent person. He pocketed it and turned the corner in the same direction the peddler had.

Fisher walked on, then turned to glance quickly over his shoulder.

The peddler was still in full sight. Fisher plunged into the nearest doorway, lingered a moment, and came out— not exactly disguised but with a sufficiently altered silhouette to be mistaken for someone else at a great enough distance along the dimly lighted streets. His snugly buttoned coat was open now, hanging loosely from the shoulders; instead of being bareheaded he had a disreputable felt hat jammed down on his head. A pair of heavily-outlined but lenseless eye-glass frames were stuck around his ears. He set out after the distant figure using a purposely altered gait and body-carriage.

When he returned to his room at three that morning, he knew where this minor bird-of-prey lived, what his name was. What remained to be found out was where and to whom he turned over the accrued profits of his transactions. That was tomorrow's job, for the peddler had made no further sales that night after leaving Fisher. Undressing, he left the little sealed packet in his coat pocket. It was probably three-quarters bicarbonate of soda, anyway.

He didn't see Joan in the morning, but he knew she had performed her usual self-imposed chore of brushing his suit before leaving, for it was neatly folded across the back of a chair just inside the door. He went back to where he had left off last night, resumed his vigil on the street corner near the peddler's room. They were ripping up car tracks on that street, and the presence of the WPA workers covered him beautifully. He dawdled on the curb, coatless, smoking and chatting with them, indistinguishable from the rest to a casual observer. Occasionally one would go out to the middle and strike a few lethargic blows with a pickaxe, very occasionally.

It was well past midnight again when he wearily climbed the rooming-house stairs, but the day hadn't been wasted. He knew now where the peddler forked over his intake, where he secured his stuff. He was creeping back up the ladder again, at least as high as when they'd sent him over after Belden.

There was a dim light still on behind Joan's door and he thought he heard a sound like muffled sobbing coming from inside, as he went by. Her hopes of landing the job she had spoken of must have been dashed, the thing must have fallen through. He stopped and rapped lightly, thinking he might be able to cheer her up.

She didn't open for a minute or two. Then when she did, her eyes were bright and hard, like mica. She didn't smile.

"Did you land the spot?" he asked tentatively.

To his surprise she nodded, almost indifferently. "Yes," she said coldly, looking him up and down as though she'd never seen him before. "I signed the contract this afternoon."

"You don't act very happy about it," he remarked uncertainly.

It was obvious something had happened to change her. "Don't I?" she said hostilely, and prepared to close the door in his face.

He threw out his hand and held the door open. "What's the matter, Joan? What's the rub? I thought I heard you crying just now—"

She flared up at that. "Don't kid yourself, mister!" she cried bitterly, "I don't waste my time crying over—over snowbirds!"

"So that's it!" He forced his way into the room, closed the door behind him.

She kept her back turned to him. "Go ahead; lie about it! Say that what I found in your coat-pocket this morning was sugar to feed the horses, or chemical to develop films! Go ahead, alibi why don't you?"

"No, it isn't," he said grimly, "it's cocaine. Now you listen to me, you little fool!" He caught her by the shoulders and swung her around to face him, and none too gently. "If you were a man I'd part your teeth in the middle—"

There were tears in her eyes again, tears of rage. "This crazy town's got to quit playing tricks on me! I can't take it any more! No wonder something threw you, no wonder something got you down! And I wasted my time feeling sorry for you—"

"I wasn't going to tell you," he said, "but if you're going to go around making noises like a kitten left out in the rain, then here goes. I was a Department of Justice agent. We were cracking down on the ring that imports and sells this stuff. They waylaid my kid brother, got him alone and unarmed, and shot him down like a dog. I got myself put on that job—I was in Texas going after marihuana smugglers at the time—I followed the man that did it to Paris. I got him, and I started back with him. What happened is too long a story to go into now. I made the worst hash of the assignment that anyone could make. He got away from me almost in sight of the dock, left me for dead. My badge was taken away from me. That was the thing that got me, that had me down when I first met you. I'm trying to come back now, trying to lick the thing singlehanded. I bought that stuff you found in my pocket purposely, from a peddler, as a means toward an end. Through him maybe I can get to the higher-ups."

He glared at her. "Now you either take that or leave it. I'm not going to back it up with papers and documents—to try to convince you. Believe it or not as you choose."

He could tell by her face she did. It was radiant again. "I might have known you had some perfectly good reason. The mere fact that what I found hadn't been opened— Why, I remember reading about your brother. It was in all the papers the day I first came to New York; it had happened that very day. Fisher, the lady begs your pardon."

"The lady's going to make some guy a hell of a wife," he assured her grumpily, "the way she goes through pockets. Now tell me about yourself."

She had the signed contract right there with her. Six weeks at fifty a week, and, if she went over, it would be renewed for another six at seventy-five. Graham was the man's name, and the formal opening was set for tomorrow night. Luckily she wouldn't have to rehearse much, she was using most of the same numbers she had at the Third Avenue place, only one new one. She had to supply her own costumes, she rattled on, that was the only part of it she didn't like. And, oh yes, it was a little out of the way, hard to get to, but she supposed she'd get used to that. Chanticler was what they were going to call it, and they had a great big rooster set up on the grounds, outlined in electric lights, and fixed so that its head swung back and forth and it seemed to be crowing—

She broke off short, stared at him. "What are you looking at me like that for? You're all—white."

He said in a strained voice, "In Westchester? Just within sight of the Sound? A low white rambling place?"

"Yes, but how did you—?"

"I followed that peddler there and back today. On the return trip he was carrying several little parcels he hadn't had when he went in. I suppose if they'd been examined, they'd have been found to be samples of favors and noise-makers for the festivities. He poses as a toy- and novelty-maker. You've signed on as singer and hostess at what's really a dope-ring headquarters."

They were very still for awhile. Finally she said, in a small scared voice: "What shall I do, Frank?" She'd never called him by his given name until now. "How'll I get out of it? I can't—really I can't."

"You take the job anyway," he told her. "Nothing'll happen to you, you'll be all right. They're just using you, and the electric-lighted rooster, and the white rambling roadhouse, as a front. If you back out now, after wanting the job as badly as you did, you may be endangering yourself. It's safer if you go through with it. Besides, I'm going to be there—tomorrow night—within call of your voice."

She went white herself this time. "But suppose they recognize you?"

"It'll be a ticklish spot," he admitted, "but it's a risk I've got to take. Trilling never exactly handed out publicity-photos of any of us around town, so I'm probably safe enough. Belden would be the only one would know me, and I hope he does!"

"But, you'e not going to walk in there alone, are you?"

"Certainly I'm going alone. I have to. I haven't been assigned to go there, because I'm not a member of the Department any more, and accordingly I can't ask it to back me up. I'll either bring them this Graham, and Belden and the rest of the outfit too, or I'll end up a grease-spot on one of the Chanticler's tablecloths."

She said, with almost comic plaintiveness, resting her hand on his arm, "Try not to be a grease-spot, Frank, I—I like you the way you are!"

At the door he said, "I'll see you there, then tomorrow night. Don't let on you know me, try not to act nervous when you see me, or you'll give me away. Little things like that count. I know I can depend on you." He smiled, and faked a fist, and touched her lightly on the chin with it. "My life is in your hands, pretty lady."

She said, "I had my costumes sent up there ahead, to the dressing room. My agent's smart as a whip, he dug up some notice about an auction-sale they were having—the wardrobe of some wealthy Iowa woman who went out of her mind and had to be committed to an asylum. I went there today and picked up just what I was looking for, for that new number I spoke of, and dirt-cheap. Wait'll you see, you won't know me in it."

Ginger ale, the little gilt-edged folder said, was a dollar a bottle. You had to pay five dollars just to sit down, anyway, whether you ordered anything or not. Fisher'd had to pay an additional ten, at the door just now, to get a table at all, because he wasn't known. Twenty dollars to rent the dinner jacket he had on, five dollars for cab fare to get out here—and oh yes, twenty-five cents for the crisp little white carnation in his button-hole. He smiled a little when he thought of the old days and the quizzical look Trilling's face would have worn if he'd sent him in an expense-account like that. When tonight was over the only coin he'd have left would be the six bullets in the gun under his arm. He hoped tonight would bring him something; he didn't see how he could come back again in a hurry.

He was up to his old tricks again—and it felt swell, like a horse must feel when it's back between the wagon-shafts—staring idly down at the little silver gas-beads in his gingerale glass, yet not missing a thing that went on all over the big overcrowded room.

They were drinking champagne, and most of them, he could sense, were just casual revelers, drawn here unwittingly to front for Graham, to aid a cause they would have shuddered at. Graham must have decided it was high time he had some enterprise to which he could safely ascribe the money he pulled out of the air—if he were suddenly pinned down. Awkward to be raking in money hand-over-fist and not be able to explain what it was derived from. By the looks of this place tonight, and the prices they were charging, he needn't worry; it could account for a big slice of his profits, with just a little juggling of the books. And it made a swell depot and distribution center, Fisher could see that with one eye closed.

That gigantic electrically-outlined rooster outside, for instance, that towered high above the roof of the building, must be visible far up and down the Sound on the darkest night. It could come in handy as a signal and beacon for, say, small launches making shore from larger ships further out, sinister tramps and freighters from Marseilles or Istanbul, with cargoes of dream-death.

What gave the whole plan away to him, what showed that it was meant for something more than just a wayside

ad to motorists going by on the Post Road, was that the
sign was unnecessarily outlined in bulbs on *both* sides, the
side that faced landward, and the side that faced the
building—and the Sound. The people around him didn't
need to be told where they were, they knew it already. He
had a good view of the sign from where he was sitting,
through a ceiling-tall French window. The side that faced
outward toward the highway was illumined in dazzling
white bulbs, the side that faced the building—and dwarfed
it—was in red. Red, the color that means *Stop—Danger*.
White, the color that means *All Clear—Go ahead*.

Here and there, spotted about the room, were quiet
watchful individuals, whose smiles were a little strained,
whose laughter rang false. . . . They sat and minded their
own business, while the rest of the guests raised the roof.
They kept their heads slightly lowered, making geometric
arrangements with the silverware or drawing designs on
the tablecloths; they were taut, waiting for something.

Ten of them in all—no more than two at the same table.
And no fizz at those tables, just black coffee and dozens,
scores of cigarettes, chain-lighted, one from the last.

That stocky man standing beaming just inside the main
door must be Graham, for he had an air of proud owner-
ship, and he looked everyone over that came in, and twice
Fisher had seen the maitre-d'hotel step up to him for
unobtrusive instructions.

Suddenly the lights went down all over the place; the
lighted rooster outside peered ruddily through the window
outlines. People shifted expectantly in their chairs. Fisher
murmured to himself: "Here she comes now. What a
chance I'd be taking, if I didn't know I could count on
her!"

He settled back.

There was a rolling build-up from the drums. Twin
spotlights, one red, one green, leaped across the polished

floor, found the door at the rear that led to the dressing
room. Joan stepped out into the green spot, and a gasp of
appreciation went all around the big silent place.

He thought he'd never seen anything, anyone, so weirdly
beautiful in his life before. But something like a galvanic
shock had gone through him just now, had all but lifted
him an inch above his chair for a moment. As though
some forgotten chord of memory had been touched just
then. Something about Joan reminded him of someone
else, made him think he was seeing someone else. Before
his eyes, a ghost from the past came to life and walked
about in full sight.

Wait, that French mannequin, Belden's girl in Paris—
that was it! No—that woman on the *Gascony*, that Mrs.
Travis, that was who it was! But could it be both? And yet
it seemed to be both. Stranger still, Joan didn't look in the
least like either one of them, not even at this moment.

The red spot remained vacant, yet followed her around
the room; the idea—and a fairly clever one at that—being
that it contained the invisible tempter whom she addressed
in her song, over her shoulder.

Slowly she circled the room from table to table, filling
the place with her rich, lovely voice, making playful motions of warding off, equally playful ones of leading on.
Then as she reached Fisher's table, suddenly she wasn't
playful any more. She stiffened, seemed to glare; there
was a noticeable break in her song.

The perimeter of the green spotlight fell across him too,
revealed his face like a mask. He smiled up at her a little,
dmiringly, encouragingly. She answered—and yet there
seemed to be menace, malice, in the parody of a smile that
pulled her lips back clear of her teeth more like a snarl
than anything else. Unaccountably he could feel the hairs
at the back of his neck bristling. . . .

Get Thee Behind Me, Satan—
Stay where you are, it's too late!

Her bell-like voice, singing the Irving Berlin tune, throbbed
down upon him; but its tone wasn't silver any more, it was
bronze, harsh and clanging. He could see her bosom moving up and down, as though rage and fury were boiling in
it.

She started to move backward toward the door by which
she had entered, bowing to the thunderous applause that
crashed out. But her eyes never once left his face as she
did so. They were beady and hard and merciless. And that
smile was still on her face, that grimace of derision and
spite and undying hostility.

The lights flared up and as she stood there a moment by
the exit door, her eyes finally left his face to travel the
length of the room to the opposite doorway. He followed
their direction, and saw Graham over there, pounding his
pudgy hands together to show that he liked her.

Fisher looked back to her just in time to catch the
beckoning toss of the head she sent Graham's way. Then
she slipped through the door.

It was so obvious what that signal meant, and yet he
couldn't believe it. No, not Joan. She wanted to ask
Graham's advice about an encore; something like that, that
was all. For more thoroughly than he realized, he had, in
Nurse Wellington's words, learned the difference between
a woman and a fire-hydrant these past few weeks, and he
couldn't unlearn it all in a flash, couldn't teach himself to
mistrust something he had learned to trust—any more than
Belden could have in Paris, or Travis on the boat. Men's
loyalty to their women dies hard—and almost always too
late.

Graham was making his way around the perimeter of the
room, to follow her back to her dressing room where she
had called him. The background music kept on vamping,

waiting for her to return and pick up her cue. A pale pink and a faint green ghost of the spotlights hovered there by the door, ready to leap out into full strength again as soon as the house lights went down.

The quiet, sullen men he'd noticed before didn't move their palms, their heads or their eyes. One of them glanced at his wrist-watch, without raising his arm. One of the gaudy women with them yawned in boredom. Outside, the rooster's red beak kept opening, closing, as its head and neck wavered back and forth, current passing from one circuit of light to another, then back again.

Fisher kept pinching the bridge of his nose, groping, baffled. Why had Joan reminded him of two other women— one dead, one vanished into limbo—as she stood before his table a moment ago? Why had he thought he was seeing Mimi Brissard, and the Travis woman, when she didn't in the slightest resemble either one of them physically— nor had they resembled each other either, for that matter. Why had she seemed to be evil incarnate, the spirit of all wickedness, when he knew her to be just the opposite? It was more than clever acting to go with her song; the very pores of his skin had seemed to exude her animosity, her baleful hatred. They couldn't be mistaken; that was an instinct going far back beyond man's reasoning power to the jungle ages.

Only a very few seconds went by; how hurried her whispers to Graham out there must have been! Graham came out again, sideward, his head still turned to where she must be standing, unseen behind the door. His face was whiter than it had seemed just now. His glance, as he turned to face the room again, arched over Fisher, purposely avoiding looking at him directly. He didn't return to where he had been. He went casually to the nearest table where a group of those silent, waiting men was. He lingered a moment, then moved on to another table. The

flamboyant woman who had been the tablemate of the man
he had spoken to, stirred, got up, moved slowly toward the
entrance as though she had been told to leave. Her companion kept his eyes lowered; but as the woman neared the
door she couldn't resist throwing a casual little look over
at Fisher.

He didn't see it. Graham had signaled the band, and
Joan had come back. The lights went down again and
Graham's movements, and the mass-exodus of the lady-
friends of the "deep thinkers," were concealed by the
darkness, while she sang.

She started her routine in reverse this time, began at
Fisher's table instead of going around the other way and
ending up at it. Began, yet ended there too, for she didn't
move on, stayed there by him, while the sultry, husky
song enveloped him.

He sat there motionless, while she moved in closer,
came around the table to his side. Slowly her bare arm
slipped caressingly around his shoulder, inched affection-
ately down the satin-faced lapel toying with the white
carnation in his buttonhole.

And again Fisher saw Mimi Brissard writhe her snake-
like way up the stone steps of the Bal au Diable, the tiny
little train wriggling after her—saw her stop and look back
at him after she had betrayed her man. Again the heady,
musk perfume of Mrs. Travis was in his nostrils; she
seemed to stand beside him in the *Gascony's* deck. . . .
Was he going crazy? Had those bullets done something to
his mind? Was it just the colors of the dress—red and
black—the cut of it—or was it something more?

The caressing hand had traveled a little lower than the
flower now, was turning insinuatingly in under his coat.
And the audience chuckled, thinking she was pretending to
be a gold-digger, playfully pretending to pick his pocket.
There was a momentary break in the spotlight-beam, as
though the switch had been thrown off then on again. For

an instant or so they were blacked out, he and Joan. Then the green glare came on again. Her hand wasn't inside his jacket any more, it was held stiffly behind her back, hidden from the room at large. A white shirtfront gleamed there in the dimness as Graham approached her from behind, then ebbed away into the dimness again.

Fisher's hand reached upward, came to rest on her shoulder. He touched the fabric of her gown. A surge of unreasoning hatred welled through him. That too seemed to be a memory out of the past. He remembered doing this, turning his hand back like this, turning the lining of a gown—

She tried to pull away, and he held her fast. The shoulder of her dress turned over as he pulled, and on it was a little silk cachet. In the flickering green light he made out dim lettering.

I'm Dangerous Tonight—Maldonando, Paris.

The yell that came from his throat drowned out the music, silenced it. His chair reeled backward with a crash, and he was erect, facing her. "It's the same one!" they heard him shout. "*Now* I know! *Now* at last—!'"

The green spot sputtered out. The lights flared up. People jumped to their feet all over the room, staring petrified at the incredible sight taking place there in full view of everyone. For the man the girl had been teasing seemed to have gone suddenly mad, was growling like a hydrophobic dog, tearing, clawing at her gown. It came off in long, brutally-severed tatters, revealing strips of white skin that grew and grew before their very eyes, until suddenly she stood there all but nude, trembling, statuelike.

They were shouting: "Stop him! He's crazy. . . !" But a mad, panic-stricken rush for the door had started on the part of all the other celebrants, that couldn't be stemmed, that hampered those who were trying to reach the attacker

and his victim. Other women were screaming while their
men pushed and jostled, trying to clear a way for them.

She alone hadn't screamed through the whole thing. She
stood there facing him quietly now, given a moment's
grace while Graham and all his silent men tried to force
their way to them.

He took his coat off and threw it around her. The
tattered remnants of the dress lay on the floor behind her.
There was a look on her face impossible to describe—the
stare of a sleep-walker suddenly awakened—then she let
out a low, fearful cry.

"I've betrayed you, Frank! I've killed you. I told them
what you were—and what you were here for—"

His hand instinctively jabbed toward his exposed shoulder holster. It swayed empty at his touch.

"I took that too," she gasped, "while I was singing—I
gave it to Graham just now—"

She was suddenly thrust aside, and they were ringed
about him—ten of them and Graham, their guns bared and
thrusting into his body.

Outside, the enormous rooster was slowly pivoting on
its base, turning its white-lighted side inward, toward the
roadhouse—and the Sound. White—that meant *All Clear—
Go ahead*. Far across the water sounded the faint bleat of a
steamer's whistle, two short ones and a long one that seemed
to end in a question-mark: "*Pip? Pip? Peep? Are you
ready?*" Some lone night-bound vessel, furtively prowling
these inner waters of the Sound instead of sticking to the
shiplane that led up through the Narrows.

"No, not in here."

Graham's crisp command stopped death, forced it back
from the very muzzles of ten guns. "Take him out where
he can get the right treatment," he said and grinned a
little.

Through the encircling ring of his enemies Fisher had
eyes for only one thing—the face of the girl who had done

this to him. She was wavering there in the background, like a sick, tormented creature, his coat still around her. He saw her clasp her hands, hold them out toward him in supplication, unseen by all the others. As though trying to ask for pardon. The coat slipped off her shoulders, fell unheeded to the floor.

He stared at her without emotion. She might have been a stone or a tree stump. She was beneath his anger. To them, scathingly, he said: "Well, get it over with. Make it fast. . . ."

One of the guns reversed, chopped down butt first, caught him across the mouth. His head went back, came forward again. A drop of blood fell, formed a splashy scarlet star.

Graham said with almost comic anxiety: "Not on my floor here! What's the water for?"

"Who's so smart now?" the girl behind them shrilled vindictively. "Use me for a stepping-stone, will you! You're going to get it now, and I hope you get it good!" She had changed again. The tattered dress was nowhere near her, its remnants lay kicked far out on the deserted dance-floor, and yet she had changed back again—to all she had been before, as though the very core of her being had become corroded with hate and malice.

Graham patted her commendingly on the shoulder. "You're worth your weight in gold, honey. You wait for us here, put something over you so you don't catch cold. Graham's going to get you a mink wrap for this, and a diamond bracelet, too, if you want. You're riding back to town tonight in my own private car. We won't take long. If you hear any screaming out on the Sound, don't pay no never mind. It'll just be the wind coming over the water. All right, boys."

As they hustled him toward the entrance, in what was almost an exact replica of the old "flying wedge" at Jack's, he glanced back over his shoulder. Again she had clasped her hands, was holding them out tremblingly toward him.

They hurried down a long slope to where black water lapped whisperingly against the gray sand. "Okay, left," Graham said tersely. They broke up into Indian file, except for the pair gripping Fisher grimly each by an arm bent stiffly backward ready to be broken in its socket at the first sign of resistance. The Sound was empty of life, not a light showing anywhere. Their footsteps moiling through the soft sand were hushed to a hissing sigh.

"Flirt a little," Graham's voice came from the rear.

Somebody took out a pocket torch, clicked it on, off, on, off again. There was an answering firefly-wink straight ahead, on the shore itself. "There they are. They landed a little off-center."

The white blur of a launch showed up, seemingly abandoned there at the water's edge; there was not a soul anywhere in sight. But a human voice crowed like a rooster somewhere near at hand, *Kri-kirri-kri-kre-e-e-e-e.*

Graham called out impatiently, "Yeah, yeah, it's us, you fools!"

Dark figures were suddenly swarming all over the lifeless launch; their trousers were rolled up to their knees. They started passing small-size packages, no bigger than shoeboxes, to those on shore.

"Come on, reach! Come out closer. Don't be afraid to get your feet wet."

Fisher spoke for the first time since they'd hauled him out of the club-house. "Pick-up and deliver. Nice work."

There was a sudden stunned silence, tension in the air. "Who's that? Who you got with you?"

"Dead man," answered Graham tonelessly. "He's going out to the ship when we get through."

"Wait a minute! I know that voice!" One of the men jumped down into the water with a splash, came wading in, stood before Fisher. A torch mooned out, upward, between them, illumining both faces.

Fisher said, almost inaudibly, "Belden. So you came back, couldn't stay away. Glad you did. You came back to your death. They can kill me ten times over, but I'm still going to get you, murderer, somehow!"

Belden lunged, grabbed Fisher by the throat with both hands, sobbing crazily: "What does it take to kill you? What does it take to make you *stay* dead?"

They had to pry him away. Graham yelled: "No, no, no. Not here. On the boat. C'mon. Break it up."

Eight of those that had come with him were toiling back, Indian file, each with a shoe box under each arm.

"Tune her up!" A motor started to bark and cough, the boat to vibrate. Graham said something about his fifteen-buck patent-leathers, went wading clumsily out, scrambled aboard. Fisher was dragged floundering backward through the shallow water, caught at the hands and feet, hauled up over the side. He watched for the moment when his legs were freed as his spine slipped up over the rim of the boat; buckled one, shot it out full-length into one of the blurred faces.

The man dropped like a log, with a long-drawn exhalation that ended in a gurgle. They floundered around in the water over him. A voice exclaimed, "Holy—! He's busted Mickey's jaw and nose with that hoof of his! Pull him up out of there!"

Vengeful blows from the butt of a gun were already chopping Fisher down to his knees; in another second he'd gone flat on his face. He went out without a sound somewhere at the bottom of the little launch. The last thing he heard from far off, was Graham's repeated cry: "Wait, can't you—and do it right? I got ideas—"

Belden was saying, in the lamplit cabin of the motionless ship, "You can give the instructions, but I'm laying it on him personally. You can even take it out of my cut if you want to, I'll pay for the privilege, that's how bad I want it!'' Fisher opened his eyes with a groan.

"So you're awake, stupid!"

Fisher said, trying to stem the weakness in his voice: "Just how personal do you want it, louse? 'Cause I want it personal too. You remember Jimmy Fisher, don't you?''

"Yep," Belden said, "we made him run the gauntlet down the stairs of an old five-story brownstone house. On every landing we put another bullet in him, but not where it would kill him. He started to die on the fourth landing from the top, so we rolled him the rest of the way with our feet.''

Fisher's eyes rolled idly upward to the oil-lamp dangling on a hook. "Jimmy's all right," he said thoughtfully, "all a guy can do is die once. The big difference is whether he dies clean—or dirty—''

His arm suddenly swept out from the shoulder in a long downward arc. The hoop of the oil lamp sprang from the hook, there was a tinny crack and a crash of glass where Belden's face had been, and then he was lathered with a lazy little flame points, giving off feeble light as if he were burnished with gold paint.

They tried to grab him, hold him, beat the flats of their hands against him. He gave a hoot-owl screech, turned and bolted out the door, and the cabin turned dark behind him. Fisher sprang after him with a quickness he hadn't thought he'd be able to muster; left all his contusions and his gunbutt bruises and his aching human weariness behind him where he'd been, and shot out to the deck after that flickering squawking torch like a disembodied spirit of revenge.

Belden was poised on the rail, like a living torch. He went over with a scream, and Fisher went over after him, hurdling sidewise on one wrist. They must have both gone in at about the same spot. He got him below the surface, collided with him as Belden was coming up, and got the hold he wanted on his neck with both arms. They came up again together—not to live, but to die.

Fisher sputtered: "Now this is for Jimmy! This!" The throb that came when Belden's neck snapped went through him. They went down again together.

When he rose to the surface again he was alone. The launch was chugging around idly near him, and angry pencils of light from torches came to a focus on his head, as he threw it back to get some air in. "There he is!"

"It's taken care of, Jimmy," he panted. "You can sleep tight."

"Save it till you get to him—you'll be right down to hell yourself!" The pencils of light now were suddenly orange, and cracked like whips, and made the water spit around his head.

Graham's voice said, "I can get him. It's a pushover," and he stood up in the bow of the circling launch. Fisher could see the white of his shirtfront.

A violet-white aurora borealis suddenly shot up over the rim of the water—behind the launch—and Graham was an ink-black cut-out against it. Then he doubled over and went in, and something banged in back of him. A voice megaphoned: "Throw 'em up or we'll let you have it!"

Distant thunder, or a high roaring wind, was coming up behind that blinding pathway of light.

Fisher wished it would get out of his eyes, it was putting the finishing touch to him. He flopped his way over to the near side of the launch to get out of the glare, caught the gunwale with one hand, and hung there like a barnacle, tired all over.

There were shoe-boxes stacked up on the tables next to overturned champagne-glasses, and a line of men were bringing their hands down from over their heads—all but Graham and a man sitting back-to-front on a chair, wrapped in an automobile-laprobe, watching everything, looking very tired, very battered—and very eager. And, oh yes, a girl crumpled forward over one of the little tables, her blond head buried between her arms. Outside the rooster was black against the dawn; the current had been cut and they were pulling it down with ropes. Chanticler would never crow again to dream-laden ships out on the Sound.

None of it mattered very much to the bundled-up man in the laprobe just then: the questioning or the taking-down of statements or Trilling's staccato machine-gun firing of orders right and left. Only two things were important: an ownerless badge laying there on a table, and the tortured, twisted fragments of a dress huddled on the dance-floor.

They came to the badge first. Trilling took time off between orders to glance at it. Then he brought it over, held it out. "What're you waiting for?" he said gruffly, "It's yours."

Fisher took it with both hands and held it as a starving man would hold a crust of bread. Then he looked up and grinned lopsidedly. "Washington?" he said.

"Washington wants results," Trilling snapped. "Well, look around you. This whole job is yours. Don't try to act hard about that hunk of tin either. I know you're all mush inside." He glanced at the girl and said, "What's *she* crying about? She got us out here in time, didn't she?"

They came to the other thing last. "Fire extinguishers?" said Trilling as he was ready to leave in the wake of the captives, "What do you want fire extinguishers trained on the floor for? There's no fire."

"There's going to be," said Fisher.

He stepped forward with a tense, frightened face, struck a match, dropped it on what lay coiled there like something malign, ready to rear and strike at whosoever ventured too near it. He retreated and put his arm around the girl, and she turned her face away and hid it against his chest. "I think I—see," she said.

"Never mind. Just forget it," Fisher murmured, "That's the only out for both of us."

A glow lit up the dance floor of the Chanticler. There was a hissing like a pit of snakes or a vat of rendering fat. There wasn't any smoke to speak of, just a peculiar odor—a little like burnt feathers, a little like chemicals, a little like sulphur or coal gas. When the flames they had fed on where reduced to crumbling white ash, the fire died down again, sank inward. Then at the very last, just as it snuffed out altogether, a solitary tongue—thin as a rope and vivid green—darted straight up into the air, bent into the semblance of a question-mark, poised motionless there for a split second. Then vanished utterly without a trace.

A gasp went up. "Did you see that? What was it?" A dozen pair of trained eyes had seen it.

Trilling answered, after a long horrified silence. "Some chemical substance impregnated in the material the dress was made of, that's all, A dye or tincture of some kind—"

Fisher just stood there lost in thought, without saying anything. There is always a rational explanation for everything in this world—whether it's the true one or not. Maybe it is better so.

THE STREET
OF JUNGLE DEATH

JUNE DALE CAME parading down the street, her heart thumping wildly, her face pale with terror under its golden tan, and a fixed theatrical smile on her lips. It was a beautiful spring evening and half of Hollywood was out airing itself on the Boulevard. People coming her way would stop short, stare at what they saw coming toward them, then leap hastily aside, the women with sqeals of alarm. Then they would close in again behind her. She had a big crowd following her at a respectful distance, and it kept growing all the time, whispering and pointing.

Manning had talked her into the stunt. He was her press agent, and he'd borrowed the leopard from a man in the hills who owned a private menagerie and made his living training and renting out the big cats to the studios. This particular one was old, toothless, practically harmless, he had assured her. It wouldn't hurt a fly. "You want your next picture to be a hit, don't you?" he had argued persuasively. "Well, then you've gotta have a build-up."

She'd given in against her better judgment. He was her own personal publicity man, not the studio's. She'd been intending to fire him all along, and now she sure she was going to, for talking her into such a risky thing.

There was something about the beast that belied Manning's assurances. The rippling play of its powerful shoulder muscles as it slithered along before her were those of an animal in its prime. It was all power and latent brute force. And no matter what Manning had tried to tell her, it had a full complement of teeth in its mouth; she'd seen them just now when it bared them at a passing car.

It wore a pitifully inadequate muzzle and leash, and her agent had provided her with a toy-whip that wouldn't have cowed a rabbit. It was like leading sudden death around on a thin strap. He hadn't even remembered to give her a gun to carry in her handbag, in case the thing should suddenly turn on her.

She reached the sidewalk-cafe where he had told her he'd have photographers planted to take pictures of her and her strange walking companion. She was to sit down for a minute, order refreshments for both herself and her pet. Immediately after that he'd drive up and take it off her hands.

She sat down warily at one of the outermost tables, keeping its circumference between herself and the leopard. A waiter edged nervously up to her, giving the beast a good wide berth.

"Bring me a cocktail, and bring it a piece of meat," she ordered, trying to sound nonchalant, and not succeeding very well.

When he had arrived with the meat, he didn't even have time to set it down on the ground near the leopard. Its ears went up, its four furled legs straightened under it with a spring and its jaws snapped like a steel trap. The meat disappeared. The waiter managed to save his arm by jumping backward.

Suddenly, the animal turned and let out a sound like the throbbing of bassdrums. There happened, luckily, to be a siphon of seltzer water standing on June's table. She barely had time to grab it up before she went over backwards, chair and all, the lightweight table on top of her as a sort of shield. That probably saved her.

June played the siphon around her in all directions, eyes

tightly shut. She could hear screaming all about her, people scampering, chairs and tables crashing over, glassware breaking. By the time the siphon was empty and she was hoisted upright again, a loping speckled form, far over on the other side of the Boulevard, was all there was to be seen of the leopard. It turned up the nearest side-street and disappeared in the gloom.

The animal had been seen to enter that side street at one end. It was a short street, extending for only a single block. The crowd that had been around June on the Bouvelard was only minutes behind it in pursuit. It should have been in sight by the time the mob surged in after it. It wasn't. It was conceivable, of course, that it had put on a burst of speed and cleared the street at the other end, before the mob entered the block. But it obviously hadn't done that either, because no one could be found at the other end who had seen it. There were even two cops standing there in perfect unawareness of what was going on.

The hue and cry came spilling out at the far end of the side street with nothing in front of it any more. The leopard had dropped from sight, disappeared completely into thin air, within the short length of one city block in the heart of Hollywood.

One or two passersby were at last found who admitted having seen it. But they all said the same thing. "Yes, I saw it coming *toward* me! But I don't know where it went. I dove into the nearest doorway. When I looked again it was gone."

The two cops had become five or six by now, shouting orders, waving the crowd back. "Move on, now. Don't block the street. It may suddenly show up again and attack." The windows of the houses lining the street became filled with tenants looking out. They were questioned fruitlessly, floor by floor. No one had been looking out in time to see it go by.

A captain of detectives named Wrigley arrived to take charge of this safari on city streets. Taxi drivers left their cabs, telegraph boys their bicycles, everyone joined in the hunt. The street, Belrose, was roped off at both ends, the crowd was driven back beyond the ropes, and a house-to-house search was begun.

Since the beast had never emerged again at the far end, the only tenable assumption was that it had found a door unfastened, entered one of the houses unseen, and was still lurking somewhere inside. All occupants along the street were ordered out immediately, and the order didn't have to be repeated; a panicky mass exodus took place, with bedding, birdcages, and even potted plants.

The police entered each successive doorway, armed to the teeth, and the crowd beyond the ropes held its breath each time. When they came out again the house was given a clean bill-of-health and the search was taken up in the next one.

The brute's trainer, the man from whom Manning had originally rented the leopard, turned up unexpectedly in the middle of the crowd. He had been afraid something like this was going to happen, he admitted. He had been on his way to the cafe to reclaim it, as soon as the publicity pictures were taken, when he heard the uproar from several blocks off, and guessed the rest. He was a lean, sinewy, almost fanatic-looking man, bronzed to the color of an Indian, with prematurely white hair. The police conferred with him, but he wasn't able to help them much. He would know how to handle it if they found it, he told them, but they would have to find it first.

Shortly after that, there was a minor flurry of excitement and a discovery, ominous rather than encouraging, was made in one of the mud-gutters along the street. The ineffectual muzzle and leash that June Dale had used were found, cast off as if the animal had rid itself of them while in full flight. It was almost incredible that they had lain there unnoticed until now, with dozens of people tracking all over the street. The only possible explanation was that nobody had recognized them in the dark. Still, it was strange.

It was midnight by the time the posse came out of the last house, its search unsuccessful. The crowd slowly melted away. The ropes were let down, the tenants allowed to go back to their houses.

Morning came and the leopard hadn't been found yet. The search went on, only now there was no longer any one particular street to concentrate on. It was harder for them to know just where to look for it. But they kept at it doggedly.

Jerry Manning, the original cause of the misadventure, had a most unhappy twenty-four hours of it. He was haled into court and fined for violation of some city ordinance or other that prohibited the displaying of wild animals on the streets without a permit. He was also fired by June Dale. She made this known to him in no uncertain terms when he tried to see her at her house. "You take your ideas somewhere else, Mr. Manning. I've got a weak heart."

"You can't can me after all these years; there's a written contract between us!"

Torn scraps of paper came flying over the transom. "You mean there *was!*"

"I've still got my copy," he scowled, trudging off, hands in pockets.

Night descended on Hollywood once more. Half a million people shivered at the thought of the ferocious leopard on the loose.

Mrs. Ramirez wiped her hands on her apron, snapped open a little change purse. "Now don't gimme no arguments," she said to her daughter. "You hustle down and get me some of that grated cheese. Your father'll be home any minute."

"Aw, mom, why couldn't you tell me before? It's too late now. The store'll be closed."

"You'll have time to make it if you hurry," said her mother, giving her a push toward the door.

The girl tugged on a hat, slammed the door behind her, went jogging down the endless flights of tenement stairs. She emerged from the decrepit house into the grubby little Mexican slum street it faced. A single wan lamp-post gleamed dismally at the far end of it, leaving the rest in shadow.

The lights were just going out in the store window, half a block down, as she rounded the corner. She gave a warning hail and started running toward it. She got there just too late. The storekeeper had just finished snapping the lock on the inside of the door as she darted up to it, breathlessly. She pounded on the glass. The grocery-woman shook her head, motioned her away, turned and waddled off into the living-quarters in back of the store.

The girl turned away disgustedly. Now she'd have to go all the way down to that other store, over on the other side of the viaduct, that was the nearest one to here. You had to go through a tunnel-like stone passageway, arched-over, to get to it. It always gave her the creeps to have to pass through there late like this, when there was no one around any more.

She took a deep breath as she approached the mouth of it. You'd think they'd have a lamp inside of it at least. Well, they had several times, but the kids always busted it.

Her footsteps began to echo hollowly as the stone roofing closed in over her. She quickened her gait instinctively. Thank God, it wasn't very long, just about the width of the boulevard that ran over it. She was halfway through now. There—she could see the opening at the other end, ahead of her. It wasn't much lighter than in here, but it sure looked good.

She happened to glance over to one side as she hurried

along and—what was that? The stones must be wet over there, water must be trickling down the face of the wall. She caught a sort of reflected gleam, a highlight, two of them, side by side. They weren't eyes, were they? No, of course not. Still, they were the shape of eyes, luminous, greenish eyes. She didn't dare look a second time; she was afraid her courage might fall to pieces. A few short steps more and the night sky opened out above her again.

The lights of the store seemed a god-send when she finally saw them ahead of her, around a turn in the crooked alley. The jangle of the bellcord attached to the door had a friendly sound as she pushed her way in.

"They shouldn't send you out alone this late," the old storekeeper said, shaking his head, as he weighed out the cheese.

"What can happen to me? This is Hollywood."

"Anything can happen," he said dolefully.

He wrapped her purchase for her in a little scrap of brown paper. The bell-pull jangled a second time and she let herself out into the dark again.

She walked at a normal gait until she rounded the turn and came in sight of that dark arched causeway again. Then she hurried up once more, to get through it as fast as possible. The excuse she gave herself was that her father might be home by now and waiting for his cheese. She knew that wasn't the real reason.

The stone oval had closed around her again. Again that hollow beat to her own footsteps. She tried not to look when she came near the place where she had imagined seeing those phosphorescent eyes the first time. If she didn't look, the thing couldn't hurt her. Probably nothing there anyway. She was afraid if she did look she might see the same thing as before.

She held her face stiffly averted, looked the other way, as she went by. It was where there was a sort of indentation or niche set into the wall. She remembered that from the daytime; you couldn't tell now, of course. In this spooky darkness you couldn't see your own hand in front of your face.

She started to say the multiplication table over to herself, to keep her mind off it. "Three times three is nine, three times four is—"

Suddenly her heart missed a beat, and her breath turned solid in her throat and stuck there. There had been a soft, blurred *pat* behind her. Not like a shod foot makes, more like something padded or bare on the ground. She nearly dropped the package, just caught it as it started to slip from her hand. She wanted to break into a run, but terror held her limbs fast. The age-old instinct to avert danger by pretending to be unaware of it asserted itself in her.

She strained her ears as she continued to move forward, rigid as an automaton. It came again, nearer this time, yet so faint she would not have heard it at all had it not been that the tunnel acted like a sounding-board, magnifying the slightest noise.

A prickly sense of being stalked, of something treading stealthily after her, ran up and down her spine. She tried to turn her head and look, but couldn't; her neck muscles refused to respond. She couldn't move her feet any more either; they trailed to a stop, terror-bound. She was trapped, held fast, as surely as a bird is by a snake.

Suddenly there was a rush of air behind her. Without any warning the whole roof of the tunnel seemed to topple down on her, crush her flat. . . .

Dunbar saw her at the morgue the next day, before her people claimed her. He went there with his captain, Wrigley, to take a look, at his own special request. This wasn't, of course, a homicide case.

"I hope you've got good strong nerves, Dun," Wrigley warned him. "You're liable to see it in your sleep for weeks to come. These people really ought to have her cremated." He tipped the sheet back, stepped aside. "Pretty bad, eh?"

His subordinate stared without flinching. He got a little white, that was all, and whistled softly.

"And it hasn't been caught yet," Wrigley said grimly.

"Are you sure the leopard did this?" Dunbar asked quietly.

Wrigley looked at him in astonishment. "What are *you* trying to say—it didn't? Her back is in ribbons. Only the claws of a jungle cat could have done such havoc. The laboratory found small bits of fuzz, loosened hairs from the leopard's coat, on her. What more could you ask?"

"Did it attempt to—?"

"Eat her?" Wrigley finished it for him. "No. It was frightened away before it had time."

"I have a peculiar feeling that there's more to this than meets the eye," insisted Dunbar stubbornly.

"What more *could* there be?"

"Doesn't it strike you as strange that a jungle animal the size and color of this leopard should remain at large, absolutely unseen by the human eye in a town the size of Hollywood, for forty-eight full hours? It hasn't even taken to the hills; it's still down here in the peopled section, judging by this attack."

Wrigley tugged perplexedly at the skin on the back of his neck. "Yeah, it is strange. But it's happened, hasn't it? Here's the proof of it."

"But where does it hide in the daytime? Where has it found refuge, with mobs of people swarming about all day long. It was seen to go into Belrose Street at ten o'clock Wednesday evening—with a crowd almost at its heels. Presto! It disappears, not another glimpse of it from then on. Now this young girl is found clawed up, in the Mexican quarter. How'd it get all the way over there unseen?"

"Maybe it has been seen more than once and mistaken for a large spotted dog, a Dalmatian for instance."

Dunbar swung his arm at him impatiently. "Now I'll tell one. Let me take a closer look at her. Can we have more light here?" When it had been provided, he bent down, peering closely at the grisly remains for a long time. Wrigley saw him parting her straight black hair, examining her scalp. He straightened finally. "Did you notice that head wound?"

"Probably the first blow from its tremendous paw did that."

"There are no claw-scratches around it; it's a *dull* wound."

"Then it was caused by her fall to the pavement beneath the animal's weight."

"How was she lying when found?"

"Face down."

"But this fracture is toward the back of the head."

"She wasn't just downed and then let alone. It worried her for some time after she was dead, probably turned her over numerous times."

"For every objection I raise, you have an answer ready. Listen, Captain Wrigley, excuse me for talking back to you, but I've seen too many of these things in my time. That fracture on her head was caused by a blunt instrument. The bruise is long and narrow, like a welt."

The captain bridled. "What are you trying to do, tell me how to run my job? What makes you keep raising vague objections, casting shadowy doubts on what's so glaringly evident? Our test tubes and analyses have been used on her; irrefutable evidence has been found, and our report has been made out accordingly. Our findings are: that Maria Ramirez was attacked and clawed to death by a leopard underneath the Bower Street viaduct at or around 11:15 P.M., Thursday night. And there's nothing further to be added." He turned and stalked off ill-humoredly.

"Except by this leopard that goes around wielding a bludgeon," said Dunbar grimly, under his breath.

"But Dolly," Mrs. Gerard protested, "you never even knew the man. Why should you get all dressed up in black and go and leave flowers on his grave?"

The girl was eighteen, golden-haired, and strikingly beautiful. "But Mr. Manning just called up and told me to. Laventino was the greatest star in silent pictures, and women were all crazy about him. Every year there's a mysterious woman in black that goes to his grave. He says it's the surest way of attracting the producers' attention, landing a big fat part, that he knows of. He's going to have photographers planted there to take my picture."

"But it's nearly dark already; why not wait until tomorrow?"

"It has to be today. Today is the anniversary of his death."

"But Dolly, I don't like you going to a lonely, out-of-the-way place like that, all by yourself."

The girl laughed blithely. "I'm not a child. I'll take a taxi out there. And Andy's meeting me there, anyway. He'll bring me back in his car." Andy Lemaire was her boy friend.

"Oh, well that's different," her mother said, reassured.

Dolly stooped to kiss the older woman. "In case he calls to find out what happened to me, tell him I was held up at the hairdresser's. I'm on my way out now."

Outside the house, she signaled a cab, got in. "To the Cedars of Eden Cemetery. And please hurry. I've got to get there before it closes."

"Yes, miss."

He drew up before the entrance in something under twenty minutes. The cemetery was one of the largest in Hollywood, a veritable estate in itself. Laurel, cypress and other trees peered over the top of the high stone wall that bordered it, as far as the eye could reach.

Dolly Gerard had lifted her veil, was anxiously scanning the curb ahead as her cab drew up, to see if she could identify Andy's little tan roadster waiting outside the entrance. It wasn't anywhere in sight. Her lips drooped disappointedly. Had he misunderstood and thought it was tomorrow she was coming? There was no sign of Manning or the photographers he had promised to bring, either, but maybe they were inside the grounds.

She dismissed her cab and went over to the gatekeeper's little booth, just inside the entrance, to inquire.

"Has there been a young man here within the past hour or so, sort of good-looking and wearing a belted tan overcoat?"

"Sure," he said instantly. "I remember him. He was asking for a young lady in black, with golden curls. Yourself, no doubt. Less than ten minutes ago, that was."

She smiled relievedly. "Then he's still inside?"

"He must be. I didn't see him come out again."

"Thank you. How much time have I?" she asked as she turned to go in.

"You better hurry, miss. We're closing in another ten minutes."

It wouldn't have been respectful to run in such surroundings, but she hastened down the long, winding pathway at the fastest walk she could manage. The cemetery was an unusually large one, and Laventino's resting-place was set far in, out of sight of the entrance, with numerous groves of trees in between. There wasn't anyone near it when she came in sight of the alabaster urn that ornamented the plot; neither Andy, nor Manning nor any cameramen. They would have had to take flashlight pictures by now anyway, it was getting so dark. Maybe that was why they hadn't waited. But then her eyes widened as they rested on the inscription engraved on the pedestal supporting the urn:

LAVENTINO
Died June 12th, 1926

Why, Manning had gotten his dates mixed! Today was the 11th, not the 12th. It was tomorrow that was the anniversary of his death. That explained why he wasn't here himself. And yet if he'd found out his mistake later on, as he must have, why hadn't he called her back in time to correct the error? That was strange. Maybe he'd forgotten to, he had so many other things on his mind, and she wasn't an important star, just a beginner.

Well, at least Andy was here. The gateman had told her so. She looked around and noticed a little marble pergola, or summer house, a considerable distance over to the left. He was probably in there, waiting for her.

She left Manning's publicity flowers and started over toward it. The sun had gone down long ago; inky shadows were lengthening ominously across the undulating cemetery sward. The pergola already looked indistinct in the dusk, a ghost-shape, as she neared it.

"Andy," she called subduedly, reluctant to raise her voice in such a place. "Are you in there?" He wasn't. She peered in between two of the fluted columns that braced the circular roof, and saw the place was empty. They had missed one another in some way, for the gateman had distinctly told her he had been here.

She was just about to turn away and go back to the gate, when she caught sight of something chalked on the back of one of the stone benches:

D.—Wait for me. Be right back. A.

Oh, then it was all right. He had been called outside the grounds for a minute for something. She sat down to wait. He would probably tip the gatekeeper to stay open a few minutes longer, so there was no need to worry. She traced the "A" of his initial fondly with her fingertip, the way a child does in sand at the seashore.

It had grown completely dark the next time she noticed her surroundings. Even the afterglow of the sun was gone now. The trees were invisible against the black sky. The white of the monuments and markers made gray ghost-shapes here and there. If she hadn't been sure he was coming back for her, it would have made her nervous to sit here alone like this.

But presently, as the minutes lengthened and the stillness deepened around her, she began to grow a little uneasy. What was keeping him so long? She had no wrist watch, but surely she had been here over ten minutes already. She had better return to the gate and wait for him there, instead. Everyone else was gone long ago.

She started out, unhurriedly at first, her footsteps crunching against the gravel of the pathway. A wind came sighing up around her, damp and mouldy, as if with the breath of the long-buried dead.

She shuddered, quickened her gait. It was so dark, it was almost impossible for her to see her way any longer. The paths were pale gray ribbons in the dark.

She started to hurry more and more, fighting to retain her self-control. She was in full flight now, pursued by that malignant wind that smelled of the clamminess of tombs and rotted coffins. She was drawing quick little sobs of breath, the gravel scattering under her flying feet like hail.

Suddenly in the darkness ahead she made out a high outline, looming palely, a little lighter than the sky. The boundary wall, the entrance! Her gasp of relief changed to a cry of alarm. The gates were closed, she had been locked in!

That absent-minded old man had forgotten about her entirely. Perhaps he had gone haphazardly around the vast place warning late visitors out, and had failed to see her sitting there within the shadowy pergola. What good did it do wondering how it had happened? It had happened, that was all that mattered!

To make things worse, the gates were not the open, barred kind usually to be met with in places of this sort. They were solid ponderous bronze, donated by some well-meaning trustee or philanthropist. She couldn't even look out through them to attract the attention of anyone on the street outside.

She pounded madly at the gates, only succeeded in bruising her hands. "Open! Open!" she wailed. "Let me out! Help, somebody!"

She found a pumice-rock used to decorate the border of the pathway, tried hitting them with that. Its sharp edges hurt the tender flesh of her palms equally as much as the uncushioned blows had. The great sheets of metal were so thick it was doubtful if more than a muffled echo escaped through them.

An occasional whisper penetrated to her—probably the sound of some passing car. It came over the wall, though, rather than through the gate itself. So near and yet so far! Oh, why couldn't she make someone hear her?

Maybe there was another gate further along in the wall someplace, a side gate, an open one that she could be seen through. But she dreaded to turn back into that maw of darkness behind her to go looking for it. The place was so vast, so lonely, yet so well-populated with those who had once been alive.

Her teeth were chattering with terror. "Help!" she screamed wildly. "Let me out of here!"

The stars were peering down at her, only adding to her feeling of helplessness and isolation. They were the only light to be seen. They seemed so far, so unconcerned. Would she have to stay in this horrid place all night? She drove her hands distractedly through the wavy blonde hair that Andy admired so, lost her hat and veil, didn't attempt to pick them up again.

Suddenly she noticed that some of the trees seemed to grow fairly close to the inside of the wall. Their branches even spanned it occasionally. Perhaps if she could find one that was not too difficult to climb, she could at least get up to the top of the wall, attract some passerby's attention.

She ran along the inside of the wall for a considerable distance, guiding herself with one arm extended out to it. The ground felt damp and slippery with moss underfoot; there was no path laid out here, but at least she knew none of the burial plots were set this close up against the wall.

She found a tree at last with a thick, massive bough projecting straight out over the wall, nearly as heavy and tough as the trunk itself, but as she stopped beneath it and peered up her hopes were dashed again. The trunk seemed so straight, so high, so far in from the wall. She tried to clasp her hands about it and draw herself up, but the tips of her stubby shoes slipped down its bark without being able to gain a hold. It was useless, she'd never be able to get up to that height. She'd only succeed in killing herself.

Then, as she stood there, whimpering disappointedly, a sound carried to her clearly from the other side of the wall. She heard a car door crack shut, and to be that distinct, it must have been standing nearly opposite to where she herself was. A moment later an engine started to vibrate. Someone had just gotten into a car out there, was about to drive off.

She raised her voice, screamed frantically, "Wait, whoever you are, don't go! Get me out of here!"

The engine stalled abruptly. There was a stunned silence. The person had heard her! She redoubled her cries. "Let me out! I've been locked in here!"

"My God! Is that you, Dolly?" a man's voice answered hoarsely. She recognized it; it was Andy himself!

"Andy," she sobbed, overcome with relief. "Oh Andy, what in the world happened to you?"

"One of the caretakers brought me a verbal message that there was a young lady waiting for me in a restaurant several blocks away. I thought it was you, of course. When I got there no one seemed to know anything about it; it must have been meant for somebody else. By the time I got back I found the gates already closed. Then I went and phoned your house and they told me you'd left long ago. I just got back now the second time. Wait, don't be frightened. I'll try to climb over there to you."

"No, don't, that won't help. I'll never be able to climb back from this side, even with you here. The only way is to get hold of the gatekeeper, bring him back with you. He has the keys."

"All right. But don't be nervous, it may take me a short time to locate him."

"I'll try not to be. Only hurry, Andy. It's so dark and spooky in here!"

The car door cracked shut once more.

The engine sang out, and she heard him go whirring off on his quest.

The first few minutes passed calmly enough, in comparison to the bad fright she had had in the beginning. There was nothing to worry about now. And what a lucky coincidence that it should be Andy himself, of all people, whose attention she had attracted from across the wall!

She grew tired standing there motionless and presently, tested the ground with her hand. It was too damp to sit down on, would have soiled her clothes. She was becoming slightly chilled, as time wore on. She began to walk back and forth to try to keep warm and make the time pass more quickly.

The hour began to toll mournfully from some distant steeple. He had been gone only a little while by then, but automatically the mere fact of the hour striking like that made it seem much longer. Little by little, uneasiness began to creep over her once more. It was so dark, so eerie in here, and that wind, swirling around her incessantly, sighed and moaned like a disembodied spirit. Then each time it would die down, the utter stillness would be even worse.

The moon had come up, but that only made her surroundings more terrible. Macabre yellow phantoms took the place of the former even darkness. Trees became gnarled shapes creeping on her, headstones became goblins rising up out of the graves. She was on the verge of hysteria from the long cumulative strain. A wailing scream was wrenched from her. "Andy! Andy, where are you?"

In the redoubled silence that followed she heard a sound, unidentifiable at first, on the other side of the wall.

It came again, a low *snuff*, as of hot breath being blown, as of nostrils being scented close against the surface of the wall. Something, someone, was present there, hidden from sight on the other side of it. Every nerve in her body, every hair-follicle in her head, told her so. And the quieter it became, the stronger the impression grew. As though, while she held her breath listening, something else was still, listening also.

She couldn't stand the suspense any longer. "Andy," she quavered, "is that you?" She knew it couldn't be. He would have come back in the car; there would have been the sound of many voices.

There was a scraping sound, along the outer side of the wall, directly abreast of her. It was like the sound a cat sometimes makes, when it tries its claws on something. She could almost detect a vibration of the ground, communicated through to where she was. As though something, somebody, had dropped heavily.

"Who is it?" she cried sharply. "Who's there?"

There was a creak, a great rustling of leaves, and yet at the moment there was a lull in the wind. Her eyes flew up to that bough that spanned the wall almost directly over her. It was thick, well-rounded, heavy enough to bear— many things. Something had happened to it; it had changed. It had stood out straight until now, well clear of the top of the wall; it had been horizontal to the trunk. It sloped downward now, was lower at the outer end, where her eyes couldn't follow it, than in at the trunk; it was all but grazing the wall. It was moving, was fluctuating notice- ably. Something had hold of it—or was on it!

She couldn't summon up any more voice. "Who is it?" she whispered hoarsely. She couldn't tear herself away, or turn and run as she wanted to. She was rooted there, hypnotized as in a nightmare, head thrown back, staring up overhead.

Through the stirring, undulating leaves that garnished the bough she caught a glint of something; pale-green, phosphorescent, peering down at her in the moonlight.

Her mouth opened spasmodically, soundlessly, as if trying to give its deathcry. . . .

Dunbar arrived on the scene almost immediately after- ward, this time. He had been at Headquarters, with Wrigley, when the flash came in.

The massive bronze gates were wide open now, too late. Inside, the cemetery had been turned into a grotesque place gleaming with high-powered searchlights, blue flash- light flares, winking pocket torches. Uniformed men were already swarming about. Red cigarette-embers showed oddly amidst the headstones here and there.

Just inside the entrance, a youth in a belted topcoat, hatless and crazed with grief and shock, was being held up between the gatekeeper and a policeman. He kept straining the upper part of his body toward a bleached spot further in along the wall, where the interlocked beams of two of the high-powered lights cast a circle, terrible in its daz- zling clarity.

It was awful, even worse than the first time. That at least had been given some semblance of concealment under the sheet at the Morgue. Dunbar stared down motionlessly from the edge of the spotlight, his face impassive but sweating profusely.

"Eye witnesses—none, of course," Wrigley snapped. "Very well, secondary witnesses, then."

The gateman was shoved forward into the circle of light. He spoke his piece in a dull tone. "—he had a hard time finding me. I had gone to the movies. Luckily my old lady knew where. He hauled me out with him. We tore back. I unlocked the gates. There wasn't a sound. We found her a minute later, lying where she is now—"

The sound of searching men calling to one another in the distance attracted Wrigley's attention. He turned his head, spoke sharply. "What are they doing? Call them back, the fools. They're just wasting their time; it's not in here any more. Anyone can see that it got out again the way it got in." His eyes flicked to the bough above. "It dropped down on her bodily from up there, in a shower of leaves. Her cries to be let out must have attracted it from the outside of the wall as it prowled by. Then it sprang up the trunk to the top of the wall again, and over. See the livid gashes on the bark from its claws—pointed *up?* Get them on your negatives."

Dunbar knew Wrigley was his superior, but he couldn't resist breaking in scathingly, "And in the face of that, you still think it's a leopard?"

"What do you mean?"

"A jungle animal would turn its back on all this protective shrubbery, the very thing its instinct leads it to seek, and deliberately go back there into the stone and cement streets?"

"There are traces of blood on the *outside* of the wall, proving it dropped down *after* the attack," one of the other operatives put in curtly. "We've already photographed them."

It was a telling blow; Dunbar's mouth opened, closed again without making a sound.

"And just for the finishing touch, look at this," Wrigley said crushingly. He stooped down over the mangled form, keeping his back to Dunbar as he did so, took out a small pair of forceps. The latter couldn't see what it was he was extracting, only the wrench of the elbow that accompanied it. He straightened up again, holding something that looked like a tiny thorn on a small piece of paper. "Hold a glass over it so Mr. Know-It-All can see."

His subordinate peered down at it.

"The tip of one of its claws, broken off short," said Wrigley mercilessly. "From her throat. And in the face of that," he parodied, "you still think it's *not* a leopard?"

"It's against all the laws of nature," Dunbar muttered disconcertedly.

There was a commotion at the gate, and the Commissioner of Police himself arrived. He cast only the briefest of glances at what lay before him on the ground, stood there glittering balefully at the quailing men before him.

"This fiend has simply got to be exterminated!" he thundered. "I want its carcass shown to me within the next twenty-four hours. Is that clear? There's a city-wide panic brewing."

Marjorie Dale, June's younger sister, turned away from the open windows with a romantic sigh. "So this is Hollywood! Now that I'm here, I'm not going to waste a minute of my time. I want to see all the sights. Let's go to that open-air restaurant in Eastland Park where all the stars go, and eat right out under the trees; and then let's take an old-fashioned carriage ride in the moonlight. It's such a swell night!"

"But that's the very sort of thing they're advising people not to do these days, go to lonely, out-of-the-way places after dark."

"Oh, June, quit kidding me," grinned the younger girl. "I'm your sister, not one of your fans. There's not a word of truth in the whole thing, is there? You and Manning just cooked it up between you, to give your next picture a send-off, didn't you?"

"I was *out* with the thing, Marj; it broke away and it hasn't been seen since. Why can't I get you to believe me?"

"Aw, June, I have to go back home tomorrow," pleaded Marjorie. "Be a sport."

June relented, began putting on her hat. "All right. Just the same, I think we're a pair of darned fools."

Marjorie opened the door. "Bring some catnip in case we run into it," she suggested flippantly.

They hailed one of the old-fashioned horse-driven hansoms Marjorie had spoken of and gave their destination. The main driveway of the park, when they entered it, was filled with taxis and private cars. In fact the traffic was fully as heavy as on some of the city thoroughfares behind them.

"Now what's wrong with this?" Marjorie queried. "Do you see anything to be afraid of here?"

"We're not out yet," was all June said, tight-lipped.

The restaurant was so crowded they even had trouble getting a table when they reached it. Under the gay lanterns strung from the trees, with music playing, waiters hustling about, and a crowd of well-dressed men and women dining and dancing all around them, it was hard to really believe there was violent death stalking about somewhere in the city, on velvety relentless paws.

Marjorie even decided to kid her sister a little. "It may be hiding out there in the dark right now, watching us through the trees. Do you suppose they pick out whom their next meal is going to be, ahead of time, and then follow it around? I heard a story once—''

''Brrh! Don't,'' pleaded June. ''I was just beginning to forget it. You had to remind me!''

But by the time they were ready to leave, an hour later, they had both forgot it. They returned to where their carriage was waiting, laughing at the way an autograph-hound had come up to Marjorie by mistake, thinking she was June. They both looked a good deal alike.

''Drive us around slowly,'' Marjorie told the coachman. ''Isn't it beautiful in here in the moonlight?''

''It's getting late and we ought to go back,'' June remonstrated. ''I have to be on the set early tomorrow—''

''This is my last night in Hollywood,'' Marjorie coaxed, never dreaming what awful truth there might be in the words. ''Turn up that way,'' she ordered the driver. ''Take us off this main driveway. It's too full of exhaust fumes from all the cars.''

They turned down an empty side-lane, stretching desertedly ahead as far as the eye could reach. The horse was going at a slow walk. Presently they spied a sheet of burnished silver, glistening like a mirror through the tress, with graceful black objects floating on its surface.

''Look at that lake with the swans on it!'' Marjorie enthused. ''Let's get out and walk down by it, stretch our legs a little. I have some crumbs here. I love to feed birds.''

''Don't you think we ought to get back where there are more people?'' June shivered. ''We're awfully far in, and there's not a soul around us any more.''

''Don't be that way. Nothing can happen to us if we stay in sight of the coach. I promise you not to stray out of its sight.''

June gave in once more. The younger girl hadn't waited, was already making her way down the inclined grassy slope toward the lake flashing in the moonlight.

June turned to the driver, warned him, "Don't you dare move from here, understand? We'll be back in a minute."

He nodded in agreement, but the horse was pawing the ground uneasily and shifting about between the traces. He had to tighten his grip on the reins to steady it. She saw its ears standing stiffly erect, as though it heard or sensed something that they didn't.

"Marj," she called, "come on back. I think we'd better get in again, I don't like the way this horse is acting."

Marjorie was already at the water's edge. In order to make herself heard and try to overrule her, June started down after her.

Marjorie was crouched down, holding out some crumbs she had brought with her to the magnificent flotilla of black swans that came streaking up from all directions. "Aren't they beauts?" she said admiringly, over her shoulder, as June joined her.

"Yes, but something's making that horse restless. Let's get out of here."

"Oh, all right," sighed Marjorie sulkily, straightening up. "I wish you wouldn't be such a wet blanket."

Suddenly the swans began to reverse, dart out into the middle of the lake again as swiftly as they had drawn in to shore just now.

"What's the matter with them? What're they doing that for?" Marjorie asked blankly.

"Something's frightened them—and it wasn't us. I told you we'd better get out of here!" She began pulling the other girl insistently by the arm.

They turned just in time to see the horse, on the driveway above, rear up on its hind legs and whinny fearfully. The coachman, nearly overturned, gave an alarmed shout. The animal dropped back again, struck sparks from its shoes, and bolted off under their eyes. The rapid clatter of its hoofbeats and the driver's excited yells both died away down the driveway.

They came running up to the lane a minute too late, stood there looking down its empty moon-speckled length, where a little dust was settling from the vehicle's headlong flight.

"Now are you satisfied?" June said pointedly.

"How did I know that was going to happen? He'll quiet the horse in a minute and come back for us."

"Well, we're not waiting here until he does!" June said sharply. "There's something around here there shouldn't be. First the swans, and then that horse—"

They started to walk rapidly along the side of the road, one behind the other, in the direction the runaway horse had taken. They were alternately in shadow and moonlight. The macadam surface was hard on their feet after awhile, through the thin-soled evening slippers they wore. First one girl, then the other, changed over to the turf on the outside of the roadway, where the walking was easier. It was when the second one had done this, and their footsteps fell silently on the soft earth, that they first became aware of something. A soft intermittent rustling sound was coming from the foliage a little behind and to one side of them. It seemed to be pacing them.

June dropped back a step so she could whisper over her shoulder without raising her voice. "Do you hear that?" she breathed. "Something—or someone—is following us through there. I told you there was something around here there shouldn't be."

They'd both stopped short, inadvertently, in order to listen the better. A moment later the slithering sound had stopped too. There was an interval of awful silence. Then belatedly a twig snapped.

All Marjorie's nonchalance had left her. "Oh, why didn't I listen to you!" she sobbed. She gave her sister a push forward. "Don't let's stand here like this! Run, quick!"

They fled swiftly down the side of the long, empty road.

The rustling had resumed again the moment they broke into motion. It was governed by whatever they did, that was easy to see. It was the pursuer, and they were the prey. It became a crashing at times, plainly audible above their pattering footfalls and hot, frightened breaths.

"Scream," Marjorie panted. "Maybe someone will hear us!"

"Help!" June wailed. "Help!" She was too out of breath to be able to give more than a thin, disjointed bleat.

The rustling and crashing were drawing slowly but surely in toward them now, coming diagonally at them instead of merely keeping parallel. There were many places where the coverage between was so thin they could have glimpsed who or what it was, but that would have meant slowing to turn their heads, and they were too frightened. Perhaps they realized instinctively that the sight of whatever it was might so add to their terror as to rob them of the use of their limbs altogether.

June was the better runner of the two. Without realizing it, she was pulling away from the other girl, first by a yard's lead, then two, then three. Marjorie's shadow, which in the moonlit stretches had fallen over her shoulder, no longer reached her. Her footfalls were dropping behind, and the sound of her breathing was no longer as distinct.

Her own pace was starting to tell on her, though. And those high heels had never been meant for protracted running like this. "I can't keep up much longer," she heaved, beginning to stagger. "Got a stitch in my side. Are you all—?" She turned her face as she spoke.

Then she stopped dead, turned completely around, stood there swaying and weaving dizzily about from the long run. The road stretched empty behind her, as far as the eye could reach. There was only silence on it, and in the thickets that paralleled it. Silence and moonlight and shadow. . . .

The other girl must have been snatched bodily off it at her very heels, too quickly even to be able to cry out.

The coachman, returning belatedly for them with his quieted horse a quarter of an hour later, found her wandering dazedly along the roadside, her dress tattered and flecked with blood, her hair straggling loosely down, a hand pressed distractedly to her head.

"Take me to the police," she whimpered numbedly. "My sister's been torn to pieces—in there."

The car stopped and the men all got out. A tiny constellation of pocket torches, further in among the trees, marked the point where the coachman and park policemen were awaiting their arrival, around the inscrutable ferns that formed the bier.

They went over and had their look. It was the same thing over: an attack of terrible ferocity that had continued, insatiable, long after death.

"This thing must be suffering from the jungle equivalent of rabies," somebody spoke up. "It oughtn't to be just shot down; it should be flayed alive over a slow fire."

"It should be caught first," seethed Wrigley.

One of the men shouted out, "Hey, Cap, I've found a print! And what a one!" They all came rushing up. He was holding his torch trained down on it. It was in a bed of moss, not far from the body; the perfect imprint of a gigantic cat's paw—somewhat like a three-leaf clover.

Wrigley turned on Dunbar almost savagely, as though taking out his own frustration on him. "Now say that wasn't made by a leopard, go ahead!"

"It was made by a leopard," agreed Dunbar glumly. "But don't ask me to change my opinion. The two girls were running along Indian file, one nearly at the other's heels. You heard Miss Dale say she didn't hear a sound behind her. There is only one way the other girl could

have been seized quickly enough to prevent at least a
dying gasp from getting out, or to prevent the sound of her
falling body being heard by the foremost girl—and that is
by prehensile human hands around her windpipe, cutting
off all sound. She wasn't felled, she was snatched off her
feet—by something upright!''

"He's still looking for a man in this!'' Wrigley motioned offensively toward him. "Don't waste my time.
You're making me lose all respect for you! Do we have to
sit the thing in your lap to get you to admit its existence?''

"Man alive!'' Dunbar burst out uncontrollably. "There
are signs all around you, big as life, and you won't take
the trouble to read their meaning, you're so dazzled by that
crusoe-like *single* footprint of yours! Look at that broken
sprig there, bent down at right angles. What does that say
to you gents?''

Wrigley curled his lips disdainfully at such an elemen-
tary question. "What is this, kindergarten? It was swept
aside and dislocated by the passage of the leopard.''

"What was the leopard doing, walking upright on its
hind legs? One of you stand over there alongside it. These
ferns all around underfoot make the actual ground-level
hard to establish, create an optical illusion.'' He fairly
yelped his satisfaction when the measurement had been
effected. "Look at that! There's a depression under them,
a trough in the ground. Your man's about five-ten and that
dangling sprig is at the tip of his ear. What a two-story
leopard that must be!''

They didn't even pay him the compliment of stopping to
draw breath. "*Must* it follow the contour of the ground?
It's not a snake crawling flat on its belly. It's a quadruped.
Those girls were in full flight. What does any quadruped
do, chasing someone? It vaulted over this ground-hollow.
Its arched back swept that sprig aside, broke it.''

Dunbar flung his hand at him exasperatedly. "You can
have your leopard! You're welcome to it. There's no use

talking to you, it's just a waste of breath. I'm going home."

"I'm sure we'll be practically helpless without you," Wrigley called after him sarcastically.

"I'm accompanying poor Marjorie's remains back home tomorrow," June Dale told Dunbar when he stopped in at her house the following evening. She was composed now, but her face still showed traces of the terrible experience she had been through. "They haven't caught it yet, have they?" she added.

"Miss Dale, it's not a leopard," he told her quietly.

She stared at him intently; her face got whiter than before, as his meaning slowly sank in.

"I know I'm right, I've got to be," he said fiercely, slapping his thigh. "But they've all been raked by claws, I can't get around that. That's why I can't get Wrigley and the rest to listen to me."

When he had finished marshalling every argument he had presented to Wrigley at one time or another, a change had come over her. There was a gleam of anger in her eyes now that had been lacking before, when it was supposedly a question of only a brute animal.

She clenched her small fists. "If I thought that," she said slowly, "I'd stay here and do everything in my power to help catch such a fiendish murderer."

"That's exactly what I came here to ask of you," he let her know.

"What is it you want me to do?" she breathed fearfully.

"Be the bait in a trap set for him." He waited, while she shared at him. "All you've got to do is say no, and I won't blame you."

"Yes," she said finally, with quiet determination.

"Good girl! Here's my idea. I am going to try to plant, in the newspapers, the idea that you are going back again to Eastland Park to feed those swans—alone. Even after what happened to your sister."

"But Wrigley's men will be buzzing around in there thick as flies, trying to track down their precious leopard."

"I can get rid of them easily enough by phoning in a false report it's been seen in an entirely different section of town. That will draw them all away from there, clear the coast for us."

"But suppose he doesn't fall for it, I mean our leopard-man?"

"He'll have to in self-defense, the way I'll word it. I'm going to drop a hint, that he alone will understand, implying that you know who he is. You don't, of course, but he won't know that. He'll think maybe you did get a look at him last night in the Park. He'll feel he has to get rid of you, to cover himself up. That's the way we'll work it. I'll arm you, of course. And I've got to get another man in on it with me. You've got to be fully protected, and it may turn out to be more than I can handle successfully alone."

"Who will you get?"

"I can't get anyone on the Squad; they'd only squeal to Wrigley. It's got to be someone I can count on. Wait, I know—young Andy Lemaire, Dolly Gerard's sweetheart! He's the right one for such a job."

He stood up, put his hand on her shoulder questioningly. "Here's your last chance to say no if you want to."

"I'm going through with it. I thought I made that plain to you from the beginning," she said unwaveringly.

"Swell girl!" he complimented. "Get all the sleep you can," he advised as he moved toward the door. "Tomorrow night's the night."

Lemaire agreed, of course; jumped at the proposition. They found June agitatedly pacing back and forth waiting for them, when they reached her house the next evening. "I was getting more nervous by the minute," she greeted them. "I'm all ready." She backed away a step to let them take in a white gown sewn with glass beads.

"Good, just the thing!" Dunbar said. "It'll glitter in the

dark and make it easier for him to pick you out. Here's a gun I brought you. Put it in your evening bag. Excuse me, Miss Dale, Mister Lemaire. Have you seen the papers? It worked! Wrigley fell for it, there's not a man left in Eastland Park. They've all been sent over to the latest danger-zone. If it ever comes out I did it, of course, I'll be broken like a stick across a curbstone.''

He gave their beautiful decoy her final instructions. "Give us time to get planted out there first ourselves. Leave here in about half-an-hour. Take an open carriage like you did last time.''

"And how long do I stay down by the lake, in case nothing happens?''

"Until you've given the swans all the crumbs you've brought alone. Smoke a cigarette after that for good measure. Try to avoid giving an impression of tension or nervousness. Oh, here's one very important point: make sure you stray *out* of the coachman's sight, if only for a short distance. If by the time you've finished your cigarette the horse hasn't been frightened into running away, you can be sure he's not around, won't show up any more tonight. Simply get in the carriage and come on back. We'll follow you in a few minutes.''

He took her hand in both of his, pressed it encouragingly. "Here goes. Now keep cool and trust us. I looked that gun over; it's in hair-trigger readiness. If it's a case of emergency, don't waste time drawing, fire it right through your bag.''

She stood in the doorway looking after them, her face white as chalk with the impending ordeal that lay ahead of her.

The slow *clop-clop* of a horse carried to where Dunbar lay hidden in the crotch of a tree. It died out momentarily, then came back again more clearly than ever in the intense silence. Was that her at last? It must be.

On it came, nearer every moment. At last he could even

make out the slight creak of the axle-joints, the hiss of the
rubber tires. He heard the coachman's voice give a low,
throaty, "Whoa!" The hoof-beats faltered to a stop, and
there was a creak from the carriage step as she descended.

He couldn't see the vehicle itself, for there was too
much interfering foliage between him and it, but a moment
later the white of her gown came into full view, corruscating
in the moonlight. She started to walk down the grassy
slope under his very eyes. Lemaire was on the other side,
on a flat stone in the middle of some reeds growing
directly out of the water.

She passed the tree that hid him without a glance over
that way. She couldn't, of course, know exactly where he
was. All she had to rely on was his assurance that he and
Lemaire would be somewhere nearby.

She reached the water's edge at last. Dunbar was now
roughly midway between her and the carriage. Nothing
could get at her from in front, across the water. Nothing
could get at her from in back, or from this side, without
passing him first. And Lemaire's position was an effective
guarantee that nothing could creep up on her from the
other side either. There wasn't a sound from the dark
masses of bushes and underbrush all around. Not a rustle,
not the snap of a twig. Nothing stirred.

The greedy birds were banked nearly solid around her, on
the water side, jostling and nudging one another aside.
Dunbar kept swivelling his head slowly, covering every
inch of ground within a 180-degree arc, his gun held
motionless at trigger-height above its holster.

Suddenly he heard the horse whinny uneasily. Its hoofs
shifted about within the confines of the traces. Dunbar's
head turned tautly around the other way—toward her. The
swans were streaking out away from her. In another moment she was standing there alone at the water's edge.

He drew his gun out further, so that its muzzle cleared
the holster. A shimmering line of brightness coursed down

her motionless back. Was she trembling at the imminence of danger, or was it just the moonlight rippling on the beads sewn to her dress?

He dropped one leg down out of the tree, let it dangle within a foot of the ground in readiness. And still the space between, from up above where the carriage was to down below where she was, remained silent, inscrutable.

She didn't look around, although she must have heard the telltale sounds from the driveway as plainly as he had. She fumbled in the small bag looped to her wrist, he heard the crackle of cellophane, and a match glowed before her face as she lit the test-cigarette he had told her to. It was the height of courage. For all she knew, something might be creeping up behind her even then. He was in a position to see, but she wasn't.

The horse took two or three abortive steps forward, as if about to break into a headlong run, then was quickly reined in, backed up again with a creaking of the carriage joints and a jiggling of the wheel rims as it crowded back on them.

She followed his instructions to the letter. She began to saunter aimlessly along the lake margin, out of sight of carriage and driver. She stopped finally and stood there as if idly contemplating the lake, arms folded across her chest and the red spark of her cigarette winking before her.

Dunbar could barely see her any more at this distance, she was just a white blur in the gloom, for she had stepped out of the moonlight into the shadow of some trees. It was up to Lemaire now to guard her, over there on the side where he was.

There wasn't a sound, except for an occasional pawing from the horse up above. Its restlessness had become chronic by now, but apparently was being kept under control by the driver. The animal's whole demeanor showed there was some unseen danger close at hand in the shadows of the park, but it stubbornly remained concealed, refused to reveal itself. The strain was almost unbearable. The tension, shared by the two hidden men watching and the visible girl smoking there by the water's edge, stretched almost to the breaking point.

At last her cigarette went out in the water with a hiss. She turned and began to make her way back. She came out into the open moonlight again and started up the slope. She passed the forked tree where Dunbar was and went on up the rest of the way, over the lip onto the roadway, and out of his line of vision.

Her thin voice carried clearly to him as she reached the carriage. "All right, you can start back now." The foot-rest creaked as she stepped in. The terrified animal instantly broke into a rapid trot that soon became a furious gallop, so anxious was it to get away from the threatening spot.

Dunbar dropped down from the tree and stood waiting for his companion to break and join him. The reeds parted and Lemaire came limping over, rubbing his hip-bone agonizedly.

"Well, it fell through," he murmured ruefully when he'd joined the detective. "He didn't show."

"But there was something around here there shouldn't have been. Didn't you notice the way the swans and that horse acted?"

"Yes, and that makes me wonder. Do you think it may be an animal, after all? They're used to human beings; they wouldn't become frightened of a human."

"You're overlooking the one thing that brought him around here tonight, and that's the hint I published that she was coming back. Animals don't read the daily papers. And Wrigley and his men cleaned this park thoroughly." They toiled up the slope side by side.

"What was that?" Dunbar exclaimed as they reached the empty driveway.

Both stood rigid, listening. It came again, a scuffling or

threshing sound, as of a large animal caught in a trap and trying to extricate itself.

"In there, across the road somewhere!" They'd both drawn their guns. The detective plunged in first, Lemaire at his heels. "Watch your eyes," he grunted, warding off branches and briars with his forearm. A moment later he went down flat and his gun nearly went off.

"Watch out, there's somebody lying here, dead or dying. I stumbled across him—"

Dunbar took out a pocket torch, played it on a bleeding face, dead now, its convulsions just over as they got there. A second later he straightened with a yell of horror that crackled through the trees. "My God! D'you know who this is? It's June's coachman, the one that brought her here! Don't you see what that means? That fiend, the very thing we're out to catch, has driven off with her right under our noses, has her with him at this moment!"

"My car, quick!" Lemaire snapped. "He's only been gone five minutes!"

The detective tore out through the underbrush without waiting to be told twice, sprinted down the road, pocketing his gun as he went. He brought the car crashing backwards out of the small grove where Lemaire had effectively concealed it, just as Lemaire arrived, gasping. He reversed it while his companion slung himself onto the running-board, climbed around in back of his shoulders to the seat on the opposite side. It shot forward like a projectile, so that both their heads snapped back with the velocity of the take-off.

Just before the desolate by-road veered in to unite with the main driveway that ran into the city, something log-like came racing toward them in the path of their head-lights. In another minute they would have gone over it.

Dunbar nearly piled the car against a tree and threw them over the windshield, the way he swerved and braked. Both had seen what it was. Neither took time to unlatch the doors. Dunbar jumped out over the back of the seat, Lemaire stood up on the door-rim with both feet and sailed down.

The log-like form was that of a dead man, lying face down. Dunbar turned him over, touched his forehead. "Still warm," he grunted. "Only just happened." He splashed his torch into the bronzed, Indian-grim face. "Know who he is?" he asked Lemaire. "The animal-trainer that owned the thing in the first place. He's been my chief suspect until now."

"What're you looking so worried about?"

"Because now—" The detective let his hands fall limply beside his thighs as he squatted there. "Who the devil *is* it? Who the blazes has her? I've been investigating him ever since the Ramirez affair, and I think he was kill-crazy from being around big cats so much. In fact, I'm almost sure of it."

"But *who killed him?* Maybe the leopard itself finally turned on him—"

"Don't start talking like Wrigley," said the dick curtly. "That's a bullet wound in the side of his head. It's easy to see what happened. He made off with her just now; killed her coachman and took his place. But then somebody else horned in along here, shot him from the underbrush as he drove by with her and took *his* place. That isn't getting her back, though! Come on, we're wasting time. She's in more danger than ever."

He sprinted back to the car, Lemaire after him. He floored the accelerator and they spurted forward.

"How can he get her into town with him, without her raising an outcry, now that she saw him shoot the trainer?" Lemaire asked.

"Easy enough. He probably stunned her with a blow at the same time, trussed her up, raised the carriage wind-break up to her chin and lowered the hood. Spooners often ride around in them that way. That isn't what's worrying me. It's *where* he's taking her—*where* to look for her if we expect to save her life!"

The lights of the town opened out before them in a wide semicircle as they reached the park entrance. Dunbar braked with a suddenness that sent a shudder through the car.

"What are you stopping for?" his companion asked.

Dunbar brought his fist down against the wheel-rim with helpless fury. "Well, where are we going to go? Our only chance was to overtake him before he got out of here. Even with just a horse pulling him, and stopping to silence her, he made it ahead of us, beat us to the city entrance. And we're working against a deadline of *seconds*. A deadline ticking off to its end—may be already over."

"Keep cool," said Lemaire tonelessly. "We haven't time to look in the wrong place, so we've got to hit it right the first time. Let's try to think of the places where this 'leopard' of Wrigley's has already appeared. Maybe that'll give it to us. The viaduct under Bower Street, the Cedars of Eden Cemetery, and here in Eastland Park, two times running now—"

Dunbar pounded the wheelrim once more, but this time elatedly. "It worked!" he yelled. "I've got it! That gave it to me! Only it's not where the 'leopard' appeared, it's where he *disappeared!* Belrose Street! It was never seen again after it went in there, so it's been hidden away in there somewhere ever since. And it's straight ahead of us down the line! Don't you see? He wouldn't dare take her any deeper into the city than that, in a horse-drawn carriage. Too many people would be liable to notice it go by."

Lemaire slammed him pulverizingly on the shoulder. "Good work! Get going!"

They flashed out of the park entrance, swerved around onto the Boulevard, and tore down that toward that fatal little side street that seemed to be the crux of the whole mystery.

"But which house?" Lemaire yelled at him above the roaring wind of their hurtling progress. "It's a block long, and that's a lot of houses."

"I've got that too—I hope. D'you remember the finding of the discarded leash and muzzle that night, a considerable time after the leopard vanished. It didn't show up until too long afterwards, to have been dropped by the beast itself in flight. It was thrown out of one of the houses, by human hands, after the leopard had already been secured inside. It was found lying nearest to Number 23. *That's* the house we want!"

"Brother, you're not a detective for nothing," said Lemaire admiringly.

They braked at the upper corner, ran down the quiet shadowy little street on foot, guns in hand.

Lemaire glanced briefly up at the unlighted face of the building as they reached the entrance together. "You mean he's got her behind one of those peaceful-looking apartment-windows up there, ready to—? Hard to believe."

"Sure it is, that's why he probably picked such a place to bring her to." Dunbar punched one of the doorbells in the entryway at random, simply to get in past the locked street door. It turned out to be that of the ground floor flat on the left side.

A family in various stages of night-attire peered apprehensively out at them. He questioned them briefly, after flashing his badge and taking a quick look around inside. "Did any of you hear a carriage draw up outside within the last ten minutes or so?"

"No. We sleep in the back, you know."

"It would have still been out there, wouldn't it?" said Lemaire in an aside to him.

"He wouldn't be that dumb. He'd give it a stroke of the whip, and it wouldn't stop running for blocks." They went outside again and closed the door after them. "Keep them in there, they'll wake the whole house up otherwise."

        *   *   *

The usual automatic elevator stood at the back of the hall, with a fire-staircase beside it.

"We'd better split up and work a double shift," Dunbar said tensely. "Every second counts. You start in at the roof and work your way down, I'll begin at the basement and work my way up. Holler if you hit pay-dirt."

He went to the back, behind the stairs, flung open the basement door without giving any warning. A maw, black as a ship's hold, confronted him. He found a light-switch on the other side of the door, cut it on, and a small, dim bulb glowed ineffectively out in the middle of the cavernous place. A rickety iron staircase led down, steep as a ladder. Below he could make out a mass of rubbish discarded by tenants—baby carriages without wheels, broomsticks without heads, empty packing cases. A couple of broken-down mattresses stood on end against one wall.

There was only one doorway to be seen, half blown-glass, half wood. A feeble light went on behind it as his feet ticked down the iron rungs, and a muffled voice called out sleepily, "Who is it? Who's out there?"

Dunbar didn't answer, went over, flung it open, and looked in for himself. He wasn't telegraphing his errand at a time like this. A scrawny individual in an old-fashioned nightshirt was sitting up in the middle of a decrepit iron cot, popping alarmed eyes at him. He was so weazened even a girl like June Dale could have handled him with one hand tied behind her.

"You the janitor?" said Dunbar gruffly.

"Yes. What's up?"

"Nothing. Just looking around." There were no recesses in the place in which she could have been hidden, no window or any other opening except the one by which he'd just come in. He went over by the cot, picked up one of a pair of warped shoes lying beside it, scanned its sole and edges for signs of recent dampness and green discoloration, such as treading on the moist soil or grass of the park might have caused. There weren't any. He dropped it with a thump, moved back to the door.

In the outer basement he made a quick circular tour of the junk-laden place, kicked a couple of packing-cases aside, punched his fist into the up-ended mattresses to see if there was anything hidden between them and the wall. They sagged limply. A cloud of dust rose and made him sneeze. The janitor's light went out again, as he jogged frustratedly up the iron steps once more.

He and Lemaire met on the third floor. They'd cased every apartment in the building by that time; there was no place further to look. They gave each other a look without saying anything, turned and went downstairs again, one behind the other.

Dunbar's face was taut, with a drop of sweat glistening at the indentation of each nostril, as they neared the street door again. "I was sure I had it right. It's no go, Lemaire. We've lost her. We went astray in our calculations somewhere along the way. This Belrose Street angle, maybe."

"Well, we can't quit, until we're sure."

"No, we can't quit," agreed the detective glumly. "But the deadline was up long ago. He's had too long an opportunity by now—"

The people in the ground floor apartment, whose bell they had first rung to get into the building, were nosing out at them through the crack of their door as they passed by on their way to the street. It was a little thing like that. . . .

Lemaire was already outside on the sidewalk. Dunbar was about to close the front door after him, when he heard a woman give a sharp exclamation somewhere inside the flat.

"What was that?" he asked alertly, turning and going back.

He pushed the partly-open door wide and looked in. The man's wife was wringing her hand, jabbering indignantly,

"He must be drunk down there! What's the matter with him, this time of year—"

Dunbar jumped inside, clapped his hand to the steam-radiator she was standing by. It stung with unexpected heat. He flung himself out into the hall again, drawing his gun as he went. "Lemaire!" he yelled hoarsely as he went racing toward the back. "This is it, after all!"

In a moment Lemaire was inside again, streaking after him. "How do you know?"

"Someone's built a fire in the furnace—in June! That means the boiler room—down below somewhere!" He piled through the basement door a second time. He didn't waste time with the iron staircase, dropped down to basement level at a single jump. "Put on that light up there by you, we've got to find the entrance. I must have missed it the first time—"

As it went on dimly, he understood in a flash and swore aloud. "The mattresses, of course—and I fell for a crude stunt like that!" The improvised screens toppled over sideways at the sweep of his arm, and both their guns rose to bear on the squat, rust-flaked iron door revealed behind them. It was less than shoulder-high. Both crouched to be able to get in under it.

Dunbar pulled it out by the iron grip that protruded, and a satanic red-and-black tableau, struck motionless at that very instant, was revealed. Those were the only two colors. The red of the furnace, with its mouth yawning wide open, the black of shadows, of night, of death. A glittering mass that swept in wave-formation high up into the two far corners was coal. A writhing, twinkling bundle that lay outlined in the ruddy pathway spreading fan-wise from the furnace-mouth, was the dress sewn with beads that had gone so gamely to its rendezvous in the park a few hours earlier. And this was the rendezvous. At least there was still life inside it, as it squirmed and strained against its bonds.

Over it were poised two feline, sleek-furred claws, stemming out of the shadows, about to descend, to tear and mangle the ivory-white skin. But between them was the red-limned black outline of a human head. A leopard-man!

Lemaire's revolver crashed out from behind Dunbar's shoulder, and the claws reared backward into the gloom, and a freshet of lumps of coal came trickling down. Dunbar jumped down, bent anxiously over the glittering, heaving dress. She hadn't been hurt yet. But in another moment—

He took out the filthy bit of waste that had been stuffed into her mouth, but she couldn't say anything at first, she had been too close to eternal silence. He raised her head from the floor, undid her bonds. Then he turned to where Lemaire was also bending down, peering closely at the body on the coal. "Who is it?" he asked.

He clicked on his torch, went over to see. He nearly dropped it again a moment later as a dead face focused beneath its beam. It was Manning, June Dale's former press agent.

"That rat!" Lemaire breathed sullenly. "He must have been Dolly's publicity man too. She told me she had one, but never mentioned the name."

Dunbar looked puzzled. "But what did he get out of it, trying to get rid of all his clients like that?"

June Dale spoke from the background. "He took out insurance on my life, to safeguard his own job. Then when he saw he was going to lose it— He expected the leopard to finish me the first time I took it out. But it didn't, and he tried again the other night, only it got poor Marj instead. He must have done the same thing with Dolly Gerard. It was in the contract I signed with him. I remember that now. But I didn't think of if in time. And after I fired him, I tore up my copy of it."

Dunbar nodded, pointed to the gauntlets on the dead man's wrists, made of the original dried hide, with the terrible claws left intact. He drew one off. It was stiff as buckram with the blood of the former victims that had drenched it. It was lined in rubber, with a small wooden wedge thrust down inside it to give the wearer's fingers a grip.

"He cut off the brute's forelegs at the joint, extracted the bone and flesh, and made these. These explain so many things that misled Wrigley: the tufts of hair found on the Ramirez girl, the claw-tip broken off short in Dolly's throat, the clawed bark on that tree in the cemetery, the paw-print in the moss at the park. Also what frightened the horse and swans. These were improperly cured, of course; he probably had them in his pocket. The scent of the original animal was carried to them on the breeze."

Dunbar pointed to two round celluloid buttons pinned to Manning's lapels. "Rubbed them with sulphur match-heads, to make them glow in the dark. The victims probably thought they were eyes glaring at them. It must have helped to paralyze them, made it easier for him to finish them off."

"But where does the Ramirez girl come in?" asked Lemaire. "She was no actress."

"That must have been the leopard's own work. That was the only one of the three Wrigley was right about. They were in cahoots with this janitor here, Manning and the trainer. The trainer was planted here ahead of time, to get the leopard back. He got it inside, with a piece of meat probably, hid it down here until the house-to-house search was over. Then later that night, as he was getting ready to smuggle it out, it broke away a second time, came on the Ramirez girl, and jumped her."

"But you told me you found a skull fracture from a blunt instrument on her."

"They caught up with it a minute or two too late, found her dying there, and the trainer probably finished her to shut her up. I told you he was kill-crazy anyway. I think that accidental killing was what gave Manning the whole idea of going out and doing the leopard's work *for* it, instead of relying on it itself. Too unreliable. So he killed it against the trainer's wishes, maybe even without his knowledge, cut off its forepaws, and probably buried it under the coal.''

''Why did he get rid of the trainer?''

''Probably afraid to trust him, once the leopard itself had been done away with. Didn't need him any more after that, anyway. But tonight he used him for the last time, as a catspaw to snatch June out of the trap we'd set; then finished him with a revolver shot and took over. He would've probably finished that janitor who led them in and out of here before long, too.''

''He has already,'' said Lemaire, coming back. ''I found the old guy strangled to death on his cot in there. What did he want this fire in the furnace for?''

''Probably to get rid of the telltale severed paws and the rest of the carcass, after they'd served his purpose. It wasn't meant for June. He probably would have dropped her body back outside someplace bearing all the vestiges of the 'leopard's' handiwork. It had to be seen so he could collect.''

''Then why didn't he finish her in the park? That would have been simpler.''

''Because we were too hot on his trail, he didn't have time. Don't worry, he must have guessed that was a trap, but he outsmarted us. Only one little thing tripped him up, a little unforeseen detail that really had nothing to do with any of the rest of it. Somebody's radiator valve happened to have been left turned on in this house, at a time of year when people never go near those things. We woke them up, and the woman happened to absently rest her hand on the thing. If it wasn't for that, we wouldn't have caught him tonight, and we would have lost the girl.''

*   *   *

He smiled a little. "Well, I guess we better get in touch with Wrigley. I want to see his face when I show him there *was* a man in it, twice out of three times anyway." He gave them the wink. "But listen, leave out just one thing, will you? That anonymous false-alarm I sent in that cleared them out of the park. I can still get in plenty of dutch for that."

Wrigley's face, when he'd finally come, seen and heard, was worth watching. It ran through a gamut of emotions that June might have envied in her screen work. But he ended up by making the amend honorable. "Yep," he said, for everyone present to hear, "I was wrong, and you were right. What more can I say? And yet right tonight a message comes in to Headquarters that it was seen in another part of town, big as life—"

Dunbar stared innocently at the ceiling.